The Dead Don't Hurt Us

P F CAIRNS

© P F Cairns 2010

Published by Astwood Publishing Ltd

Astwood House
Carnoustie
Angus
DD7 6LW

Website: www.astwood.org.uk

ISBN 978-0-9566732-0-6

Cover design by Sanctus Media
Tel: 01506 827217
Website: www.sanctusmedia.com

Disclaimer
The characters of this novel are all fictitious, and any possible likeness to anyone living or dead is purely accidental; each character has been developed from the author's imagination. Similarly, the village communities are entirely fictitious, and, at times, the geography of the region has been intentionally scrambled.

Prepared and printed by:

York Publishing Services Ltd
64 Hallfield Road
Layerthorpe
York YO31 7ZQ
Tel: 01904 431213

Website: www.yps-publishing.co.uk

This book is dedicated to

My mother, Freda, for her love and prayers

Contents

	Acknowledgements	vii
	About the Author	viii
	Preface	x
	Reviews	xi
	The Street Boys	xiv
Chapter 1	What if?	1
Chapter 2	Shattered Lives!	14
Chapter 3	Only Dressed in Shorts!	20
Chapter 4	Learning Curve!	28
Chapter 5	White-knuckle Ride	34
Chapter 6	Just Waiting and Waiting!	42
Chapter 7	Clearer Picture	49
Chapter 8	Snatched!	53
Chapter 9	On the Third Dive!	59
Chapter 10	No Survivors	69
Chapter 11	Commando Sortie	76
Chapter 12	Shocking Impact	84
Chapter 13	New Friends	93
Chapter 14	Diplomatic Incident	102
Chapter 15	Search Plans	109

Chapter 16	Culture Shock	123
Chapter 17	Poor Reception	136
Chapter 18	Jungle Wasteland	146
Chapter 19	Touch and Go	159
Chapter 20	Ruled by Fear	167
Chapter 21	Too Much to Bear	179
Chapter 22	Saved by Love	187
Chapter 23	Nimrod II	204
Chapter 24	Brutal Encounter	214
Chapter 25	Black Hole	226
Chapter 26	Street Life	230
Chapter 27	Miracle	240
	Epilogue	250

vii

Acknowledgements

My grateful thanks go to;

My husband, Alan, and our family for their love and support.

My many friends who have read the manuscript, corrected, advised and encouraged me to publish 'The Dead Don't Hurt Us'.

To Morag Bramhall for patiently proofreading.

Albert Bogle, Willie McPherson of The Vine Trust and Paul Clark of Scripture Union Peru – for opening my eyes to the plight of street children.

Duncan Beal and staff at York Publishing Services.

To Neil MacLennan and Rae Manger at Sanctus Media for preparing the cover and creating the book's website www. donthurtus.org

About the Author

Pam Cairns was brought up on a small farm in Dumfriesshire, Scotland. The author was educated at Lockerbie Academy and, later, at Edinburgh University, where she studied medicine.

While working as a general practitioner in Kirkcaldy, Fife, Pam and her husband Alan had the opportunity to lead a team of medical volunteers to the Amazon jungle of Peru. This was the first UK medical team that The Vine Trust charity had sent to work on their vessel, Amazon Hope. The medical staff delivered primary health and dental care to the villagers on the banks of the river Amazon.

The three-week trip to Peru had a huge effect on Pam. Resigning from her medical practice, she became the volunteer Medical Director of the Vine Trust. Over the next two years, she and her husband worked, with others, to develop and promote the Amazon Hope Medical and Dental Project. (See www.vinetrust.org)

It was while in Peru that the author first came across street children and learnt of their struggle for survival. Pam began to understand the factors responsible for their ever increasing numbers worldwide. Deeply shocked, she discovered that not only did the children have to contend with hunger and disease, but also the cruelties and abuses of adults and the authorities.

Now retired from medicine, Pam lives with her husband on their small holding in Angus, Scotland. The couple have three adult children. Pam is a committed Christian and an active member of Soroptimist International. She is enjoying her new career as a writer.

Preface

This is a fast moving, contemporary adventure story based in the hot and dangerous Amazon jungle and the Peruvian city of Iquitos

A .highly stressed, arrogant British oil executive and his wife search for their children who are missing in the rainforest. During the rescue mission, the parents come face to face with the terrible destruction of the rainforest by oil exploration and mining. They come to realise the huge impact this has on the village communities and an ancient way of life.

The children experience the hardships of jungle life, encountering witch doctors and cocaine smugglers along the way. Reaching the jungle city of Iquitos, they are mistaken for street rats. Pursued by the authorities, they hide in the sewers.

Reviews

Readers of all ages will be moved by P.F. Cairns' debut novel which follows the fortunes of two British children lost in the dangerous Peruvian jungle. Its fast-flowing plot contains as many twists and turns as the Amazon and shows how love, courage and optimism can overcome adversity and evil. Its strong moral message is all the more powerful as many ideas for her story are based on her involvement in charity work in the area. Readers can gain an insight into problems facing street children and feel some satisfaction that profits from her novel will help children like those we encounter in the story.

Secondary school teacher

A great adventure story which cleverly weaves facts with fiction. The messages about strength of the human spirit, compassion, hope, love are what make this a compelling read.

Head teacher

Reviews from younger readers

Really sad to think children felt safer in a cemetery than anywhere else. A cemetery would scare me.

Sad, exciting and shocking. I wanted to keep reading it.

Let me know about how the children felt being so alone and without their parents. Had to survive and use things they had heard and read about, amazing.

Really sad what people think of the street children, they are treated like animals or worse.

Dramatic, descriptive and kept me on the edge of my seat.

Gave us a lot of information particularly about life in the jungle in South America and what it was like to be a street child.

The children had a belief in God which helped them get through the terrible time they had.

I am 14 and I have read a lot of stories but I have never read a story quite like this before. The characters are well developed throughout the story and the suspense is built up well. A lot of information is given on the topic of South American life, in the jungle and on the streets. Although I was vaguely aware of guerrillas, drug lords and other South American hardships such as these, I never knew how bad life is there if you are in the wrong place. The contrast between upper city life to street and jungle lives is very clear.

The story can be taken at different levels for different readers. Younger readers can read the story at face value while older readers can appreciate the deeper concepts. This book is well written and I recommend others to read it.

The Street Boys

Curled round in a little ball,
A small rag thrust to his nose.
Shivering, feeling no warmth at all,
The pain within doesn't let him doze.

It's dark down there but safe,
Other kids are huddled round, trembling too.
Deep cold shows in the blue-lipped face.
The pain within is nothing new.

No food today but some 'garbaged' pasta.
Disturbed by the police they had to run.
Their little hearts pounding faster, faster.
The pain within lifts when threatened by a gun.

Down the broken manhole to the sewer.
A place police never follow – the stench!
The rats scurry here, there, then fewer.
The pain within makes the stomach wrench.

This is home for them, all thirty.
Some are seven, eleven or even four years old
They're hungry, ill, smelly, dirty.
The pain within makes them very, very cold.

They all think they've done something awful,
That's why they were thrown out and are all alone.
Adults hate them, make them fearful.
The pain within reaches to the bone.

They exist in stinky sewers, lonely graveyards.
The rats, the dead, they are their friends.
There are thousands around the world. Oh it's hard!
'Cos the pain within kills them in the end.

© P F Cairns 2007

CHAPTER 1

What if?

Katie's screaming brought Tim to his senses. He looked across and saw her blood-spattered face, but she was not screaming because of pain but at the lifeless body of Aunt Susie strapped in her seat across the aisle. Tim couldn't see much more as smoke filled the whole area, but he could see the flames a few metres in front of him.

He ripped off his oxygen mask and shouted to Katie, 'We have to get out of here, and fast!' But she just kept on screaming.

Tim looked to his left. The old lady who was in the seat next to him was motionless – too quiet, too pale. Tim nudged her, but her head fell forward onto her chest.

'We have to get out of here, now!' Tim yelled, as he reached across and unclipped Katie's seat belt and pushed her into the aisle of the plane.

At the beginning of the flight, Tim had listened to everything the flight attendant had said about emergency procedures. He knew that the exit door was just a row behind them. He had wondered why the attendant had shown them how to put on a life jacket because their flight north from Lima to Bogotá was over the mountains and dense jungle.

Things had gone wrong about an hour after take off. The captain had spoken over the intercom and said that there was a severe thunderstorm ahead and that he was expecting some turbulence. Everyone had to put on seat belts. About ten minutes later, the plane began to shake violently. Tim's bottle of Inka Cola, his favourite Peruvian drink, flew off his little table and onto the lap of the old Peruvian lady next to him. She grunted at him in a language he didn't recognise, but he knew she was annoyed.

Tim also knew about turbulence as he had flown many times before. His parents had worked in Lima for three years, so he had flown with them several times, back and forward to Britain. Usually they would fly from Lima to Amsterdam, but the decision to go to Scotland had only been made the previous week. Aunt Susie had agreed to accompany the youngsters as their parents couldn't get the time off work to make the trip. So, Tim and his younger sister, Katie, and their favourite aunt were all travelling to Scotland to visit Granny and Papa Mitchell. Their grandparents lived on a small farm near Edinburgh. The only flight available, at such short notice in the tourist season, had been up north to Bogotá, Columbia, then via Madrid to Glasgow. This was not the best arrangement, but for the vacation to go ahead they had needed to put up with all the flight changes.

Katie had been very excited about the trip. She was ten years old, tall and thin for her age, with long brown hair and deep brown eyes. She loved visiting her grandparents' farm. Nothing excited her more than rising early in the morning to help Papa with the feeding of the animals. Katie hoped that Papa would have some pet lambs to bottle feed or maybe even some new piglets from Patsy his black sow. Tim, on the other hand, was thirteen and a little short and plump for his age; his teenage hormones had not quite fired up yet. He liked going to Scotland but, at times, found the farm boring. He had wondered how he was going to fill the time. After all, Papa didn't have a computer, so no chance of the internet! He did like to ride Coringo, Papa's old horse. His grandfather bought the horse, a ten-year-old ex-hunter, about five years ago. Katie was always annoyed because she was too small for such a big horse, and there were no ponies for her to ride on the farm. But Tim was much stronger and rode Coringo well, always under Papa's supervision though, as the horse could be a bit 'prickly' at times.

* * *

When the flight attendants rushed to strap themselves into their seats, Tim did get a little worried. Aunt Susie must have been frightened too, because she reached across and tightened Katie's seat belt and told Tim to tighten his. Aunt Susie then closed her eyes and clasped her hands. Tim had seen her do this before at home when she was praying. She always prayed when she was worried.

Tim could remember the plane shaking violently, and the lights of the cabin flashing off and on. Then as the front of the plane tilted violently downwards the oxygen masks dropped from the ceiling. That was when the screaming started! The plane lost more and more height, and then there was a tremendous crash! Tim must have blacked out then because he could not remember the fire starting or the plane filling with smoke.

Tim and Katie found the door, guided by the emergency lights. Tim tried to turn the handle, but his right arm was so painful he didn't have the strength to unlock the door. Katie grabbed the handle too and together they struggled, but nothing would move. Behind them a figure came out of the smoke. It was Julie, one of the flight attendants. She was holding her side, blood oozing through her fingers. She could hardly stand, but she pushed past them and pulled at the lever. The door flew open and the escape chute shot out in front of them down to the ground. Katie thought it was like a giant slide at the park.

'Jump onto the chute!' Julie yelled to the children.

'Once you're on the ground get away from the plane as fast as you can – it may explode. I'll go and see if I can help anyone else. Now jump!'

Tim quickly pushed Katie onto the slide, and then jumped himself. They both landed in a heap at the bottom. Tim's ankle was hurt in the fall but Katie helped him up and they hobbled away from the plane, as Julie had told them to do. The plane seemed to have landed in a small clearing in the jungle. The nose of the aircraft had smashed deep into the trees, the tail sticking up in the air.

They struggled as fast as they could to reach the edge of the jungle. Suddenly, the noise from the burning plane became incredibly intense followed by a huge explosion. Katie and Tim were thrown to the ground. They huddled together with their hands over their ears, to shut out the roar of the blast, and cowered from the intense heat that enveloped them. The smell of burning fuel was overpowering. They were terrified!

After what seemed like forever, the noise died down, but the heat from the fire was so fierce that the two had to move further away. They were at the edge of the clearing, but the trees and undergrowth were so thick that they couldn't see a way to escape from the heat. Fortunately, Katie spotted a small opening just a few metres to the right, so they scrambled over. It seemed like the beginnings of an old path but it didn't look as if anyone had used it recently. Katie helped Tim as they fought their way through the creepers and fallen branches that blocked their way. They struggled on for about a hundred metres, falling exhausted at the foot of a very tall tree.

The children sat stunned. Shocked by the horrible experience they had just lived through. Katie was sobbing again, overwhelmed by their terrifying ordeal.

Tim held on tightly to his little sister as her young body trembled uncontrollably. She was too young to have witnessed such shocking scenes he thought. And even though he tried to be strong himself, he couldn't stop the tears streaming from his eyes onto his sister's dark brown hair.

After a while, Tim calmed down and began to consider their plight. By now it must be late in the afternoon, he thought to himself. Their flight took off on time at four thirty, about an hour and a half ago, so it would be dark soon. He had lived in the tropics long enough to know that darkness comes suddenly; one minute you can see in front of you and the next you cannot see your own hand!

'It's so hot here. We must find some water and somewhere to spend the night. It'll be dark in about half an hour, so we don't have much time,' Tim said, gently shaking Katie to gain her attention.

'Where's everyone else?' Katie sobbed. 'Where's Julie? She was behind us at the door.'

'Julie went to help others but she hasn't made it. I think we're the only ones to get out of the plane alive,' Tim muttered, in disbelief.

'We should go and look for others. There must have been over a hundred and fifty people on the plane. Surely they can't all be dead! 'What about Aunt Susie? Was she really dead or just sleeping?' sobbed Katie.

'She was dead, and so was the old lady next to me. Both their heads just hung there. They weren't breathing. No one could survive that explosion. If they didn't get out of the plane, they're dead,' Tim answered, trying to hide the tremble in his voice. 'We can't go back to the plane to look for others; it's too dangerous. There might be other explosions! We just don't know,' he continued. 'We must go on!'

He tried to stand up but fell back as his ankle had stiffened up and was really sore now. Katie was startled by Tim's apparent helplessness and even more shocked when she realised from his red eyes that he had been crying too. She hadn't seen her big brother cry since his best friend drowned three years earlier.

'I'll look for a stick for you, Tim. Remember when Mum twisted her ankle; the nurse at the hospital gave her a walking stick."

'Don't go far! Stay close! There'll be snakes around here. Try that tree just there,' Tim said.

Katie looked at the tree but didn't know which branch to break off as they were covered in creepers. She spotted a branch just above her head that was not all tangled, but how was she going to reach it? Just then, Katie heard her Mum's voice in her head; 'Never say never until you try.' Her Mum always said this when Katie was stuck with her homework, so Katie would go back and try again and, usually, she would manage to solve the problem.

She crouched really low under the branch and then leapt as high as she could, but only just touched the branch. Next time she tried just a little harder and managed to grasp the branch to swing it down. Tim had to use his good hand to help her break the stick away from the tree. It was just the right length. Tim quickly learnt to use it and was able to walk a good bit better.

The children could only follow the path. The jungle was so thick on either side that at times the branches scratched their faces and made Katie cry with pain. Tim fell over a couple of times as his bad ankle caught on the tree roots, but he always managed to get back up without crying. He knew he was really close to sobbing again; he was so frightened. Tim knew the jungle was a very dangerous place to be after dark. Uncle Hugh used to tell him about his expeditions to the jungle when he came to visit. Tim loved to hear his stories. Uncle Hugh was an army officer and had been in the Amazon jungle and in the African jungle many times. Tim wished his uncle was with them now; he would know what to do.

Katie was very hot, her face sore and her legs scratched and bleeding. She wished she had put her trousers on instead of shorts, as her mother had wanted. Tears began to fill her eyes when she thought of her Mum.

'Who's going to help us? No one even knows where we are?' she cried. Tim stopped to comfort his little sister; both of them sobbed.

'Mum said that God is with us all the time, wherever we are. He knows where we are, so we are not lost. He knows everything, let's ask Him for help. Dear God, please help us!' Katie prayed, wiping her eyes.

'Yes, God, if you are listening, as Katie says, please help us,' Tim echoed, although he was not quite so convinced that God would help them. Why had He let the crash happen in the first place and allowed all these people to die!

The pair walked slowly on. Suddenly, the path turned to the right and started to go down steeply, really steeply. Tim grabbed the branches of the nearest tree as his feet were starting to slip. Katie could see he was frightened.

'What's wrong?' she shouted from behind.

'The path drops over this steep edge. I don't think we can go any further'.

'Listen!' yelled Katie. 'That sounds like a stream or river down there.'

'Yes, you're right, but it is too steep; we can't get down. It must be over a hundred metres and there's mist at the bottom,' Tim squeaked. 'I'm feeling sick. You know I don't like heights; we'll have to go back!'

'Go back where?' yelled Katie. 'We need water or we'll die like all the rest of the people on the plane. We have to go down!'

Katie was the strong one now. She looked around and saw that the path didn't go straight down the slope but round behind a big boulder. She walked carefully over and saw that at the side of the path were long strands of creepers woven together like pieces of cord. Someone had made these to act as a rope to climb down the slope. The strands looked quite worn in places so they must have been there a long time.

'Look Tim, over here! We can get down this way; we'll be alright,' Katie called.

Katie led the way down the narrow steep path. At first she was nervous but she began to relax when she realised it was no worse than walking on the beam in her gymnastics class. Katie loved gymnastics. Tim, too, was making good progress, more confident when he saw his little sister leading the way. Tim knew that had it not been for his sore ankle, he would be leading his sister!

It took a long time to reach the bottom of the ravine. But, sure enough, there was a river and a small clearing on the bank. Just at the back of the grassy area was a hut or, rather, the remains of a hut. The floor was a platform raised up on short wooden piers, five steps up from the ground. Half of the roof was missing but there was a place at the back of the hut that would offer some shelter for the night.

'I need a drink of water,' cried Katie. 'I'm so hot and thirsty. Do you think it would be safe to take water from the river? Dad said we should only drink bottled water when we are in South America because the tap water isn't good and we'll be sick, but I'm so thirsty now.'

'Me too! I'm going to dangle my feet at the edge of the river,' Tim said, slipping off his shoes and lowering his feet into the river. The coolness of the water made his sore ankle feel so much better.

'What about those small fish that'll eat you? They live in the Amazon rivers! Or crocodiles!' screamed Katie, as she imagined her brother being dragged into the river and disappearing forever.

'You mean piranha. Don't worry, silly! The water is clear here; I can see the bottom, and there are no fish here just now. They're not called crocodiles in the Amazon but camen and they only lie in the dark waters. Come and see for yourself,' Tim said confidently.

'What are we going to drink? What are we going to eat? I'm hungry!' Katie said, as she sat down beside Tim on the bank.

Tim thought for a minute wondering what his Uncle Hugh would do.

'We'll have to drink the river water. If we don't drink it, we'll die, and we'll have to drink a lot of water. Uncle Hugh told me a story about a soldier who had to be rescued by helicopter because he hadn't drunk enough water; it was on one of his missions in the jungle.'

'Tim, will they send a helicopter for us, to rescue us?' Katie asked.

'As soon as they know that the plane is late, they'll start looking for us. There will be planes and helicopters all over this area very soon,' Tim replied confidently.

'But how will they find us in the dark? You said it would be dark soon,' Katie questioned.

'They won't! We must stay here tonight. Look, the sun's almost setting. Let's have a drink then have a look in the hut,' Tim said firmly, trying to hide his own fear.

They both cupped their hands and lifted water to their mouths for several minutes. Katie washed her face, cleaning off the dried blood. Tim could see it had only been a small cut to her nose, probably from something that had fallen out of the overhead lockers. His arm was badly bruised but he could move it in every direction so he decided it was not broken, but his ankle was still very painful when he walked. He knew that if he had been at home his mother would have taken him to hospital for an X-ray, just in case it was broken.

Katie helped Tim up the steps into the hut. There was nothing much left inside: a broken three-legged stool and some ash piled on the floor where a fire had been. Something caught Katie's eye as she went to the back of the room; up in the rafters was a pot jammed in-between the beams. Tim reached up and pulled it down.

'We could wash this and use it to carry water from the river. You go Katie, before it gets dark, so we can have water for during the night. But be careful; the water is dark and deep away from the bank. Don't slip!'

Tim carried on looking around their new home. He spied an old piece of blanket lying in the corner. When he lifted it with the end of his stick, a huge spider crawled out from under the rag! He shot back towards the door with a yell!

Katie was coming up the steps with the water when she heard Tim scream. 'What is it? What is it?' she shouted.

'I think it's a tarantula! You know … the big poisonous spiders. I frightened it off though. It's gone over the edge of the floor and now it's on the ground crawling into the jungle,' Tim said reassuringly.

'I wish I'd seen it. My teacher was talking about jungle spiders on the last day of term. These big hairy spiders can damage your eyes. They can make you go blind, as well as bite, you know,' Katie said, as she laid down the pot of water.

'How can a spider make a person go blind?' Tim said, doubting his sister.

'If you get too close, they flick their hairy legs. The hairs have barbs on them like fish hooks, so if they get stuck on the front of the eyeball they're very painful and hard to remove,' Katie explained.

'I hope there are no snakes in here, Tim. Let's look all around and up in the rafters before it gets dark,' Katie suggested, as she started to search the room, straining her eyes into the dark corners.

Tim joined in the task. In the corner he found a piece of wood that looked like a paddle. It was just over a metre and a half long, with a huge leaf-shaped bit at the bottom. Nothing like a paddle he had seen before, but what else could it be? Maybe there's a canoe near here he thought. Probably unlikely, as the native people would never leave a canoe; they are too valuable and take so long to make. A canoe is the pride and joy of every village man, just like a flashy car back in the UK. But, if there was a boat, they could float down the river. All the rivers on this side of the mountains run into the Amazon. His geography teacher had told the class about the Amazon region last year. He had loved learning all about the jungle, the people and a little about how they lived. If they could drift down river, they would be bound to come to a village or town where they could get help. He didn't say anything to Katie as he didn't want to dash her hopes about being rescued by helicopter. This was definitely plan B.

'I'm hungry, what are we going to eat?' Katie grumbled.

'We'll have to wait till morning now. It's too dark to leave the hut. Come on let's sit over in this corner. At least there's a roof over our heads and we've some water.' Tim shuffled over to the corner and lowered himself carefully onto the floor, trying not to hurt his ankle or arm.

Katie sat down beside him, sliding up to lean on his shoulder.

'Do you think it's going to be completely dark? It's much noisier outside now. The birds are chattering loudly, and listen to all the frogs; what a noise they make!', Katie marvelled. '… What's that strange call? Are there lions in the jungles here?' Katie whimpered.

Tim put his arm round his little sister. 'No, there are no lions in South America. The jungle comes alive at night. That's why we're not going out of this hut till morning. The sky is quite clear just now, so the moon might shine tonight.' Tim didn't tell his sister about the big cats such as jaguars that did live in South America or the blood sucking bats he had learned about while surfing the internet recently. Actually, he was too frightened himself to talk about them, just in case some of them came round their hut tonight.

'Tim, do you remember we asked God to help us when we left the burning plane? He has! Look we have a house and water. I'm going to ask Him to keep the bad animals away from us tonight.' Katie prayed, 'Dear God, please, please, keep the snakes and spiders away.'

Katie was exhausted and fell asleep quickly. Tim wanted to stay awake to look after his sister. He thought over everything that had happened that day; he even pinched himself to make sure he was not having a nightmare. How could all these people be dead? Why did we survive? If we hadn't moved from our front seats to the back of the plane to sit with Aunt Susie, we would be dead! If the passengers who had booked those seats at the back hadn't missed the flight, we wouldn't have been able to move seats at all! Tim shuddered as he thought of what might have been.

Tears filled his eyes when he thought about his Mum and Dad being told that the plane had crashed. Dad would know that they were bound to be alive. He would come looking for them. He would never give up. In the morning there would be helicopters all over the place and by tomorrow night they would be back in Lima and he would be surfing the net on his new laptop. He did not want to go to Scotland anyway. He wanted to be at home when Uncle Hugh came to visit next week. Dad and Uncle Hugh were going into the jungle on a wildlife trip and Tim hoped to persuade his Dad to let him go with them on the expedition.

Katie nudged Tim in the ribs. 'What's that?' she whispered.

CHAPTER 2

Shattered Lives!

Sarah knew there was a problem when Alex arrived in her office before six o'clock. He always worked late. Even though his office was in the tower block across the street from her own, she could count on one hand the number of times he had been able to give her a lift home since they moved to Peru three years ago. Sarah accepted reluctantly that, as a senior Executive of Petro-Explore NMW, an oil exploration company, he would always be busy. She had never liked the long office hours that Peruvians work or the short holidays. Fortunately, as she was a part-time editor of a woman's magazine, she had time for the children. Alex, on the other hand, hardly ever saw them. He didn't seem to realise that Tim was a teenager now, and needed more time than ever with his Dad. Katie loved her father dearly, but even she had complained that he was never around at weekends to take her pony riding. Alex had changed into a workaholic since he came to Lima, and Sarah knew she would have to tackle him about it soon, or the entire family was going to suffer.

But this was not the time to challenge him about his excessive working. The look on Alex's face made Sarah shudder.

'What's wrong? What is it?' she asked anxiously.

Alex tried to speak, but his words just stuck in his mouth.

He tried again. 'I've just received a phone call from Aero Inca. They have lost contact with the flight somewhere over the jungle, and it's now overdue in Bogotá by an hour.

'No, no it can't be! My babies. My babies!' Sarah screamed. Alex grabbed her and held her tight as she wept into his shoulder.

'We must go to the airport to see if there is any more news. Quickly, I have a car waiting downstairs,' Alex helped Sarah gather her things.

The Lima traffic was as awful as ever, cars honking at any excuse. Over-laden lorries with goods, and often people, frequently changed lanes without any warning.

'Señor Baxter, there are still road works on the main road to the airport,' the driver shouted through to Alex. 'It would be best to take a detour. I've heard from other drivers that, at this time of night, there can be delays of up to two hours.'

'Just get us there as fast as you can!' snapped Alex.

The car turned off the main road and travelled through poorly lit streets, over rough bumps. Sarah could see lots of people hanging about on the street corners, especially groups of boys, scruffy looking kids. Alex's bodyguard in the front seat seemed tense. All foreign high-ranking executives had a body guard in Peru; too many had been kidnapped in the past few years.

'What's wrong Pablo?' asked Alex.

'I don't like coming this way, even at this time of night. Last week another of our cars was set upon at traffic lights by the "piranha" of this area.'

'Did you say "piranha"?' Sarah questioned.

'Si Señora Baxter, they are street boys, kids who live wild on the streets. They hunt in gangs, robbing and sometimes killing people. The police are supposed to keep them under control but there are so many of them.'

'They are just vermin!' Alex snapped. 'I don't know why the government doesn't deal with them once and for all. Only last week, one of my juniors was robbed by them. He ended up in hospital with a fractured skull.'

'Alex, that's a terrible thing to say! They're so young. This country is really getting to you, to all of us! Why did we ever come?' Sarah sobbed.

'Never mind all that! We have to get to the airport as fast as we can. The traffic is lighter in this area. José, do not stop at traffic lights, just slow down,' Alex instructed the driver.

The Mercedes pulled up at the VIP entrance to the airport after a rather tense journey through the back streets of Lima. The Baxters were met by a high-ranking police officer who escorted them to the airport manager's office.

'Señor, Señora Baxter, I am so sorry. I understand your two children are on the flight with your sister, Señora,' the manager, Señor De Silva, greeted them. He took them, immediately, over to a large wall map.

'The last contact the air-traffic controllers had was here,' he said, pointing to the map. 'Right here in the jungle near to the township of Intuto, on the Tigre River. We think the plane has come down in this area, which is very remote with no roadways at all. We have aircraft up looking for the plane already, but we are not optimistic. I think it will be tomorrow before we hear any news.'

'Does anyone know what has happened? Why has there been no radio contact? Maybe it's only a communications fault,' Sarah blurted hysterically.

'Señora, the traffic controllers have lost the plane on the radar. It's not just radio contact that has been lost, I am so sorry,' Señor De Silva said softly.

Sarah began to sob. Alex was fighting to control his tears as well.

'You can stay here tonight if you would like to. If there is any news, you will find out straight away,' the manger offered, as he showed the couple through to his large private lounge, which overlooked the main terminal.

'I'll have my secretary organise some food and refreshments for you,' he closed the door and left Tim and Katie's parents alone, trying to come to terms with all they had just been told.

'So, if they have survived the crash, they will be lost in the jungle. Is that what he is saying? Is that what he is saying? No, no please God do not take my children!' Sarah sobbed.

Alex put his arm round his wife. 'You're jumping to conclusions. Maybe a skilful pilot might have been able to find somewhere to put the stricken plane down. Perhaps in a clearing, you've heard how much of the jungle is being cleared for timber, and so there are lots of survivors, including our kids. We must not give up hope!'

Alex realised his comments were wishful thinking. He knew what the jungle was really like, wall to wall dense forest, and, although timber operations were under way near the Brazilian border, he didn't know of any up in the region of the crash. He knew he was grasping at straws.

'We must contact Hugh so he can go and speak to your father Alex, and I'll have to phone my brother Bob so he can go to the farm and tell my parents. It would be terrible if any of the grandparents put on the TV and heard the news that way. Your father will know the flight numbers and everything; you know what he's like with the internet now that he's retired. Hugh is home on leave just now isn't he?' Sarah asked.

'Yes, he's just home from Iraq. You're right, it would be terrible for them to find out from the media. What time will it be in the UK? ... It is seven thirty here, so it'll be around one thirty in the morning back home but I think I'll phone anyway; the morning news is bound to feature something like this,' Alex said as he reached for the telephone.

'Hugh. Hi Hugh, it's me, Alex. I know it's the middle of the night! The children's flight has come down, probably somewhere over the jungle in north of Peru, although we are not sure exactly yet. I wish we knew more. ... No we don't know about survivors, just that they have lost all contact both radio and radar. It's the not knowing that is so hard,' Alex's voice started to waver.

'Would you drive over and speak to Mum and Dad, we don't want them finding out on the television. ... We're at the airport so we can get any news straight away. Thanks Hugh. ... Yes, I'll ring back as soon as we hear anything. We can't do anything till they locate the wreckage. ... Is there? Thanks I'll remember that, a commando unit. But, as I say, until they pinpoint the plane there is nothing any of us can do here. ... No, the Peruvian authorities have moved in to action. ... Speak soon. Bye.' Alex hung up.

'Hugh will go over to the cottage straight away and wake Granny and Gramps. They'll take it hard. He says that he will come to Lima as soon as he can. You know he's really fond of our kids, I suppose it's because he has none of his own. He says that there are some UK commandos on exercise in the Amazon basin in Columbia, somewhere due north of Iquitos he thinks, might be worth remembering.

'Oh! How I wish we knew a bit more,' Alex said, holding his head in his hands.

'Alex, would you phone Bob? I'll not manage to ...' Sarah mumbled.

'It's alright Sarah. Of course I'll contact him,' Alex agreed as he reached over to comfort his wife.

Another sad phone call was made. Bob agreed to go straight over to the farm.

Alex and Sarah sat in the office for at least two hours before the manager returned with two officers from the Peruvian air force. They explained how they planned to step up the search at first light with at least five fixed-wing aircraft from the air force base just north-east of Lima and three helicopters from the Iquitos base. The officers were very pessimistic about finding anyone alive. They did think there was a slim chance the pilot had found some sort of clearing, but in this area, one of the most remote in the Peruvian jungle, clearings were few and far between. They hoped that the signal from the plane's black box would help locate the crash site.

Alex suggested to Sarah that maybe she would be better to go home and rest as it would be some time before there was any news, but she refused to leave.

During the morning, they watched the news reports. All the graphic details were discussed, including the number of passengers, the severe thunder storms over the region and the possibility of electronic failure if struck by lightning.

The efforts of the rescuers were hampered by bad weather in the area. It was just after midday before they heard anything more; a preliminary search had failed to show any sign of the stricken plane, but the spotter aircraft would continue systematically searching the area until nightfall.

All Sarah and Alex could do was sit and wait.

CHAPTER 3

Only Dressed in Shorts!

'What noise? I didn't hear anything different. The insects are making an awful noise that's all,' Tim said trying to get himself comfy. 'Get some sleep Katie.'

'Listen there it is again! There's something outside, down by the river.'

'I hear it,' Tim struggled to his feet and peered out. It was a beautiful moonlit night, the moon and stars glistening on the river. Tim couldn't believe his eyes, there was a big cat and her cubs silhouetted in the night, drinking at the water's edge.

'Shh! There's a mother with her cubs down at the river. She mustn't find us! I think it's a jaguar.' Tim motioned his little sister to the back of the hut and grabbed his stick, while he continued to watch through the empty door frame. Katie cowered at the back, too frightened to move even the tiniest muscle, in case the cat heard them and came looking!

Tim was so stiff and sore by the time the jaguar moved away. He watched her as she walked slowly back into the jungle, her young skipping playfully behind her, paying no attention at all to the hut.

'Phew! Thank goodness she didn't pick up our scent. You go back to sleep for a while Katie and I'll keep watch, then you will have to be 'on watch' while I sleep. Have another drink before you lie down, Uncle Hugh said that people in the jungle have to drink plenty of water to survive,' Tim sounded more relaxed now.

Katie fell into a deep sleep so Tim didn't waken her. In the early hours he too drifted off to sleep, exhausted.

Katie was the first to stir as the bright sunlight streamed through the door of the hut. The birds were in full, beautiful, song. The jungle once more became alive with the sounds of hundreds of species of wildlife as they greeted the morning. Fortunately, the insects were fewer than the night before as most mosquitoes come out at night.

Katie tiptoed quietly passed Tim and went outside to look around. When they had arrived at the hut the night before, they only had a few minutes before darkness. Katie wanted to look around and see if she could find anything useful. Down at the water's edge she could see some logs tied together at the side of the river. Perhaps this was where the people who lived here used to wash their clothes, she thought. She had seen something like it on a television programme. Under the hut she could see another old pot that looked as if it had been on the fire, an old sandal and a piece of rope. Katie also found a path leading from the side of the hut down the hill back into the jungle. The path seemed quite clear so Katie set out. Maybe I can find some fruit to eat she thought. As she turned the corner she could see that the path led down to another part of the river so she went on to explore. As Katie approached the water's edge, she saw what looked like a canoe sticking out from the undergrowth, but it was just out of her reach. She hurried back up the path to tell Tim.

He was awake and just about to take a drink from the water in the hut.

'Oh Gross! The water is covered in dead insects. Look Katie, there are hundreds of them, it's disgusting! You should have put something over the pot to keep them out,' Tim said trying not to be sick.

'Like what?' Katie replied slightly out of breath.

'Where have you been? I told you to stay close?' Tim demanded.

'Tim, I think there is a canoe down by the river. I could just make it out in the weeds, but I couldn't reach it. How's your ankle?'

'Cool, a canoe! That would be great! We could row down the river and find help,' Tim rushed to the door, but yelped with pain. He had forgotten about his sore ankle!

'Use your stick stupid!' shouted Katie. 'It's not going to get better just like that, remember when Mum sprained her ankle playing tennis? She had a crutch for nearly a month.'

'Don't cheer me up! Come on show me this boat!' Tim hobbled down the path to where Katie had found the canoe.

'I'll have to wade into the river and grab the end of the canoe,' Tim said thoughtfully. 'The river is very fast though.'

'I know. Wait Tim, and don't do anything, I'll be back in a minute,' Katie advised, and then rushed back up the hill, scrambled under the hut, remembering to watch out for the tarantula, and grabbed the rope.

'Where did you get that? It could be very useful. I'll tie it round my waist and then to that tree. It should be long enough to let me walk out and just stretch to the canoe.' Tim tied the rope with the best knots he knew from the sea cadets. He didn't want to be swept off into the river and provide a fresh meal for the piranha. Gingerly, Tim stepped into the water, trying not to put too much weight on his bad ankle, but he was quickly out of his depth and had to swim. The current was so strong; he had to swim at his best.

'Keep going, Tim, you're almost there!' Katie yelled encouragement from the bank. Two more metres and Tim was there holding onto the canoe looking very proud of himself.

Katie cheered!

Tim clambered into the canoe and started to pull on the rope. The canoe gently pulled free of the reeds and he guided it to the bank.

The children were delighted. The boat seemed to be sound, with no holes! When Katie looked into the boat she couldn't believe her eyes; under the seat neatly coiled up was fishing line.

'Look Tim a fishing line. We won't be hungry now!'

Tim smiled as he securely tied the canoe to the tree.

'That must be the oar we found in the hut.' He said. 'I wonder why the boat was left here?'

'Maybe the fisherman went back to the main village,' Katie suggested.

'If that's so, how did he get there?'

'He left in a bigger canoe, with his family.'

'I don't think so. This canoe has been carved out of one big tree trunk. It probably took someone a long time using only a few simple tools. They showed us a film one day in class. No one would spend hours making something as good and useful as this and leave it here to rot. There has to be another reason,' Tim argued.

'I'm hungry now, what are we going to eat?' Katie asked.

'Let's see if we can find some fruit,' Tim suggested.

The two set off down the river bank as there seemed to be a way through, as long as they stayed close to the bank. After about fifty metres, Tim spotted a banana tree. He could see the fruits high up in the branches.

'We'll never be able to get at those,' Katie moaned.

'No! Even if my leg was OK, I wouldn't be able to get up there,' Tim replied. 'Uncle Hugh told me that not all bananas grow on tall trees, so let's keep looking for some lower down.'

Slightly further on – success! Bananas were hanging only about two metres off the ground.

'I'll give you a leg up Katie and you can knock them down'

'OK, but don't drop me,' she said nervously.

The hungry youngsters quickly devoured three fruits apiece!

They set off back to the hut carrying the remainder of the bunch. Half way back, Tim noticed another path leading off into the bush.

'Let's have a look along here, Katie.'

Tim hobbled ahead as Katie carried the fruit on her shoulder.

'Ahhhh…..' screamed Tim scrambling back to Katie.

'What is it? What is it?' Katie yelled to her brother.

'There's a body … a skeleton sitting up against a tree through there,' Tim shouted.

'Are you sure? No! You're not kidding me. I can see by the look on your face,' Katie acknowledged.

The children hurried back to the riverside and flopped down on the bank.

'It must've been the fisherman. I wonder what happened to him. There were 'just bones' wearing a pair of shorts. He must have been dead a long time,' Tim concluded.

'That must've been awful to see! Glad it wasn't me who found it,' Katie moaned.

Tim was still shaking ten minutes later. Katie could see her big brother had been really scared.

'We need to get away from here. I hate it! That dead man – he's frightened both of us. Why are there no helicopters? It has been light for at least two hours now,' Katie began to cry.

Tim pulled himself together and put his arm round Katie.

'Come on little one, let's get out of the sun and eat some food. We'll need to change the water as well. Just forget about the body.' Tim was trying to reassure himself as much as Katie.

Katie's right! Where are the helicopters he thought? They must know where the plane came down by now.

The heat of the sun had become much greater and the children were glad to be back in the shade of the hut.

'I think we should stay here for another night Katie. We're not far from the crash site so we are bound to hear them searching. We have food, water and shelter, so we need to stay put!' Tim said assertively.

'How will they know we're down here? Remember we came down that steep slope. I don't think they're ever going to find us!' Katie snivelled.

'Don't cry Katie. Dad and Uncle Hugh will never leave us in the jungle,' Tim said confidently.

'But how do they know we're alive. The front of the plane where we were supposed to be sitting has been completely destroyed. You saw it after the crash,' Katie pointed out.

'Dad will know. He will sense we are alive! Although, we need to have some way of signalling that we are here, but how?'

'You could take off your white T-shirt and we could wave it at the helicopter if it came nearby,' Katie suggested.

'No, that'll never work,' Tim moaned.

We have no way to start a fire, so that's no use as an idea, Tim thought. Just then, he looked up at the wall of the hut.

'Look Katie! There's a small mirror jammed in the door frame!' Tim struggled to his feet.

'It should be big enough, but there's a bit broken … Careful it's sharp! We could use this to catch the sun and the pilot will see the reflection. Yeah that'll work,' Tim was getting enthusiastic now.

'Couldn't we use the mirror to set dry grass on

fire? I saw them do that on a film once. It was about a shipwrecked family trying to survive on a desert island,' Katie suggested.

'Why didn't I think of that? Let's have some more fruit then we'll try an experiment!'

Katie went down to the river to collect some fresh water, but she kept looking along the path to where the corpse was found, just in case something or someone moved.

'What do you think happened to that man, Tim?' she asked, when she returned.

'Maybe he died of malaria, many people in the jungle die of malaria.'

'What is that? Katie asked. 'How do you get malaria?'

'Remember the mosquitoes that were flying around last night, and the dead ones in the water pot?' Tim reminded her.

'Yes,' she nodded.

'When they bite you, they suck your blood and they put tiny bugs into you. These bugs make you really unwell a few days later, with very a high fever,' Tim said, sounding very knowledgeable.

'Can you get treatment?'

'Yes, there are medicines, but not out here in the jungle,' Tim answered. 'That's why so many people die from malaria.'

'How come you know so much about it? What is it called … malarye?' Katie wondered.

'Malaria. The last time Uncle Hugh was here, he told me about it. When he was in the jungle with his marines, they all had to take tablets to stop them catching the disease. Even then, some of his soldiers became ill with other illnesses caused by insect bites.'

'I've some bites on my legs from last night. Look!' Katie pointed out her bites to her big brother.

'Those are just little bites. Mosquito bites have a blood

centre where the mosquito has bitten into you,' Tim advised.

'You mean like these here on my arms?'

'Yes like those. I have them too. There's nothing we can do about it. We don't have any mosquito nets or insect spray to keep off the little beasties. Remember we used nets and spray 'stuff' when we were in Africa last year on holiday?'

'Yes, Mum kept putting sunscreen and that horrible smelly 'stuff' on us every five minutes, it seemed. We don't have any sunscreen here though; we must try not to get burnt,' Katie sounded worried.

'Mum was worried that we would get skin cancer if we had sunburn. Her friend's husband died last year of skin cancer and it really freaked Mum out,' Tim remembered.

'When will Mum and Dad find us Tim? I'm frightened. That body has really scared me.' Katie said trying not to cry.

Tim tried to comfort his little sister, but all the time he was thinking about the skeleton as well.

How had that man died, he wondered. Perhaps he had been bitten by a snake, or injured in a fight. But who would he fight with here? Maybe he died of old age. Yeah that's it; he probably died of old age.

'Katie that man most likely died of old age, you know,' Tim suggested.

'You're just saying that so as not to frighten me, it might have been a snake bite, or a vampire bat for all we know!' Katie argued.

'Come on Katie, cheer up, and let's see if we can start a fire with this mirror. Tim grabbed the mirror and clambered gently down the steps of the hut.

CHAPTER 4

Learning Curve!

'Look it's smouldering, Tim. Blow it gently. Now it'll light.'

Sure enough, the dry grass burst into flames. No sooner was it alight than the children were throwing water on it to put the flames out!

'Right Katie, that's worked OK. Now all we need to do is prepare a fire here, out in the open, so if we hear any planes or helicopters we'll be able to light it,' Tim said sounding very confident now.

Tim and Katie worked together for about half an hour piling up bits of dry stick and grass. They checked the undergrowth every time before grabbing the grass, just in case some viper lay curled up ready to pounce.

'That should be enough,' Katie said, as she flopped down in the shade. 'I'm so hot!'

'It's almost midday now, we should get in out of the sun before we get sun stroke,' Tim said, hobbling towards the hut.

'What's sunstroke?' Katie asked.

'I don't know, but Mum used to say if we didn't get out of the sun we would get sunstroke. I think it's when you get so hot that you become ill and have to go to hospital.'

'It is very hot now and I am hungry again. What's for lunch?' Katie asked.

'What do you think Katie? I bet you can't guess!'

'Bananas! Great they're my favourite!' Katie said cheekily.

'When it gets a bit cooler, I'll try to fix up the fishing line, and then maybe we can have fish for tea,' Tim said optimistically.

'What are you going to use for bait … banana?' Katie asked.

The two children sat down on the floor of the hut eating their fruit. 'Tim, what is that wrapped round the rafters, over there at the back?' Katie said, pointing to a bundle tied round a beam.

'I don't know. How come we didn't see it before?'

'I suppose last night it was too dark, and in the morning that part of the hut was in the shade. Do you think it's a hammock? Usually the Peruvians wrap these into tight rolls,' Katie suggested.

Tim knocked it loose with his stick; sure enough it was a hammock.

'I'm going to sleep in it tonight,' Katie asserted.

'I don't think so! I think it is big enough for both of us. Me at one end, and you at my feet! If we manage to do that we won't be bothered by ants and other creepy crawlies,' Tim explained.

'Listen, Tim! Listen!' Katie ran outside. 'It's an aeroplane!'

Both children rushed out of the hut to their fire. They tried to light it with the mirror but it was so slow. Eventually the grass started to smoulder but they couldn't see or hear the plane any more.

'Do you think he saw us?' Katie asked anxiously.

'No, I think he was too high. I think that was a normal plane crossing to the north. Come on, let's get some rest,' Tim said, as he climbed slowly back into the hut and flopped down on the floor. He relived the last few minutes in his mind. Why couldn't we have been quicker? Surely that was a rescue plane, but Katie mustn't know; she'll start crying again. She's been very brave for a ten-year-old.

'Tim, I know where we can get some bait,' Katie said excitedly. 'Remember all those insects on top of the water container from last night? Where did you throw the water?'

'Over the edge of the floor, at the back of the hut, onto the dirt. That's a great idea. Some of the beasties were quite big.'

The pair crawled to the edge of the hut at the back and looked down onto the ground; sure enough, the carcasses were lying there. Some of the dead insects were being recycled, eaten by ants. The children would have to grab the bigger ones fast, before they were devoured by the greedy attackers.

'Katie, you'll have to go and pick them up. My ankle is sore again. Watch those ants though,' Tim said, rather naughtily as he knew that Katie hated creepy crawlies.

'OK,' Katie replied, with a false self-confidence. 'I'll go right now.'

'Watch out for the tarantula!' Tim shouted after her, as she disappeared out of the doorway.

Katie bravely crouched down at the back of the hut and lifted the first big, dead, black, horrible insect into her left hand. She dropped it straight away and shook with disgust! She tried again. This time she knew what it felt like to have a tickly, frightening creature in the palm of her hand but she knew how important it was to collect the insects if they were to catch any fish… so this time she held on tight! One, two, three, little beasties safely in her hand.

Katie returned triumphantly to Tim to show off her prizes. He tore a small piece of material from his t-shirt and wrapped the insects in it carefully.

'Just in case we lose them,' he said.

It was now very hot, and they were both feeling very tired.

'Let's see if we can get into this hammock,' Tim suggested.

Enthusiastically, and without thinking, Katie jumped in first but landed right out the other side, feeling rather stupid. Tim laughed so much tears started running down his cheeks. Katie was upset at first but then saw the funny side and joined in the laughter.

'You're so smart! Let's see you try,' she said cheekily.

'I think I saw one of my friends do it like this.'

Tim straddled the hammock, sat down then lifted up his feet.

'That looked easy,' Katie said. 'But how do I get in now?

'Just put your leg over my feet and I'll pull you in,' Tim said reassuringly.

Katie lifted her leg over the end of the hammock and Tim pulled, but rather hard so that Katie lost her balance and both of them spun round the hammock and landed on the floor!

Laughing at themselves, Katie said, 'I think we should just sleep on the floor.'

'No, let's try again,' Tim said.

This time they succeeded. They found the hammock very comfortable and before long they both fell fast asleep.

Tim woke first. Two parrots in the near trees were making such a noise he thought they were in the hut with them! He struggled out of the hammock to see if he could see the birds. Katie was wakened by Tim's toe catching her nose!

'Hey! That was sore!'

'Sorry, I'm trying to see the birds,' he said cheerfully.

'Look Katie, they aren't parrots but toucans. Their colours are great, bright yellow and red.'

'Oh, they're cool!' Katie stood beside Tim just watching the birds calling to one another. 'Look there's a beautiful blue bird on the other branch. Is that a macaw? It's a gorgeous colour.'

Suddenly the birds flew off.

'I wonder what startled them?' Katie whispered, as if whispering would bring them back again.

'Look Tim! On the next tree. Something moved. It's a monkey, and behind it there's another one! They're so tiny. I wonder if they are marmosets,' Katie pointed excitedly to the trees just next to where the toucans were.

'Do you think big monkeys eat toucans?' Katie continued.

'No, how would they ever catch one? I suppose, if one had a broken wing and couldn't fly, then maybe,' Tim said thoughtfully.

The children watched the monkeys for ages; they seemed to be a happy family group. Finally, they moved off into the jungle.

Later in the afternoon, the clouds began to darken, and then came the rains. Heavy tropical rain! Soon streams of water were flowing from under the hut into the river. The kids were delighted though, as they danced under the downpour cooling off.

Thoroughly soaked, hair dripping but refreshed, they returned to the shelter of the house.

'We could collect some of the rainwater to drink. It's bound to be clean. I'll get the pot,' Katie suggested.

'Yeah, OK.' Tim was busy now trying to find the fishing line to see if he could attach the insects.

'Where did we put the fishing line Katie?'

'It's still in the front of the boat.'

The children had left the boat on a piece of muddy bank. As Tim walked down the now treacherous slope towards the canoe, he slipped on the wet mud landing in a heap alongside the boat. He quickly tried to grab a fallen tree with his right hand to stop himself sliding into the river but in doing so he rolled over the log. He disturbed a thin black and green snake, which was about a metre long. It looked straight at him. Tim couldn't move! Katie came out of the hut and saw Tim lying absolutely still … petrified!

'Tim, what is …?'

He nodded with his head towards the log. Katie tiptoed over to Tim and realised that he was in grave danger. Without hesitating, she picked up a branch and used it to flick the snake into the river. Katie did this so quickly the snake had no time to strike. Tim rolled away, scrambled to his feet and hobbled back to the hut, terrified.

Katie looked carefully round the canoe with her big stick to check for more snakes. Once she was happy there were no more horrible creatures, she picked up the fishing line and returned quickly to the hut. Tim was still shaking.

'That was incredibly brave Katie,' Tim said drying his eyes. 'You saved my life.'

'I don't suppose every snake bite is poisonous, but in the jungle here they probably are. A good job that stick was handy and that flicking it worked! Here's the fishing line,' Katie said, as she handed Tim the line. 'It seems a bit cooler now that it's raining, but it's really cloudy and misty. It will make it hard for the rescue planes to see the wreckage,' Katie continued. 'Do you think it will take them long to find us Tim?'

'If the weather improves, hopefully they will find us tomorrow,' Tim answered, as he tried to fix the bait.

CHAPTER 5

White-knuckle Ride

Tim eventually managed to tie one of the flies onto the hook, but it was not easy.

'Ok, we're ready to go fishing!' he said triumphantly.

'The river is really fast, Tim! What if we cannot paddle back to the bank? We'll be swept down river,' Katie cautioned.

'No, it'll be alright. I've canoed before. If you want something other than bananas to eat, we'd better get a move on before it's dark. We probably have two hours, so come on let's get going.'

'Why can't we fish from the river bank, here?' Katie asked innocently.

'Because I think we are much more likely to catch some fish over at the other bank, where the water seems to be a bit slower and deeper. We can drop the line from the boat and it'll drift behind us, but if we try throwing it from the bank it will get caught in the trees,' Tim replied, a bit annoyed at his sister's lack of faith in his decision.

'Katie, run and get the paddle. It's in the hut.'

The river was fast flowing because it was in a deep gorge.

Over millions of years it had carved out the steep ravine that the young survivors had clambered down from the crash site. From where the children were in the clearing, it was only about twenty metres to the other bank. The jungle came right up to the bank on the other side, with the branches overhanging the river.

'Katie, you'll have to push the canoe into the water as I'll have to get in first because of my ankle,' Tim suggested, as Katie handed him the paddle.

The pair untied the canoe and pushed it into the water, and then Tim managed to get in without too much difficulty. He used the paddle to keep the canoe by the bank as Katie jumped in.

'Steady!' Tim shouted. 'You almost tipped me out!'

Before they knew it, the canoe was in the middle of the river being carried by the strong current. Tim was doing his best to steer the boat to the other bank but the river was far too strong for him. Within a few minutes they were disappearing round a bend in the river, and they could no longer see the clearing, or the hut that had sheltered them the night before.

'Tim! Look what you've done!' Katie screamed at her brother. 'I knew we should have stayed on the bank!' Katie started to cry.

'Oh shut up, you little wimp. How was I supposed to know, that the river was this fast!' Tim said, trying to conceal the panic in his voice.

For half an hour the terrified youngsters were carried helplessly in the river. Tim kept trying to steer the canoe to the bank, but it was hopeless; the current was just too powerful. It had never been like this when he was canoeing in the sea cadets; he had even passed his first three canoe badges. Suddenly, he noticed that the river was narrowing even more, and the water was swirling round the boat. The sound of the river was growing louder and louder. It was hard to hear the jungle above the noise of the river. Tim could feel his heart starting to pound in his chest as he realised what was happening. Rapids!

'Hang on Katie! It's going to be rough!' he yelled.

Katie was gripping the sides of the boat with both hands, her face white with fear. She, too, had worked out what was coming next. The canoe was moving faster and faster, twisting and turning as it found its way down through the rapids. At one moment it was almost up in the air, then it was plunging deep into the water; the children were almost thrown overboard! Katie was screaming. Tim was trying his very best to keep the canoe away from the huge boulders that rose up out of the river bed, like giant knuckles ready to smash their little boat. Suddenly, Tim realised that the river was about to disappear in front of them over a waterfall. He tried to paddle backwards, but he didn't have the strength to overcome the current. The canoe leapt through the air, turned over and threw its occupants out into a deep pool of very peaceful water. Katie surfaced first. She managed to swim to the canoe, which had miraculously turned itself and was gently floating ten metres away from her. Breathless, she clung onto the canoe but where was Tim?

'Tim, Tim where are you?' she cried frantically. Then she saw her brother clinging to a branch that overhung the water, slightly downriver from where she was.

Katie knew her brother would be terrified. Although he could swim, he hated it now, ever since one of his classmates drowned at the beach back in the UK. Since then, Tim had lost all confidence in the water.

'Tim, I'm coming!' Katie shouted, as she held onto the canoe and kicked with all her might downstream towards him.

Tim was so relieved to grab hold of the boat and heave himself inside again.

'Give me your hand, Katie, and I'll pull you in,' he said, regaining his cool.

'But wait! Grab hold of the tree again or we'll be off down the river once more,' Katie shouted.

The river was much calmer now, so between them they managed to get Katie back in the boat and throw the rope from the canoe over the branch. At least for now they were not going anywhere! The pair said nothing for at least five minutes, both just sat exhausted in the canoe.

Katie spoke first. 'We were almost killed. Tim, you did really well avoiding those huge rocks. If we had hit one of those, the canoe would have been smashed and us with it.'

Tim looked up to the waterfall. 'Look how the river has come over that waterfall, like a drain pipe going into a barrel. Just as well it was no higher than that or, you're right, we would have been killed! Mum would have said that our guardian angel was looking after us.'

'What are we going to do now?' Katie asked. 'We must have come a long way from the hut and the plane. We must have been on the river for over an hour. They'll never find us now! We really are lost!'

'Yes, and it's going to be dark very soon. We can't stay here because there's no clearing, and the jungle is so thick all the way to the river bank,' Tim noted.

'The river is quite gentle now though, we could paddle on for a little longer. Tim where is the paddle?'

'Oh no! It must have fallen out when we were tipped over. What are we going to do now? How many more things can go wrong?' Tim grumbled.

'We must look for the paddle, or find something else to use instead,' Katie asserted.

The pair scanned around the pool, down one side of the river as far as they could see then up the other. The light was fading fast making the task even more difficult.

'Look, Tim, just over by the waterfall. Look in the sand by the fallen branch. It must have landed with a real thud to get caught like that in the sand. But how will we get over to it? It's upstream from us by about twenty metres. The water is still and dark, so it's probably quite deep,' Katie said.

'I'll swim over and get it! I am the best swimmer,' Tim said bravely.

'What about your ankle?

'It's much better now, and a little water therapy will do it good. One of the ways football stars get back to fitness is by working out in the swimming pool.'

Before Katie could reply, Tim pulled off his T-shirt, dived into the water, quickly swam over and grabbed the paddle. Trophy in hand, he returned just as fast and clambered back into the boat.

Katie gave her brother a big hug, and then she screamed, 'Look Tim! Your back is covered in insects; they're everywhere.'

She picked up Tim's T-shirt and began knocking the insects off his back, but they landed in the canoe and started biting their feet. Both youngsters fought with the little beasts until all were squashed, but by then both had battle scars, Tim on his back and Katie on her legs and feet.

The children sat with heads bowed over their knees, recovering their strength. Any effort in the heat of this place exhausted them.

'I think we should tie the rope securely to the tree and sleep here for the night. At least we won't be bothered by a jaguar like last night. Maybe in the morning we'll be able to go on downstream and find a village,' Tim said, recovering his breath.

'We're too near the trees, Tim. I don't want to sleep here. Listen to the noise of the jungle. It's getting louder as darkness falls.

'Ow, I've just been bitten again. We're being attacked Katie. You're right, there are beasties everywhere. The same thing happened last night when it got dark. I think it'll be much worse if we're right under the trees. Snakes could climb into the canoe from the trees as well. Let's hope this rain stops soon and the clouds will clear. If it's a clear night we could go on down the river a bit further. We might find a clearing or a village,' suggested Tim.

'I suppose we've lost the fishing line as well?' Katie moaned.

'Oh! I forgot all about the line,' Tim turned round and felt over the back of the canoe. 'No. It's still here. I fastened it onto the boat when you went back to get the paddle.' Tim pulled up the line; amazingly, there was a small fish on the hook.

'Well that's not much use, is it?' Katie said, thinking of food.

'Yeah, it is! I've seen fishermen use smaller fish to catch bigger fish.'

'That's disgusting! But I'm hungry so … if it works,' Katie added.

As usual in the tropics, darkness came down as if someone had just switched off the light. The noise of the jungle grew louder as the creatures crept out of their hides to enjoy their time of day – night time. For them, it's safe, the time to look for food, away from predators of the sky and out of the heat of the sun, but for Tim and Katie it was a frightening time. Unable to see around them because of the pitch dark, every noise seemed threatening.

Was the stirring in the leaves above them an anaconda making his way from the high canopy down to the river? An anaconda can crush and eat a goat, so a couple of kids would just be a snack, Tim thought to himself. Then there were splashing noises a short distance from them, or so it seemed. Was that a camen dragging its prey to the deep to drown it before eating it?

'Katie, you're definitely right. We need to get out from under these trees. We can't stay here too long or the insects will eat us alive. Just pray that the rain will stop and the sky will clear. We need the moon to shine!' Tim said, with a slightly anxious voice.

'The rain has kept us cool for a while now, but I do wish it would stop soon. I think the mosquitoes will be really bad once the heavy rain dies down,' Katie added.

The two youngsters sat very still in the canoe. They were frightened that a sudden movement would tip them into the deep water, frightened that a camen might toss them out, frightened that a snake might slither in beside them.

'I'm really scared,' Katie said trying not to cry.

Soon the rain died down. At first, the moon only peeped through the clouds, but soon the sky cleared to allow the moon to light up the river, enough for the children to decide to move on downstream.

'Look, Tim, the stars are glinting on the river,' Katie said, in a happier voice.

'I've never seen the stars reflected in a river like that at home; it's so beautiful,' Tim observed. 'Hey what's that?'

'Where?' Katie asked.

'Look darting just above the river towards the other bank. I think it's a bat, picking up insects as it flies.'

'Tim! Look at the bright green dots flying around us. Look up there! Now beside you!'

'"Glow in the dark" insects. I wonder what they're called,' Tim said. 'Maybe they're fireflies.'

The canoe drifted gently on the current, requiring only a little steerage from Tim.

'I hope we can find a clearing where we can stop for the night, well away from these awful insects,' Tim said, frustrated by the little beasties.

'Yes, I hope so,' Katie replied, as she smacked another insect from her left arm.

It was good that the river flow was much slower now than during their terrifying ordeal of the afternoon, and this helped the children relax a little bit.

But where would the river take them? Further away from the crash site and therefore the rescue teams, but in the direction of the sea so closer to villages and help. How long would it be till they met another human being? A day, a week, or perhaps even longer? And where exactly were they?

CHAPTER 6

Just Waiting and Waiting!

Sarah watched with tears streaming down her cheeks as darkness fell over the long black runway and concrete terminal buildings of Lima airport. Alex tried to comfort her.

'When are they going to find them? Surely with all the sophisticated equipment on planes these days they would be able to find the wreckage quicker than this,' Sarah mumbled.

'It's a huge area they have to check. The lightning may have destroyed the plane's equipment before it came down, so it's possible they're looking in the wrong place,' Alex suggested.

Just at that, the office door opened and in came a grim looking air commodore, the same officer they had spoken to in the morning.

'I am sorry to say that we still have not located the plane. There is a storm blowing up north just now, coming down from the Andes into the Amazon region, so the visibility is very poor. It is now dark so we have had to call off the search till morning,' he reported.

'I have been looking at the map on the wall. Is it possible that the plane has 'limped' along further to the east, driven by the weather system which blew from the mountains? Perhaps a greater distance than first thought and is lying up near the Columbian border? After all, the report we received earlier indicated that visibility was good, but even after the first sweep there was no sign of the aircraft,' Alex commented to the officer.

The tall, greying officer who was wearing an impeccably smart air force uniform, approached the wall map, and tapped authoritatively on the chart.

'This is the position of the last radar contact we received. The area is part of the Amazon rainforest, and there is very thick jungle in this region. Wreckage will be difficult to spot. In answer to your question about the plane's position … Yes, it is possible that the plane is further to the east. We have considered the effect of the storm on the flight path. It is our intention to widen the search tomorrow. At first light we will send aircraft over this area of jungle here,' the commodore explained, as he pointed out the region to Alex and Sarah.

'Thank you for your help, Commodore. We realise that it is a difficult job,' Alex acknowledged, as he shook the officer's hand before he left the couple.

'I think we should go home now, Sarah; you are exhausted. We're not going to hear any news till tomorrow.'

'Yes, you're right. I'll not sleep, but at least I can lie down,' Sarah conceded.

The journey to their up-market apartment in the San Isidro district of Lima was surprisingly uneventful. Both were completely wrapped up in their thoughts as the car sped through rundown districts of the capital where the majority of the poor inhabitants lived. They were even oblivious to the bright lights of the smart restaurants and clubs as they approached their home.

Bruno was the doorman of their tower block. His white, gloved hand pulled open the door as usual for the Baxters but he must have realised something awful had happened to them, because his friendly, respectful, evening greeting was met with downcast eyes and sunken shoulders. He had missed the news when he left for work at six in the morning. He knew nothing of the plane crash.

Shortly after returning home, the phone rang. Sarah had been staring out of their top floor penthouse, over the city lights towards the Pacific Ocean, in deep thought. She jumped with fright. Alex answered the call.

'Hi Hugh, it's you… No we haven't heard any more news. The air force has searched the region where radar was lost and found nothing. I think I have persuaded them to look further east – you know how far some of these aircraft can glide even after they have lost power, especially with such a storm blowing from the mountains.

How are the old folks coping? … Yes, I thought Dad would know the flight number, even for a small company like Aero Inca … You're breaking up Hugh. What did you say? …

Yes, we would really appreciate it if you could come. Who knows, we might end up in the jungle ourselves at this rate! When will you get here? … Around six thirty tomorrow night, Lima time. Good. Give our love to Mum and Dad. Tell them not to give up hope. Thanks for coming Hugh. We need you … Bye for now.' Alex hung up the phone.

'What do you mean you might end up in the jungle?' Sarah asked.

'If there are signs that the children did survive we'll need to find them. The jungle is so vast the Peruvian army will only search for so long. When I was in the marines, I led many exercises in the jungle in Belize. I haven't forgotten about life in the jungle.'

'Alex that was over ten years ago!' Sarah said in disbelief.

'I'm still quite fit, you know that. Besides, Hugh will be coming with me – but it might not come to that.' Alex paused looking out of the window into the large private grounds surrounding their apartment building, remembering the times he, Tim and Katie had played football on the grass. Katie loved football as much as her brother. Only last week she was out there playing.

'I'll never rest till I find them or someone can prove to me beyond doubt that they didn't survive.' Alex's voice began to quiver. Sarah ran over to comfort *him* this time.

'They'll find them. I know they will. I just know in my heart they're alive.'

Alex and Sarah tried to get some rest, but sleep just wouldn't come. Around midnight, Sarah rose and went downstairs to watch the news. There was nothing she didn't know already. She kept flitting between channels to see if any reporter knew anything more, but there was no new development. Exhausted, she fell asleep on the settee, her arms wrapped tightly round a cushion.

Alex found Sarah still asleep. He could see by her face that she must have cried herself to sleep. He bent down and kissed his wife gently on the forehead.

An hour later, Sarah woke up with a start.

'What time is it? Is there any news?' she asked anxiously.

'No, nothing as yet. I don't expect we'll hear anything for a while. I've made some coffee. Would you like some?' Alex asked.

Sarah's best friend Amy came round for a while to offer support. Later on Pastor Jim came over. He had heard the news on his flight down from Seattle where he had been home on leave. Jim was more than their pastor; he was a personal friend. The Baxter family had come to love and respect him over the three years they had lived in Peru. He listened to Alex's account of the tragedy so far. By this time Sarah couldn't bear to talk about anything. She just sat quietly on the settee with her legs drawn up under her, still cuddling the cushion.

As Jim stood up to leave, having felt quite useless, Sarah asked in a very soft voice, 'Jim would you pray for us, for the kids. I just cannot find the words.'

Alex said nothing. His mind was full of thoughts, angry thoughts. He couldn't pray; he was too angry with God for letting this terrible thing happen to his kids. How could He! How could a loving God allow these people, men, women and children, to die? Surely not innocent children! Why did He not take me instead of them? I'm the guilty one, not them. Alex wept.

Around two in the afternoon the phone rang. Alex rushed to answer it.

'Hello, yes, Alex Baxter speaking … You've found the wreckage! In the jungle. How badly damaged is it? … Oh, no … I understand … Yes, we'll be here. Thank you. Goodbye.'

'Have they found it? Are there survivors?' Sarah asked, almost hysterically.

'Yes they've found it in the jungle close to the Columbian border,' Alex said softly.

'How badly damaged is it?' Sarah persisted.

'Sarah, where were the children sitting in the plane?'

'The kids had seats together near the front, but because we booked late Susie had a seat at the back. Why?'

'The information from the commodore is that the plane has been extensively destroyed by an explosion and fire on impact. Only the tail section is visible from the air now. There will be very few survivors, if any,' Alex tried to stay calm. 'The Peruvian search and rescue are dropping in a small team from a helicopter in the next hour, so we should know more then.'

Sarah started to sob quietly again.

'I still think my babies are alive. I just know they're not dead,' she whispered.

Alex didn't reply; he was in deep thought. The children wouldn't be happy at the front of the plane, if their favourite aunt was away at the back; they would have moved if they possibly could. Maybe, I'm just clutching at straws! Alex did not say anything to Sarah; he didn't want to raise her hopes.

'Hugh will be arriving at the airport soon,' said Alex, breaking the long silence.

'I'm going to meet him. Why don't you phone Amy and ask her to come and keep you company till I get back?' Alex had an idea but didn't want to upset Sarah further if he drew a blank.

'No, I'm coming with you! Alex, don't keep anything from me, not now, not ever!' Sarah shouted at him, something she rarely did.

'You know me too well!' Alex said, embracing his wife. 'Like you, I have a strong feeling that the children are alive. I have a hunch that, if there were two seats at the back of the plane near Susie, the children would move to be near her. I thought that, if I went to the airport, I could see the passenger list and see if the seats at the back were free.'

'But the plane was fully booked. That's why I couldn't book the seats together in the first place,' Sarah explained.

'But what if someone, or a couple, cancelled at the last moment, or someone took ill, or they were held up in the roadworks on the way to the airport? Who knows? Anything could have happened. We have to hope; we cannot give up hoping!' Alex slumped down in the chair.

'Let's both go. We need to be together. Promise me you'll not keep anything from me. I know you're just trying to protect me, but I'd rather know it all, no matter how bad! Promise me please!' Sarah pleaded.

'I promise.'

The couple arrived at the airport half an hour before Hugh was due to touch down. They met with Señor De Silva again, who happened to have the passenger list on his desk. He listened to what they had to say, but didn't hold out much hope.

'The flight was fully booked,' he said, reading from the list. Two people failed to make the gate. Their seats were 26B and 26C.'

'Where is that in the plane?' Alex asked quickly.

The manager shuffled through the charts on his desk.

'Those seats are right at the back just in front of the back doors,' he said.

'Where was Susie sitting?' Alex asked Sarah.

'I don't know the exact number, but right at the back. Her name is Susie Mitchell you must have her on the list.'

'Let me see. Mitchell, Susie … 26D.'

'It's just possible, just possible,' Alex said, excitedly hugging Sarah.

'We'll have to wait to hear from the search and rescue people first to see if the tail section is intact,' Señor De Silva said, bringing Sarah and Alex back down to earth.

Shortly afterwards, the telephone rang. Señor De Silva looked troubled by the phone message.

'I am sorry to have to tell you that the helicopters have not been able to take off due to strong winds and heavy rain. They will not be able to reach the accident site till tomorrow.'

'Oh no! Not another night without knowing. If they're alive, how will they cope? They will be terrified. They may be injured'… Sarah shrieked.

Alex and Sarah felt as if they had just been kicked again.

CHAPTER 7

Clearer Picture

The arrival of the KLM flight from Amsterdam to Lima was announced over the airport speakers, interrupting Alex and Sarah's dark thoughts.

'Hugh will be through the gate in about forty minutes, by the time he collects his luggage and clears immigration,' Alex commented to Sarah.

'No, Señor! What is your brother's name? I will send someone to meet him at the foot of the aircraft's steps and bring him straight here,' the airport manager interrupted.

'That would be very kind,' Alex responded.

'Señor, it is the least I can do. I, too, have children.'

Alex and Sarah greeted Hugh, with hugs and tears, about ten minutes later. He was brought up-to-date with the situation very quickly.

'Show me exactly where the wreckage was found, Señor,' Hugh said courteously to Señor De Silva.

The four stood round the wall chart. Hugh wrote down the coordinates, much to the surprise of the Peruvian.

'I have a detailed map in my luggage; we will be able to look again at the location when we return to your house, Alex. What is the plan for tomorrow Señor?' Hugh enquired.

'The commodore said that a rescue team would be sent in at first light, depending on the weather of course.'

'Thank you. I think we should go home and get some sleep. There is nothing else we can do here. What do you think Alex?' Hugh turned and winked at Alex.

'Yes, I'll call our driver right away,' Alex replied, looking at Sarah and raising his eyebrows in a way that she understood only too well.

Sarah hated the way Hugh always took over; he didn't seem to be able to help himself. He treated every situation like an army exercise. No wonder he had never married! Alex usually kept his younger brother in check, but today he didn't. Sarah wondered why?

Nothing very much was said on the journey back to the house, other than polite chat about Hugh's flight. Each seemed to be engrossed in his or her thoughts. Sarah started to weep quietly to herself as she thought that, if the children were alive, they would be spending another night in the jungle. Katie would be really scared by all the noise and insects of the forest, and Tim would be trying to be brave for his sister. Sarah suddenly thought, what if Katie was alone, and something had happened to Tim? Maybe they're both dead? She shook her head and refused to consider that possibility until she had seen the evidence.

Once they had all settled in the sitting room, Hugh and Alex started to chat over the situation, while Sarah busied herself in the kitchen making some coffee.

'Why didn't the Peruvians send a small group down to the wreckage yesterday afternoon?' Hugh asked.

'We were told that bad weather had prevented the helicopters from taking off. I don't know for sure where the nearest airbase is to the crash site, but I would have thought somewhere near Iquitos,' Alex replied.

'The crash site is very close to the Colombian border. One of my young officers is just back from that area; he was working with the Colombian army trying to keep the militia under control. The region is bandit country really. The terrorists are thought to be remnants of the Shining Path. Remember the Maoist group of the 1980's? They're now thought to be making their money from cocaine smuggling. The local villagers either work willingly with them or are forced to support them. A recent increase in pressure from the Colombian government, with US and UK backing, has meant that there has been a large military presence on the Columbian side of the border. As a result, many of the terrorists have moved over into Peru. Sadly, the Peruvian government doesn't see it as such a high priority, so the military are underfunded and undermanned in that part of Peru. Most of the Peruvian military activity is against the few remaining pockets of the terrorists in the south, near Lake Titicaca,' Hugh continued.

'Did I hear you say Shining Path?' Sarah asked, as she came through with the coffee. 'Please don't tell me they're still around! They terrorised and killed thousands of Peruvians when they were at their worst. I thought they were all in jail!'

'There are still some groups causing problems in the Puna area and other regions around the Bolivian border, but none as far as I know near the crash site,' Hugh replied, giving a worried look to Alex.

'Don't worry, Hugh. Sarah and I have had this out already; she wants to know everything, the good and the bad. It's the only way we can get through this together. So, if you have anything on your mind, let us have it,' Alex asked.

'I'm just a bit concerned, you see, since you told me the location of the crash site. I contacted "friends" in HQ in London to get up to speed with the current 'situation' in that area. There is a lot of terrorist activity at the moment. Some of our lads were involved in a fire-fight only last week, somewhere along the Napo River. Several of the militia were killed, and a cocaine factory was destroyed,' Hugh continued.

'That's all we need.' Alex slumped back in the settee.

'I think the Peruvian army didn't want to go anywhere near that area until back-up arrived. To be honest, I wouldn't want to take an undermanned squad in there either. One of my SAS teams at night, that's different! It's bread and butter to them. These rebel groups can be really nasty, so you have to be prepared to hit them hard.'

'Do you think, if the children are alive and one of these groups found them, they would look after them?' Sarah asked, nervously.

'Yes, I think they would, but only because they would want to make money out of them. Gringo kids in the jungle, they know the parents want them back, so they have 'value'. They will find out from the children about Alex's work and smell big bucks! So don't worry, they will be looked after. I am tired now. I know tomorrow is going to be a long day, so I'm off to get some sleep. You and Sarah look exhausted. Go and get some rest. You'll be no good to anyone if you can't function,' Hugh cautioned, as he headed for his room.

'Good night, Hugh. Thank you for coming so far to help us,' Alex said.

'I love your kids. You know I would go right round the world if I had to for them. Good night.'

CHAPTER 8

Snatched!

The children's eyesight had adapted well, so they were able to see their surroundings quite clearly. The noise of the jungle intensified as the creatures of the forest moved throughout the high canopy or slithered in the dense undergrowth. Bats flew across the moon, adding an eerie slant to the near idyllic picture. Katie had to pinch herself just to make sure she wasn't dreaming. Then the horror of the last twenty-four hours ran through her mind. *Why can't I wake up? Has all this been a dream?*

'Tim, what do you think Mum and Dad are doing now?'

'Looking for us, stupid!'

'But I was thinking…When the rescuers find the plane, they'll think everyone has been killed in the explosion. How will they know we're alive?'

Tim hadn't thought of that! Katie was right. When they looked back at the plane it looked completely wrecked; no one could have survived the explosion.

'They'll send experts to the crash site; they will realise we have survived,' Tim said, confidently.

'But remember, we were supposed to be in the front of the plane. Everything was destroyed at the cockpit end when we crashed,' Katie argued.

'I suppose. Stop worrying. They will find us. Dad and Mum will never give up! Uncle Hugh will come and help too!' Tim shouted, trying to control his fears.

'Let's bait this hook and see if we can catch something for breakfast,' Tim suggested, changing the subject.

The children drifted slowly down the river keeping quite close to the bank where the water was slowest, but far enough away from the trees to be safe from snakes and insects. After a few minutes the line went taught and the pair pulled in a fish of about twenty five centimetres in length.

'That was sore!' Katie yelled. 'The line has cut into my fingers, well almost – but it was sore!' she complained.

'We'll have to be careful, but the Peruvians fish like that all the time,' Tim pointed out.

Over the next half hour the children managed to catch five good-sized fish – enough for a meal – and they were really hungry now, but they knew they would have to wait until they found somewhere to land.

'You should try and sleep, Katie. I'll do the paddling just now.'

Katie made herself as comfy as she could in the front of the boat and soon fell asleep.

Tim was very tired too; he began to nod off.

'What was that?' Katie shouted. 'Tim, wake up! It sounded like a gun. Listen! There it is again. There must be a village up ahead.'

Tim gave himself a shake.

'Sorry Katie. I must have dozed off. Some soldier I'll make. What did you hear?'

'It sounded like a rifle, coming from that direction.' Katie pointed downstream to where the river curved to the right. Tim was fully alert now.

'We must get into the river bank, under cover,' he said softly.

'Why? What's wrong? There must be a village near here, somewhere we can get help.'

'Have you not heard about the guerrillas, the terrorist groups who hide in the jungle, especially near the Columbian border? There are often news reports about them fighting the Columbian army. We were in the air for about ninety minutes, so I reckon we could be near, very near, the Columbian border. The local villagers have no need for guns. We must check and see what's up ahead before we just sail up the river for all to see. If it is a band of guerrillas, they'll capture us and hold us hostage!' Tim warned.

'We'll keep the canoe close to the bank, under the trees for cover, and edge slowly downriver to see what's up ahead. It'll be dawn in about two hours. We need to know if it's safe to go on before then, or we are in real trouble,' he added.

As silently as he could, Tim guided the canoe close to the bank. At times the branches scratched Katie's face but she said nothing. She had listened to what Tim had said, and she was scared! Even the mosquitoes, irritating as they were, did not make Katie cry out. This was not the time.

When they rounded the bend, they could see the village about one hundred metres downstream, on the opposite bank. There was a large fire burning on the open ground in front of half a dozen huts. Several men were pacing up and down the bank with rifles over their shoulders. They were not dressed like village people, but seemed to be in military dress. Others were sitting round the big fire. Over to the left by the trees, Tim saw what looked like four native people tied to posts, their arms pinned behind their backs. Tim shuddered. We must get out of here, he thought.

Tim paddled backwards constantly to keep the canoe right under the trees and as well hidden as he could from any lookouts.

Suddenly, and without warning, two figures jumped out of the trees straddling the canoe, one behind Katie and the other behind Tim. The children struggled pointlessly. The two attackers were strong and held on tight, each with a hand over his captive's mouth. A third attacker was in the water at the bow of the canoe pushing the vessel upstream, round the corner out of sight of the village.

Katie's young body started to shake as she sobbed, terrified but unable to cry out, the tears streamed down her face. Tim just couldn't move; he was convinced they were going to be taken to the village, kidnapped, or worse still…they were about to die.

The young man holding Tim spoke to his companion in a language Tim couldn't understand. There was urgency in his voice, yet not in any way threatening towards the children. He relaxed his grip slightly, making Tim more comfortable. Once they had gone upstream a couple of hundred yards there was a clearing by the bank. The canoe was pushed firmly into the mud.

To Tim's huge relief the Peruvian holding him gave him a gentle look, smiled, then said in Spanish, 'Gringo, come with us. The men in the village are bad; they will hurt you just as they have hurt many of our brothers. Quickly now, keep quiet, we will not harm you. But we need to get away from here as fast as possible. We will go into the jungle, to our village.'

Tim glanced at Katie. She had stopped crying now but still looked confused.

'Are they going to help us Tim?' she whispered.

'I think so. I think it's going to be alright.'

The three 'captors' helped Tim and Katie up the steep, slippy bank, which was just as well; even though Tim's ankle was much better he still found the climb difficult.

'What about the fish we caught?' Katie asked Tim at the top.

Tim used his Spanish to speak with the leader, a dark-featured handsome lad of about eighteen years, although it was hard for Tim to guess exactly how old he was. Tim told the boy, whose name was Miguel, about the fish. Miguel laughed and pointed to the smaller youth at the back of the group who was looking very proud of himself, because he had the fish stuffed into the bag over his shoulder.

'This is Pablo; he is my little brother, and he is always hungry; he never misses food. Come quickly, gringo kids,' Miguel said as he hurried off down the jungle path. After a few metres he stopped at the foot of a large tree, moved some branches and retrieved three large machetes that the trio had stashed earlier.

The noise in the jungle seemed to really intensify as they walked, or rather trotted, deep into the jungle. Tim thought it was a sign that dawn was not far away. The children felt more confident now, as the natives had shown them only kindness. The quiet Peruvian, who so far had not really related to Tim and Katie, stopped at the foot of a tree, climbed up about three metres and cut down some strange looking fruit. The children couldn't see the colour, but when it was sliced open with a machete the flesh was really moist. Everyone had a slice of the fruit. Tim and Katie thought it was so tasty. Miguel saw the way the youngsters had gulped down the food. He realised that they must be very hungry so the quiet one, who was called Ronaldo, was sent back up the tree for another!

The group didn't stop long as Miguel was keen to get going again. Katie found it hard to keep up. At times the path was steep and slippery; sometimes fallen logs blocked the path and they had to climb over them, but the young men always stopped to help her and Tim.

'How much further do you think we will have to go?' Katie asked Tim.

'I don't know but they seem to be in an awful hurry. Now that the sun is up they're going even faster!' Tim added.

The group trudged on and on. The jungle was much quieter now. Most of the animals were resting after their night adventures, but there was still a lot of bird song from the high canopy. The path was becoming really difficult now. The native boys were using their machetes to cut a way through.

'I don't think this is a path they use very often,' Tim said. 'We seem to be going off the track we have been on, deeper into the jungle'.

After about half an hour of pushing through the thick jungle they arrived at a big waterfall. It must have been well over thirty metres high, plunging into a dark deep pool. The sound of the cascade was so loud that Katie had her hands over her ears, at first causing the native boys to laugh and laugh.

Tim asked Miguel if they could rest for a while as he could see that Katie was exhausted, but he was told quite firmly that they had to cross the river first.

'How will we do that?' Katie grumbled.

Before Tim could answer they were on their way again up the side of the river slithering over slippy rocks, climbing up a steep, dangerous bank. Both children were holding on as tight as they could, as they realised that the river was very deep. Tim was behind Katie, trying to encourage her. He stepped across a gap between two large boulders, but his bad ankle gave way and he fell into the river which was about five metres below them. Tim screamed as he fell; then he was silent. Katie could see that his head had struck a rock on the way down. He disappeared under the water. Katie was screaming for her brother, but he had completely gone from view.

CHAPTER 9

On the Third Dive!

Miguel who was up ahead, turned as he heard the cries. He quickly realised what had happened and dived off the rocks into the pool. He too, disappeared from view for several seconds then reappeared for air, but there was no sign of Tim. Katie was hysterical shouting for her brother. Miguel dived again. He was out of sight for what seemed like eternity to Katie. He surfaced again, looked round the pool and dived once more. This time he found Tim and dragged him to the water's edge. Katie slithered down beside them.

'Tim, Tim!' she shouted. 'Wake up, wake up!'

Miguel slapped Tim on the face to try and rouse him.

'He's not breathing. He's not breathing!' Katie roared but no one could understand her.

Katie realised that she had to act quickly if she was going to save her brother's life. The First Aid she had learnt at Guide Camp flashed into her mind.

'Please God, help us,' she prayed.

She rolled Tim onto his back, tipped up his chin to clear his wind pipe, pinched his nose, and then as cool as a cucumber, sealed her lips over his and breathed two slow breaths.

Tim coughed and spluttered. Quick as a flash Katie pulled him onto his side as he spewed up the water he had swallowed.

The Peruvian lads let out a big cheer. Katie wept with joy. It took Tim a few more minutes to come round completely.

'What happened?' he asked. 'The back of my head is so sore.'

Katie explained the whole drama. Tim squeezed his sister's hand. 'That's twice you've saved my life. First the snake, now this.'

Miguel came over and shook Tim's hand. The other two young men gathered round patting Tim and Miguel on the back. Miguel would only let the group settle for a few more minutes before they had to move on, back up over the rocks.

'Why can't we rest a bit longer?' Katie asked Tim.

'I don't know, but don't worry I'm fine now,' he said as he struggled to his feet.

But Tim wasn't alright. He was quite wobbly and Ronaldo had to grab him before he fell in a heap. Miguel spoke to Ronaldo in their native language. From then on he was to help Tim, but they had to get moving. Katie could see that Miguel was nervous and wanted to get going.

'Ask Miguel what's wrong,' she said to Tim.

Tim spoke to Miguel.

'He has noticed some changes in the behaviour of the animals behind us; they are much quieter now and he is worried that we are being followed?' Tim informed Katie.

'Who could be following us?' Katie asked anxiously.

'Maybe someone saw us back at that village?' Tim suggested. 'Miguel wants to cross the river and then we'll rest. He said that, once we are on the other side, one of them will watch the trail for a while.'

'But how are we going to cross the river? We don't have a boat, and it's too dangerous to swim!' Katie complained.

'Miguel has a plan,' Tim replied. 'We have to trust him. He saved my life and put his own life at risk so I think we can trust him. In fact, I know we can trust him.'

The group continued their climb up over the rocks to the huge waterfall. The noise of the water was fearsome, so loud they couldn't hear each other speak. Miguel waved to them to follow him, and then he disappeared behind a large boulder, right at the edge of the waterfall.

Pablo was just in front of Katie now and urged her to keep going, but with the spray and the noise she was scared stiff. She could hardly make her legs move, and now the rocks were wet, slippy, and covered with green moss which frightened her even more. Tim was right behind with Ronaldo supporting him. Pablo realised that Katie was going to freeze so he grabbed her hand, and helped her down behind the boulder which had hidden Miguel. To her horror, Katie saw that there was a deep crevice across their path which must have been about one metre wide. Miguel was on the other side, with the waterfall thundering above him; he was right under the cascade. Katie could see the crevice was dark and deep; she knew if she fell, she would be lost for ever! She knew they couldn't go back because the guerrillas were probably following them. Her heart was pounding in her chest and her legs were like blobs of jelly. Miguel was gesticulating to her to cross, but she couldn't do it! She knew it was irrational because, had it been the long jump at school, she could easily clear that distance, but it wasn't. She knew to fall would mean certain death.

Miguel jumped back across to where Pablo and Katie were standing. He spoke with Pablo then both boys held on to Katie and ran with her towards the crevice. Katie's screams were lost in the waterfall. They all landed safely in a heap on the other side. Miguel then went back to help Ronaldo get Tim across.

Once all were over, Miguel took the lead again and gingerly continued on the slimy path behind the huge flow of water. The path became very narrow, so much so that for about five metres they had to walk with their backs to the rocks. Again, Pablo and Miguel took Katie by the hand and eased her along the ledge. At times, loose stones disappeared over the precipice.

To cross behind the fall seemed to take forever, but Tim and Katie were so relieved to be safely on the other side. Miguel escorted them round the side of the rock face and through a very narrow opening, which the children would have easily missed, into a large cool cave. Miguel spoke to Tim and said that they would rest here for several hours. This would keep them out of the noon-day sun.

'What else did Miguel say, Tim?' Katie asked.

'That he was going to send Pablo to watch the trail in case we were followed, but he thought that we were safe, as only his tribe knew how to cross the river behind the waterfall. Strangers would not know of the secret path. Ronaldo will go and look for food. We'll need to rest, eat and drink plenty as it will be another four hours, at least, before we arrive at their village,' Tim answered.

'I wonder why the boys were so far away from their village, and why did they rescue us Tim? What are we to them that they should risk their lives for us?' Katie continued.

'I don't know. Maybe they took pity on us because they saw that we were so young,' Tim suggested. 'When Miguel comes back, I'll try and ask him a few more questions.'

'At least they've looked after us. It's lovely and cool in here. Tim, I was so frightened under that waterfall; the noise was awful! I just kept praying.'

'Yeah, I must admit, I was praying too. It's funny, God seemed really close when we were under that waterfall.'

'Tim, you should lie down and get some rest after all that has happened to you.'

'Katie you've been great. You saved my life back there, such quick thinking. I don't think I would have remembered what to do if it had been you,' Tim said thoughtfully.

'You would!'

'Would what?'

'Would have remembered how to give the "Kiss of Life".'

'Na! You know me! I'm not into that kissing thing,' Tim said, as he put his arm round his little sister and gave her a thankful hug.

'Ah get off! I can't cope when you are being too nice to me,' Katie replied, teasingly. 'Anyway it's Miguel you have to thank. He dived into the pool from the rocks, from about ten metres up I reckon. Even then, he had to dive under the water three times to find you. That's really brave! There could have been piranha, electric eels, and all sorts of nasty creatures in there.'

'I know. I owe him a lot,' Tim acknowledged.

Just at that, Miguel arrived with some fruit folded in his T-shirt, a kind neither Katie nor Tim had seen before. They were blue berries about the size of grapes, and they tasted delicious.

After they had eaten, Tim thanked Miguel for all he had done for them and especially for saving his life. They chatted in Spanish for about half an hour. Katie was desperate to know what they were talking about, but her Spanish was still quite poor. Her understanding was better than her spoken language so she realised that the boys were talking about Miguel's village and his family. Their conversation ended when Miguel went to give Pablo a break from watching the trail.

'What did you find out?' Katie asked excitedly.

'Lots. Miguel, Pablo, and Ronaldo are brothers. Miguel is eighteen, Ronaldo fifteen and Pablo is twelve. They have two older sisters who are married and have moved to different villages down the Napo River with their new husbands.'

'Phew, quite a big family,' Katie said.

'There were more. A younger sister died last year of malaria; she was eight years old. A brother died about fifteen years ago when he was two years old; he fell into the river and drowned,' Tim continued.

'Oh that's really sad. I thought Miguel looked upset when you were talking,' Katie added.

'Yes, his little sister was called Marie. He misses her very much. There's more. Remember the village where we saw the guerrillas? Well, that was where the family used to live. Two months ago, the bandits arrived at the village and beat up many of the men because they would not help the gang by planting coca plants to make cocaine; you know the one the drugs addicts use? The headman was told that, if he didn't convince the villagers that they had to help the gang, he would be killed. The gang left but said that they would be back in a few days and expected the right answer.

The leaders of the village met to discuss what to do. Everyone in the village was frightened. They had heard stories from other villagers, especially those up north close to the Columbian border. Many people had been killed by the bandits for not co-operating with them; some had even been tortured. Others had heard that those who had agreed to plant coca, and help to make the drugs, ran the risk of being shot or sent to prison by the army. The headman, who is the uncle of the brothers, thought for a while, and then he suggested that they leave the village by creeping out at night and travelling deep into the jungle, well away from the guerrillas. They would live as their forefathers had done, surviving off the forest.'

'Many of the men folk were unhappy, because their children were going to school now. Also, their families were receiving health care from the nurse at the health centre, and the doctor from Bella Vista visited every three months. If they went into the deep jungle, they would lose all this. Others were very frightened, and told more tales of the horrible things these bandits had done elsewhere.'

'The headman called for a vote. The majority decided to leave for the deep jungle. However, four of the older men were determined to stay; they had founded the village twenty-five years ago, and would not leave for anyone. They were the four men tied to the posts that we saw. Miguel said that they were dead.'

'Oh, that's awful!' Katie interrupted.

Tim continued, 'Later that evening, the village folk took to their canoes and headed down river for about two hours then turned up a small river travelling for another three hours until they found a suitable place to make camp. It was an abandoned village left by some other tribe a few years earlier. We are going there now.

'Miguel and his brothers were sent by the headman to sneak back to the village to see what was happening. They had been right up to the edge of the village, hiding in the undergrowth and could see exactly what had happened to the old men. That was why Miguel was so upset when he was telling me about it; he said the men had died in a horrible way but wouldn't tell me any more. The brothers were on their way back when they spotted our canoe.'

'But why did they stop to help us?' Katie asked.

'I asked Miguel the same question and he said that it was because the sentries might have spotted us all,' Tim replied. 'Miguel said that they could see we were gringo children and knew that we would not realise how much danger we were in. When Pablo was really sick last year, a ship with gringo doctors and dentists visited the village. They gave Pablo 'gringo' medicine, and within two days he was better. Miguel and Pablo were so happy because they thought he was going to die like Marie; the village shaman had not been able to help him.'

'What's a shaman?' Katie asked.

'The witch doctor! Also, Miguel had very bad toothache which he had for many days. The dentist from the ship pulled out his bad tooth and the pain was gone,' Tim continued.

'So that explains why they've all been so nice to us,' Katie said.

'Yeah, and Miguel is cool, really cool,' Tim added.

The group rested in the cave for a couple of hours. Pablo returned to report that there was no sign of the guerrillas, so Miguel decided it was safe to move on. Hopefully, they would reach the village by nightfall. Before they left the cave, Miguel spoke with Tim again.

'What did he say?' Katie asked, impatiently.

'He was checking that I was feeling OK to move on; if not, we could stay here for the night,' Tim replied.

'Oh no! I don't want to stay here; it will be pitch dark at night. There are probably bats in here, you know, the ones that suck your blood when you're sleeping!' Katie said, as she jumped to her feet to leave.

'That's what Miguel said! Let's get going.' Tim pulled himself up as quickly as he could.

When they left the cool of the cave the heat hit them like a blast from a furnace. 'It's really hot now!' Katie said. 'I hope it's not too far to the village and not too difficult.'

Five minutes along the route, and the path headed up a steep slope, criss-crossed with creepers. Miguel chopped furiously to clear the way. Both Tim and Katie were beginning to struggle but Pablo and Ronaldo helped them up the track. The path was wet and squidgy at times, so their feet often slipped in the mud. At least twice, Katie fell her length and had to be helped up by Pablo. The jungle was noisy with birds and other creatures. Miguel who was about twenty metres up front suddenly stopped. The brothers shouted to one another in their own language. Katie could see Miguel had raised his machete above his head.

'What is it?' she whispered to Tim.

'I don't know. But Miguel looks quite worried,' Tim replied, nervously.

'Yes, and so do Pablo and Ronaldo,' Katie whispered.

Miguel waved at them to stay back, but on he crept. Stealthily he moved forward, like a hunter, muscles taught, machete raised to strike. Suddenly, he lunged forward at what looked like a stick across his path. A quick swipe and then a cry of excitement leapt from his mouth. He turned with a huge grin on his face. They rushed forward to see, as Miguel picked up the headless body of a three-metre snake. The snake was thin and black with greenish stripes on its back. The younger brothers were quick to congratulate their big brother, chatting excitedly with him.

Pablo came and spoke to Katie and Tim, in his best Spanish, the first time he had felt confident enough to speak with them.

Tim translated for Katie. 'The snake was very dangerous. It was just as well Miguel had seen it before it had the chance to strike. A bite from this snake would have killed him in ten minutes. The boys are very proud of their big brother.'

'Do you think there will be more snakes on the paths? I thought they only came out at night?' Katie asked, now quite worried.

'They say that there are more snake bites in the rainy season because the snakes are swept inland by rising rivers; as this is the rainy season, we had better watch out!' Tim cautioned.

The group trudged on and on. Katie was feeling awful as the heat was exhausting her. Tim could see that his sister was tired; she slipped repeatedly in the mud. Fortunately, Pablo was always close by to steady her. Miguel realised that the young girl was beginning to slow up the group and he knew it would soon be dark. When they stopped to drink by a river, he spoke with his brothers and then Tim.

'Katie, Miguel and his brothers are going to take turns giving you a piggy back because you are exhausted. Miguel says we have to make it to the village tonight and it is not long now till nightfall.'

'OK. I suppose so,' Katie said, feeling a little embarrassed. 'I can't go another step.'

Katie was helped onto Miguel's broad shoulders and off they set again at such a pace that Tim found the going really hard as well. Somehow, he managed to keep pace, despite all his aches and pains.

It was almost pitch dark when they came out of the jungle into a clearing. They could smell the smoke from the cooking fires, the harsh sound of a cockerel crowing and the laughter of children. They had arrived in the village!

Miguel took them to the largest hut. There, he gently lowered Katie to the floor. Tim collapsed in a heap beside her. This was the headman's hut, which belonged to Miguel's uncle. The villagers looked stunned at the 'gringo' children lying in front of them. There was a great deal of chatter between the boys and the head man, and then he signalled the woman folk to attend to Katie and Tim. They sat Katie up and gave her some water to drink and some of the food they had prepared for supper. Tim managed to prop himself up against the wall of the hut, and his new friend Miguel brought food over to him.

Miguel said to him, 'My uncle, the headman, welcomes you and Katie to our village. You will be safe here. We're all tired now and must sleep. You can rest here in this hut; my brothers and I will return to our father's house, but will come for you in the morning. My aunt and uncle will look after you. They are Christian, and will not let anything happen to you.'

Katie was too tired to even ask Tim what Miguel had said. She fell asleep on the floor where she was. Tim lay close to his sister and was soon fast asleep too.

CHAPTER 10

No Survivors

Sarah and Alex managed to get some sleep, but by the time they arrived in the kitchen for breakfast, Hugh was already up and dressed.

'Good morning both. Did you get some sleep?' Hugh enquired.

'A little,' said Sarah sleepily. 'You look bright and surprisingly cheerful, all things considered.'

'Yes, I've just been speaking with George in HQ in London. Apparently, we have an active unit only forty miles from the crash site. All very top secret as the Peruvians don't know we're there. Well, they know we are working along the Columbian border, but they think we are in Columbia. But every now and then we have to make an 'excursion' over the border to tidy up one or two of the militia groups. He has offered to send in the boys if necessary to search out the crash site, but obviously would prefer the Peruvians to get a move on and do the job themselves. He has said that the unit will be active in the region for at least another couple of weeks, so if we need their help we can call on them.'

'That's excellent Hugh, but I realise it could be politically sensitive,' Alex said. 'So what do we do just now?'

'We wait till we hear from the commodore again; in the meantime, I'm going to prepare for a trek into the jungle, just in case,' Hugh replied.

'Well, if you go, I'm coming with you,' Alex volunteered. 'Give me a kit list and I'll get it organised.'

'I thought you would remember from your marine days! Are you fit enough for several days in the jungle? You are carrying a bit of flab,' Hugh teased, as he slapped Alex on his stomach.

'I'll be fine!'

The two men continued their preparations just in case they had to go looking for the children themselves. All three felt, in their hearts, that somehow the kids had survived. About four in the afternoon, they were summoned back to the airport as the air commodore had asked for a meeting prior to making a statement to the press.

Hugh was introduced to the commodore who was obviously in a sombre mood. Sarah held on tightly to Alex as the officer began to speak.

'Our men have been winched down to the wreckage and have just reported back. I am very sorry to tell you there are no survivors. The plane exploded on impact and has been consumed in a fireball.'

Sarah screamed, 'No, no, not my babies!' Alex tried to comfort her.

'Do you have any photographs?' Hugh asked.

'Yes, Colonel. We have some that were taken from the helicopter and also from the rescue team. Here they are.'

Hugh took the photographs, and then walked over to the window to get a better look at them.

'Could we have a copy of these photographs, Commodore?'

'Certainly. It will take only a few moments.'

'What are the recovery plans? When will the crash investigators be going in?' Hugh asked.

Sarah and Alex were too stunned to ask any questions. They had been so convinced that their children were alive.

'The crash site is very remote,' the commodore said, pointing to the wall-map. 'We will have to call on the navy to transfer men and recovery equipment up the Napo River from Iquitos. At this point here, the village of Santa Maria, they will have to cut a road through the jungle to the site, a distance of around thirty kilometres. This is all going to take time. It will be at least a week before men and materials reach the aircraft. Our advance team did recover the black box, so crash investigators will be able to start work as soon as possible. I am so sorry it is going to take such a long time to recover the bodies, but the location is so deep in the jungle.'

'We understand Commodore,' Hugh acknowledged. 'A dangerous part of the country for your men; so close to the Columbian border. Have you had much trouble recently?'

'Not that I have heard of, but the air force is not usually involved in fighting the drug barons. It is the responsibility of the army or drug enforcement officers. I will leave you now, as I must speak with the press.'

'Mr and Mrs Baxter, may I offer you my sincere condolences,' the commodore said, turning to Alex and Sarah.

'Good afternoon Colonel Baxter. If I or any of my colleagues can help in any way, please let me know.' Hastily, the commodore left the room.

'What did you say to him that sent him off in such a hurry?' Alex asked.

'A bit touchy about the drug barons I'd say. Let's get home,' Hugh replied.

The trio arrived back at the apartment within the hour. Again, the car journey had been very quiet, each deep in thought.

'Why did you ask for the photographs?' That's a bit gruesome is it not?' Alex asked.

'Gruesome maybe, but I just want to check the air commodore isn't keeping anything back. Have you a magnifying glass Sarah? I'll have a proper look at these now,' Hugh replied. Hugh put the three photographs out on the table and spent several minutes looking at them.

'That's interesting. From this aerial picture I can see that the front two thirds of the plane has been completely destroyed but the structure of the tail is intact, although it looks scorched. The back door is missing, perhaps blown off. Pass me the magnifying glass please.'

'What is it? What can you see?' Alex asked excitedly.

'Come and look. What do you make of that, by that tree, about thirty metres from the fuselage?'

'Do you mean that grey coloured, tortuous line? I'm not sure. Is it in any of the pictures taken on the ground?' Alex asked.

'No, these pictures are looking at the aircraft and don't show much of the surroundings. I think it could be part of an escape slide, maybe the one from the back door,' Hugh continued. 'There's no sign of other doors having been open or slides activated automatically.'

'What are you saying, Hugh?' Sarah asked as she rushed across the room to look at the pictures.

'I think it is possible that the back door has been opened and the escape chute activated manually, which therefore means that there has been at least one survivor!'

'Are you sure? Why haven't the Peruvians noticed this?' Alex asked.

'I think we have the advantage of the aerial photograph. Remember, the rescue crew would be looking at the aircraft. If they landed on the right-hand side of the wreck, where the clearing is bigger, they wouldn't see the slide over here. I'll contact the air commodore and ask if his people could look at the photographs again. It's just possible some passengers escaped before the fireball, in which case, they will need to send in some rescue teams to search the area, and quickly! It's three days since the accident.'

'I need a drink!' Alex said, striding over to the drinks cabinet. 'A whisky for you, Hugh? Sarah, you should have one too; it'll settle your nerves a bit.'

'Fine for me thanks,' Hugh said gathering up the photographs.

'Count me out. I'll go and order in some supper. No doubt we'll have to hang around a while before we hear anything more,' Sarah said disconsolately.

Hugh contacted the commodore and explained his findings. The commodore agreed that his experts would review the pictures and get back to them as soon as possible.

The family spent a very restless two hours, picking at a Chinese meal they had ordered, before they heard any more.

Hugh answered the telephone. 'I see, yes I understand… An artefact, something on the camera lens perhaps. The commander of the rescue team did not see any escape slides at all. Thank you for your help.'

'Did you hear that? His 'experts' don't believe it's the remnant of an escape slide. He has spoken with the officer in charge of the rescue who clearly states that there was no evidence of any survivors or slide activation at any of the doors.'

'So we are just kidding ourselves. It's not a slide we're looking at, just some scratch!' Sarah said as she slumped in the chair.

Hugh and Alex pored over the photograph again.

'But the more I look at this, the more convinced I am that it is an escape chute,' Hugh said.

'Do you think it is likely that the kids moved to the back of the plane to be with Susie? Looking at the wreckage of the plane, the people likely to have opened that door must have been at the back,' Hugh continued.

'The children adore their Aunt Susie. If they could have moved beside her, they would, and we know from the boarding list that the two passengers next to Susie missed the flight. So I'm certain the children would have moved to be with her,' Alex confirmed.

'Right, we need to be sure that this is an escape slide we are looking at. Let's scan this photograph and electronically send it to HQ in London. I'll speak to James and ask him to push it through as top priority. The 'boys' in his department have all the most up-to-date equipment. With the war in Afghanistan, they are used to looking for 'needles in haystacks' as much of the terrain is rugged mountain and all looks the same. There might even have been a satellite over the region in the last twenty-four hours that will have taken some new pictures; it's quite possible, actually, with the marine unit in the area. The HQ guys use satellite a great deal these days for their intelligence. It lets them see new campsites or drug factories; there is so much detail available. Hopefully, we'll have an answer in a couple of hours. I'm pretty convinced someone escaped from that plane, and if the Peruvians won't buy it then we'll have to check it out ourselves. I'm going to arrange contact with the special unit in Columbia and warn them that I'll be joining them tomorrow, provided I get confirmation from HQ about the photograph.'

'Count me in, I'm coming too!' Alex was quick to confirm. Hugh looked at Sarah 'Will you be alright on your own?'

'Yes, you must go. I'll ask Amy to come and stay with me till you get back. The three of us have a deep feeling that the children are still alive, so we cannot wait a week until the authorities recover the bodies and discover some are missing, lost in the jungle. So both of you get ready to go,' Sarah encouraged.

Alex rushed over and hugged his wife.

Later that afternoon, Hugh received the confirmation he had been waiting for. There had been a satellite over the region within the last twenty-four hours taking up-to-date pictures for the commando unit. The crash site was located, and London was convinced that there was a piece of the escape slide caught up in the trees, at the edge of the clearing.

Hugh organised a rendezvous with the commando unit. He and Alex would have to fly to Bogotá in Columbia and rely on the help of the Columbian military. Both would be in military fatigues. Alex would have to squeeze into his old uniform, so he was hoping he had not put on too much weight. It was over six years since he left the army, and regular exercise was not always easy to achieve with the demands of his new job, not to mention too many business lunches. He had reached the rank of major after a fourteen-year career in the marines, so in 'the field' he knew he would have to acknowledge his little brother's superior rank, which could just be a little difficult for him. Sarah reminded him to behave and not upset Hugh, as he had in the past; the children were all that mattered, not the sibling rivalry of the older generation.

As far as the Columbian army was concerned, they were reinforcements for the special unit. The Brits didn't want to upset Anglo-Peruvian relations by letting the Columbian's know the real reason for their visit to the commando group. The Columbians just might have used the information to embarrass the Peruvians, something the UK government would not want. The flight to Bogotá left at ten in the evening, so there was much to do and very little time.

CHAPTER 11

Commando Sortie

Alex and Hugh rendezvoused with the British commando unit, deep in the Columbian jungle, about twenty-four hours after leaving Lima. The Columbian army had transported Hugh and Alex by helicopter to a clearing an hour's walk from the base camp. They were met by a very keen and energetic young lieutenant who quickly briefed them on the journey ahead. By the time they reached the camp, Alex's lack of fitness was beginning to show. He was sweaty and exhausted.

Hugh had worked with the officer in charge, Captain Peter Jones, so they were well received by the team. Pete, as he was known by his fellow officers, was a career soldier from Wales. He was a tall ginger-haired, young man, who, after graduating from Sandhurst Military Academy, gained his first commission in the Welsh guards. The young officer then transferred to the Special Air Service, or SAS as the unit is known. Pete was one of Hugh's junior officers when their SAS unit was deployed to Iraq three years earlier. Hugh thought highly of the younger man, and was confident the current mission would go well.

Captain Pete welcomed them at the camp, and then ushered the two men into his tent to discuss the task ahead.

'I'm very sorry to hear about your children, Alex. The 'not knowing' must be unbearable for you. From the coordinates you have given us, Hugh, we are about three hour's trek from the crash site. We'll cross into Peru at this point on the river, which should take us about two hours to reach. Then we'll use our boats to travel upstream as far as we can. If all goes well, there should only be about a half-hour jungle climb to the site.'

'When do we leave?' Hugh asked impatiently.

Capt. Pete looked at Alex. 'At first light. In the meantime, get some rest. Oh, and remember to collect your weapons from Sgt. Patterson. There has been a lot of guerrilla activity over the last month. Only last week we raided a coca 'farm'. There was a firefight and we took out several of their guys, including one of their regional commanders. Right now, they are really mad with us 'gringo' soldiers.'

'Where was the "farm"?' Hugh asked. 'Anywhere near the crash site?'

'No, but it was in Peru, thirty kilometres in this direction. We had Columbian drug enforcement men with us; thought we were still in Columbia,' Pete said with a smile.

'Yea, I suppose the guerrillas think you will not pursue them over the border. Do the Peruvians not offer you any support?' Hugh asked.

'The Columbians and Peruvians have never seen eye to eye. They've had occasional skirmishes over the years. But I think it is more down to costs. The Peruvians are fighting Marxists groups in the south and cannot afford to have a heavy military presence up here as well. They know we are operating in the area, but turn a blind eye as long as we don't attract attention to ourselves,' Pete continued.

'What time are we off?' Alex asked.

'Be ready at dawn. Corporal White will show you to your tent. Good night,' Pete said, saluting politely to the senior officers.

The tent turned out to be nothing more than a hammock strung between a couple of trees with a tarpaulin as a roof from the tropical rains and a mosquito net encasing the hammock to reduce the risk of malaria.

'Remember and take your anti-malarial tablet, Alex,' Hugh said.

'Yes, I won't forget. The Amazon region at this time of year is very bad for malaria, especially the serious one … falciparum I think it's called. If the kids are alive they won't have any protection, but I suppose that is the least of our worries,' Alex replied, as he settled into his hammock.

Next morning twenty men, including Alex and Hugh and two local guides, set off for the crash site. They followed tracks to start with, but then, in order to reach the river as soon as possible, they slashed their way through thick jungle. Hugh was in his element; he had always enjoyed expeditions in the jungle. The heat and the sweat were all part and parcel of being a soldier, trekking in the tropics. Alex, on the other hand, was older, less fit and distracted. He was thinking about what they might find when they reached the aircraft. Would there just be a burnt-out shell? Would they find the children's bodies, or would they find evidence that somehow they had survived? If they had lived, how could they cope with five days in the forest? Yes, it had been five days since the accident.

After about an hour had passed, a signal came back from the lead scout who was about one hundred metres up ahead. He was at the bank of the river in the undergrowth. He had stopped because, on the other side, about eighty metres away, a fast boat had tied up, and six heavily armed fighters had gone ashore. It looked as if they had stopped to stretch their legs, make a comfort stop and eat. Capt. Pete crept forward to the scout to take a look for himself; Hugh was right behind him. The entire platoon was now silent, crouched down with safety catches off!

'They're guerrillas alright. Looks like there's cargo in the back of the boat, probably drugs,' Pete whispered, as he looked through his binoculars. 'We'll have to wait till they load up and set off again. I don't want to engage with them; we have another job to do just now.'

The team was held up for over an hour before the guerrillas climbed back in the boat and sped down river. Alex was quite glad of the rest. Hugh and Capt. Pete watched as the drug runners disappeared round the bend in the river.

'Sorry you couldn't have a go at these guys, Pete,' Hugh said.

'Don't worry. I think we'll be back sometime soon. I'll bet it's not the first time they've been on this river. It's a drug route we don't know about, so we'll be back, back very soon,' Pete answered, as he signalled to his lads to bring up the inflatables.

The expedition made good time as they sped up river, in two separate boats, as far as they could. Alex and Hugh were resting in the back of the second boat, each deep in thought, no doubt wondering what they were going to find when they reached the crash site. Capt. Pete was in the lead boat.

'What do you think we'll find, Hugh?' Alex asked, above the noise of the outboard motor.

'Not sure. Hopefully, confirm that what we saw in the aerial photograph was an escape slide and evidence that at least some folks have escaped with their lives. Not long now I think.'

The river was beginning to narrow from the eighty metres or so it had been when they started to nearer thirty metres. The marines were looking more alert, and it was not just the lookouts paying attention; every commando was ready for action in case of an attack from guerrillas on the bank. The river entered a narrow gorge, the rocks climbing higher and higher. Pete signalled that the lead boat would go in first to check there was no trouble lurking; soon his boat was out of sight of the other.

'I hope there is no trouble up ahead,' Alex said nervously.

'No. Pete has always been a cautious guy. He's a good officer,' Hugh replied.

Ten minutes later, the signal came back to follow into the gorge. Number two boat drew alongside the others in a large pool at the bottom of a fifteen-metre-high waterfall. It was a beautiful spot. With the engines cut, the jungle cacophony was loud and clear, with birds calling, monkeys gibbering in the trees, and large frogs croaking on the forest floor.

'This waterfall wasn't on the map,' Pete explained. 'I'm going to send three lads up and over to see if it's worth taking the boats or if we should leave them here with some of the boys till we continue onto the crash site. In the meantime, we'll have some rest and food; shouldn't take too long.

'Sgt. Patterson, take a couple of the lads and see what's up ahead. I'll send Cpl. Smith and two other lads back in boat number two to the entrance of the gorge to watch the river. We don't want to be caught in here, or we'll be like rats in a trap!' Pete instructed his NCO. 'Right Hugh and Alex, let's get to dry land and stretch our legs,' he continued.

Those not on guard duty or scouting took advantage of the down time and had a plunge in the pool. Alex and Hugh followed suit; they were so hot and sweaty, and the cool of the pool was wonderful.

One of the younger marines approached his commanding officer. 'Sir, I've found these over on the other bank.' The soldier handed over six spent rounds of ammunition.

'So someone has been here before! Look, Hugh. Six rounds. Look Russian to me. What do you think?' Pete handed the bullets to Hugh.

'Yeah, these are the same ones the rebels were using up north in Belize,' Hugh confirmed.

'Cpl. Menzies, pass the word round the men that this place is visited by guerrillas, and by the look of these bullets not so long ago. So keep weapons at the ready!' Pete snapped out his orders for his men.

The relaxation was over! Everyone was tense again. Sgt Patterson returned after half an hour.

'Sir, I think we will have to proceed on foot; the river above the fall is too narrow for the inflatables.'

'Right, thanks, Sergeant. I think it would be safer to stow the boats and keep the group together. We have found some rounds here so fighters are in the area. Organise the men. I want to be out of here in twenty minutes,' Pete replied.

'How long to the crash site now?' Hugh asked.

Pete dug out his map. 'The boat would have been faster and more comfortable for you guys, but you can see how the river loops round. We are headed for this point which is just across this narrow neck of land so distance is actually quite short. Hard work for the scouts though as they will have to hack a way through the jungle with their machetes, but they are young fit lads! I'd say an hour's march.'

'Ok Pete, Alex and I will get ready for the off,' Hugh said confidently.

It was hard going. Alex was soaked with sweat, streams of moisture running down his forehead into his eyes. 'I don't remember it being this bad in the jungle before.'

'You were ten years younger then,' Hugh replied teasingly.

'Yeah, I guess I was. Look! Pete's trying to speak to us,' Alex said as he gestured up the path.

Pete was sliding back along the path to the two men.

'The scouts have located the plane up ahead about one hundred metres. It's not going to be easy. Are you sure you can go through with this Alex?'

'I'll go with Pete and the lads, and check the plane over, Alex. You wait here with one of the marines,' Hugh said protectively of his big brother.

'Absolutely not! I am looking for my children and I'm not stopping now, not for anything or anyone!' Alex replied forcefully as he pushed past Hugh on up the path.

Hugh and Pete exchanged glances but said no more.

As the squad entered the clearing, they could see the tail of the aircraft high above them, blackened streaks of fire damage on the tail fins. Walking on and to the right of the clearing, the extent of the damage to the wreck was more apparent. The fuselage was black and scorched, windows blown out. The cockpit was barely visible, smashed deep into the jungle, entangled in blackened trees and dead foliage. Doors on the right side were twisted and buckled but still in place.

When they walked round to the other side of the plane a large vulture flew off the top of the fuselage into the forest, then another flew out of the rear door.

'Oh, no! That's horrible! Shoot the vultures!' Alex cried distraught.

'There's no need Alex,' Pete replied putting his arm round Alex to steady him. 'They're scared off now.'

'Sgt, secure the clearing. Get two men up on the fuselage to lower a rope down from that back door. We'll then send up a party to examine the wreck.'

'Sir!' Sgt Smith, a stocky and able NCO accepted his orders.

Quickly, the commandos carried out their instructions. Hugh and Alex were wandering round the clearing while the lads attached the ropes.

'Look Hugh, you were right! There's what's left of the escape chute,' Alex said as he pointed to the fabric caught in the trees. 'No other slides have been activated; so surely someone has escaped from the plane!'

'I hope so, I really do hope so,' Hugh said shaking his head.

Just then, one of the scouts reported to Capt. Pete. 'Sir, there's a path leading away from the clearing to the north. It looks as if it has been used recently.'

'Thank you Corporal. Maybe the Peruvian army came in that way.'

'I don't think so, sir. A platoon would have trampled the path much more than this,' the scout replied.

'The Peruvians were winched down, Pete,' Hugh interrupted.

'OK Corporal, take three men and follow the path. See where it leads and who is likely to have been using it. Maybe this clearing has been made by drug barons to drop chemicals or lift drugs out by air. So keep a close eye.'

'Sir!' the corporal saluted as he left.

'We need to get a move on as it'll be dark in three hours,' Pete continued.

'Captain, the ropes are in position now,' Sgt Smith called from the door of the plane.

'Alex, Hugh are you ready? It's time,' Pete signalled to the two men to follow.

CHAPTER 12

Shocking Impact

Pete was pulled up to the back door of the plane first, followed by Hugh, and then Alex. In all, five men stood looking into the devastation that had been the cabin of the modern jet. The two young marines, who could only have been in their early twenties, used strips of cloth as masks. This was an attempt not only to protect them from the stench, but in part to conceal their emotional response to the horror they now witnessed. It was obvious from their eyes just how awful they found the scene before them, and they were battle-hardened young men.

Pete spoke first, 'These poor souls didn't stand a chance!'

Once Hugh had recovered from the shocking sight, he remembered the reason they were there. They knew no-one was alive here. But what had happened to the children? Had they escaped or were they among the twisted corpses in the fuselage.

'I'll go to the front and see if there are any children among the dead. Alex, which seats should the kids have been in?'

The second row from the start of economy class, seats C and D, across the aisle from one another,' Alex replied, through a croaky voice, fighting for composure.

'You stay put,' Hugh said, nodding to the marine to hold onto Alex.

'I'll come with you Hugh,' Pete volunteered, as both men put handkerchiefs round their noses.

'Yeah, OK,' Alex whimpered, as he slithered onto the floor of the cabin near the door.

The two officers edged their way up to the front of the plane. They discovered charred bodies still strapped to the seats. The gangway was strewn with pieces of hand luggage that had fallen down from overhead lockers. They managed to reach the partition that marked off the first class section at the front of the plane, but could go no further as twisted, gnarled metal blocked the way. The stench was overpowering.

'This must be the first row then,' Pete said. 'These seats are occupied on both sides. Now let's look at the second row.'

'Which seats did Alex say the kids were in?' Pete said excitedly.

'The ones on either side of the isle,' Hugh answered.

'They're empty!'

'Are you sure? Have you got a torch? We need a closer look. I don't want to give Alex false hope.'

'No sign that anyone was sitting in either of these two seats!' Hugh confirmed.

The two men made their way back up the plane to speak to Alex.

'If the children had moved seats to be with Aunt Susie which seats should they be in?'

'The row in front of the door here; on the left I think,' Alex replied, his head in his hands, too numb to think straight, too frightened to look in the seats, where the children might be.

This area of the plane was less damaged than the front. Hugh could see clearly that there were two empty seats on the left.

Hugh's heart was thumping in his chest. He could see that the pocket in front of the middle seat had something sticking out of it. He reached across to pull it out. It was a charred book but he could just make out the title Harry Pot… It was in English!

'Alex did the kids take any books to read for the journey?'

'I don't know, Tim was always reading about that wizard boy, what do you call him, Harry something?' he said wearily. 'What does it matter, everyone's dead, nobody survived this hell,' Alex replied, as he started to weep.

'Harry Potter! Look, Alex. Is this Tim's book? I found it in this empty seat!' Hugh said excitedly.

'Alex, are you listening man! There are two empty seats on this side,' Hugh was crouching down beside Alex now, trying to get through to him. Alex was fully Tim and Katie's father at this point, not a seasoned soldier; he was totally overcome by the situation and not able to take in Hugh's discovery.

'Alex, listen to Hugh,' Pete said gently. 'The children may have escaped. There are empty seats next to Aunt Susie.'

Alex looked up through deep red, moist eyes. He stared Hugh straight in the face and there he recognised the smile of hope.

'The children have survived this hell?' Alex mumbled, almost incoherently.

'We believe so,' Hugh replied softly.

'I think the body there, is Susie. Sarah said she had a new pair of specs, red rimmed I think. This lady has twisted glasses on her face. I can just make out small areas of red on the battered frame.'

'Oh dear! Sarah will be so sad. She and Susie were really close,' Alex muttered.

'Come on let's get out of here,' Hugh urged. 'We've found out more than we had hoped.'

The young marine helped Alex to his feet, secured the rope around him and lowered him gently to the ground.

When they had all returned from the aircraft, the officers and men were emotionally exhausted. They sat down and had some food and a drink. No one spoke, each deep in thought, the scenes inside the aircraft playing over and over in their minds like a DVD on repeat.

The silence was broken by the returning scouts. 'Sir! The path goes steeply down to a river. There's an abandoned hut and two hundred metres from the hut are the remains of a man. He has a bullet wound to his head.

It looks as if someone has been in the hut recently and inside there are footprints on the floor, on the dust. Sir, I think you should come and see as the footprints are of someone with small feet, possibly a child, and wearing a shoe. I don't think these would be native children, perhaps a survivor.'

'Thank you, Corporal. Firstly, how long do you think the man has been dead?' Capt. Pete asked.

'Hard to tell, Sir. In this heat it's anyone's guess; there is nothing left but a pair of shorts over bones, but the bullet hole is in the right side of the skull,' Cpl Menzies explained.

'So the guerrillas have done their worst in this area too, but at least not recently. Even so, I want everyone to be on guard. We may not be on our own as the drug men are obviously around. Sergeant, brief the men. Oh, and Sarge, watch out for these two young marines Smith and Fletcher; they have witnessed a ghastly scene today,' Capt. Pete instructed his NCO.

Hugh and Alex were up on their feet now; the news that perhaps children's footprints had been found had lifted their spirits. Pete could see they were keen to set off.

'Just give the men ten minutes to secure the equipment and we'll go down to this hut. It'll be dark in about half an hour so perhaps it'll be a suitable place to camp for the night. I would have preferred to return to Columbian soil, but that's not possible now, so we'll have to head back at first light.'

Corporal Menzies, a Highlander through and through, led the group down the steep path to the hut. He was like a mountain goat, as he walked confidently down the path, hardly noting the sheer drop to the valley below. Alex had difficulty keeping his footing as, after the rain, the path was treacherous. He wondered how the children had coped, if indeed they had come this way. To his great embarrassment, one of the young marines had to grab him to stop him disappearing over the edge to the water below. Alex knew that would never have happened to him ten years ago when he was at peak fitness and leading his own platoon in the jungles of Borneo. Physical fitness disappears so fast once you stop doing active exercise, he thought to himself. I really must get back to the gym once this is all over and we get the children home. Work at the office has just mounted up and up; I hardly ever manage to see Tim play cricket anymore. Katie is always asking me to take her riding, but Sarah has to go as I'm always too busy. I taught her to ride as well. Guilt gripped Alex. He could feel the tears welling up in his eyes, and he had to fight hard to prevent embarrassing himself again.

Pete was emerging from the hut, in deep discussion with his sergeant who scurried away to organise the sentries. The captain despatched two scouts to go further down the river and make sure there was no sign of guerrillas.

'Hugh, Alex, come and have a look at this.' Pete shouted across to the brothers. The two men rushed into the hut.

'Slow down guys or you will spoil the evidence!' Pete pointed to the floor over at the back of the jungle house. It was thick with dust. 'Nobody has had the vacuum cleaner out here recently,' Pete joked. 'Have a look at these; I think the corporal is right.'

'He's spot on! These are the footprints of a child, and it's not a bare foot!' Hugh shouted excitedly. 'But look there are other footprints alongside bigger than those, but not quite a man's size. It could be a trainer sole. Alex what was Tim wearing on his feet?'

'I don't know, we would have to ask Sarah. She helped the children get ready for the trip. I know he has trainers, in fact I remember discussing the credit card with Sarah only about a month back. She seemed to have bought a lot in a store I didn't recognise. I was worried someone had stolen our credit card details, but it was one of these new stores from the US, a fancy designer outlet in downtown Lima. Sarah said she had bought new clothes for both kids so they would be smart to go to their grandparents. Does it look like a trainer sole?' Alex asked.

'I think it does,' Hugh replied.

'Then they must have survived the crash!' Alex screamed with delight. 'There were no other children on the passenger list.'

Alex slumped to the floor and began to sob. He couldn't control his emotions anymore.

'Our kids are alive; they're alive!' he cried.

'Alex, don't build your hopes up too much. We still have to find them. They are not here now and it's five days since the crash. It's a wild, dangerous jungle out there,' Pete said, as he crouched down to comfort Alex.

'Captain, you had better come and see this.' A marine leapt up the two steps of the hut.

Pete grabbed his weapon and followed the soldier. Hugh watched as they disappeared along the river bank heading upstream. He could see there must be a problem as the platoon was alert, each man running for cover with his weapon at the ready.

'We had better stay here just now, Alex; something is up!' Hugh warned.

The young marine who had obviously been instructed to take care of them made a dart for the hut to join them.

'Capt. said you were to have these if we hit any trouble,' he said as he handed them both assault rifles.

'Thanks,' Hugh replied as he checked over the weapon. 'It seems a bit heavier than I remember,' Alex commented, as he familiarised himself with the recent model of army-issue rifle.

'I told you that you were not keeping yourself in shape these days. Working at a keyboard all day doesn't keep up the muscles,' Hugh said, teasingly to Alex.

The young marine grinned enjoying the joke between the brothers.

Two hundred metres up the track Pete and the marines were examining the remains of a fire.

'Captain these logs are still smouldering. It's not that long since this fire was abandoned, maybe this morning,' the sergeant said.

'The footprints round here are all boots; this has been a military force,' the captain added. 'Perhaps they were Peruvians looking for the wreckage.'

'Captain, over here, Sir,' a heavily camouflaged scout beckoned him. 'Someone has been firing off rounds, lots of them.'

'A search party wouldn't be shooting the place up,' the captain commented. He examined a couple of the bullets. 'These are Russian too. The Peruvian army are supplied legally by the United States, but the militia buy their arms from the dealers with the best prices, usually the Russians or Chinese. We have to assume these guys are militia. We don't want to have a skirmish on Peruvian soil if we can possibly avoid it.'

The commandos searched round the campsite. The footprints led to the river, the militia must have come and gone by the boat. Returning to the hut, Capt. Pete briefed Alex and Hugh. 'We can't stay here tonight; we must move under cover of darkness. We don't want to engage the enemy at all if we can avoid it while we are on this search and rescue mission, and certainly not while in Peru. So we must have some food, then we'll move out in about an hour.'

'Where are we going? What about the children? Do you think the militia have taken them?' Alex asked.

'I don't think the militia have them. They stopped up river from here, but I don't think they knew this place was here otherwise they would have made use of the hut and the greater space. My guys made a clean sweep of this site as soon as we arrived; they have not reported any evidence of soldiers having been here. The only footprints are children's, hopefully your children Alex.'

'But where do we look for them now?'

'The boys report that there are lots of footprints down by the river. I was going to go there with you when all the commotion started, so let's go now. Keep your weapon with you at all times now, Alex; the platoon is on red alert.' Alex picked up his rifle as he, Hugh and the captain left the cool of the hut and made their way down to the river.

'It certainly looks as if they've come down to the river and not returned to the hut, at this point,' Hugh offered.

'Maybe the guy that lived here had a canoe. He didn't leave with it did he?'

'No, he didn't. He's probably the corpse along the bank,' Pete agreed. 'The lads think that the children left by canoe, and on their own, as there are no other footprints. The current is quite strong so they have probably gone downstream.'

'Tim is very keen on geography; he'll know that going with the current will take them nearer the sea and therefore out of the jungle, and eventually to villages and communications. So I agree, I think they'll have gone downstream. But what if we're wrong? They are just kids. They won't survive out here that long…' Alex's voice tailed off.

'We go downstream in a couple of hours,' Pete said, authoritatively with nods of agreement from Hugh and his fellow commandos. 'But first, we have to retrieve the inflatables from the other river. Sarge, take six of the lads and recover the boats. Watch yourselves though.'

CHAPTER 13

New Friends

The children were wakened by the sun streaming through the window opening. It took Tim just a little while to work out where he was. Propping himself up on one arm, he looked around and saw two women sitting on the floor, with legs crossed, eating some food. Over in the other corner was an old lady sitting, rocking gently to and fro in a hammock; she seemed to be in deep thought gazing out through the open door of the house.

Katie nudged him. 'Oh I'm so sore lying on this hard floor, but I seem to have been asleep for ages,' she said, as she rubbed her eyes.

The women heard them speaking and beckoned the kids to go over to them. The children were given fruit and some porridge-like substance to eat. The fruit had strange pinkish flesh, very sweet and enjoyable. Katie thought it was a bit peachy, but it didn't look anything like a peach. The porridge, on the other hand, was disgusting.

'That tasted just like wallpaper paste,' Tim whispered to Katie, yet disguised his dislike from his hosts.

'Oh yeah! When did you ever eat wallpaper paste?' Katie teased.

Although it tasted awful, the youngsters felt much better after the meal. They smiled thankfully at the two women and thanked them in Spanish, not sure if they understood or not.

Just as they finished eating, Ronaldo arrived at the door. He greeted the women in his native dialect, chatted for a minute then disappeared again. Five minutes later, he arrived with two young girls. One looked to be about the same age as Katie, the other two or three years older. Ronaldo brought the girls over to Tim and Katie. He introduced them in Spanish.

The younger girl was called Maria, the other Mayu. Both girls were grinning and took Katie by the hand. Ronaldo explained that the girls were going to take Katie to wash by the river, show her round the village and introduce her to the other girls. Tim was a bit reluctant to let his sister out of his sight, but he felt confident that the girls would look after her. Ronaldo reassured Tim when he said he was going to show him round the village as well, but really it was best if the girls went off and did their thing while the boys saw to some of the more manly chores that needed to be done.

'I'll be OK, Tim. The girls seem very friendly. I'll see you later,' Katie said confidently.

'Cool. I don't think we're going too far away anyhow,' Tim acknowledged.

The girls ran down the steps of the hut into the village square. Katie counted five or six houses round the edge of a grassy area. The huts were all built the same way, with the bases raised on stilts about a metre off the ground. The walls were made of wood, which only extended halfway up the wall; the rest was just open, probably to let any cool breeze blow through the house, Katie thought. The roof was made of dried palm leaves, thatched together to provide protection from the rain in the wet season, and of course shade from the sun.

The girls took Katie to the hut in the corner of the square, laughing all the way. Inside were four or five other girls, sitting cross legged on the floor. Maria greeted and cuddled the woman who was with them. She called her a word that Katie didn't understand but then used the Spanish word 'Mama'.

Katie had been learning Spanish at school in Lima but was still shy about using it. However, when she realised the girls knew some Spanish she realised that she might be able to communicate with her new friends. Mayu indicated to Katie to sit down. The 'Mama' passed Katie, Maria and Mayu a piece of fruit to eat; the same as the other girls. Katie was a bit unsure at first. The fruit was about the size of a plum and was blood red in colour, but the skin was covered with scales. She could see that the other girls were eating bright orange flesh. Everyone was watching Katie to see what she was going to do. Katie put her lips to the hard outside and took a bite. She nearly broke her front tooth! The girls burst into peals of laughter. Katie soon saw the funny side and laughed as well. Maria showed Katie what to do; taking a small knife she scraped off the red scales exposing the orange flesh beneath. Once finished she passed the fruit to Katie who gently bit into the soft, sweet fruit amid cheers from her new friends. Katie could feel herself relax and realised that she was going to get along with her new chums really well.

When the snack was over, the girls left the hut and trooped down to the river to wash. Katie was surprised at how fast the river was flowing; it was a dirty brown colour and looked to her to be in flood. She remembered that Tim had said that this was the rainy season. There were large branches spinning down the river at great speed. Katie wondered how they were ever going to wash in that torrent. Mayu led the girls along a path on the river bank then she turned off to the right as if going away from the river. After twenty metres or so, the path disappeared over a slope down into a small valley that had been gouged by a little tributary that flowed into the main river. Here, the smaller stream was gently flowing. The villagers had made pontoons by tying logs together. Village children were diving off the logs into the river. Katie heard Tim calling to her but she couldn't see him. He called again; this time she caught sight of him as he and Ronaldo set off up the small river in a canoe.

'We're going fishing. Ronaldo is going to teach me how to fish "Amazonian style",' Tim shouted.

'Bring back something for supper, won't you,' Katie replied cheerily.

The other girls had jumped from the bank onto the nearest logs, and from there straight into the river to swim. Katie hesitated for a moment, then followed suit, but landed somewhat unsteadily on the floating logs; she had not anticipated the movement of the wood. An old lady sitting on the bank washing her clothes looked when she heard Katie's shriek and laughed at the newcomer's attempts to balance on the logs.

The girls were having great fun splashing each other. Katie was keen to join in so launched herself into the pool, clothes and all, just like the locals. The water was lovely and warm, so refreshing. The girls played together for a while, and then concentrated on washing their hair before clambering back on the logs, to lie and dry in the sun.

It was still quite early in the morning, probably around eight o'clock, Katie thought. The sun was just pleasant, although still much warmer than back home in Lima. As Katie lay there, she wondered about her Mum. It was almost four days now since the crash. Did her Mum and Dad know that she and Tim were alive? They would be very sad, and Granny and Papa would be very unhappy too. Tim and Katie should have been enjoying their holiday in Scotland, visiting cousins, seeing their old dog, Sky. Katie loved Sky. She was a Scottish bearded collie and had come to them as a puppy five years ago. But when her father had been sent to Lima by his company they had to ask Papa to look after her. Katie could feel tears filling her eyes, but she was suddenly distracted by something biting her toe, and then another bite and another. She looked down to see an ant or rather many ants crawling up her legs eating as they went. Quickly she jumped to her feet, screaming. Mayu, who was dozing next to her soon realised the problem, and she had the answer. Springing to her feet she grabbed Katie by the arm and the pair plunged into the pool. The other girls were quick to leave the floating logs for the bank knowing only too well that these ants could give a very painful bite. For Katie relief was quick; even so, the pair splashed about for a while before returning to the land.

The old lady who had been washing her clothes stood up from her work and shuffled over to Katie to look at her feet. She shook her head, smiled sympathetically, and then rattled off something in her native tongue to Maria. The young girl ran off into the forest with one of the other youngsters in hot pursuit. Within a few minutes she returned with some pink berries and handed them to the old lady. Taking some of the berries into her mouth, the woman chewed them to a pulp then took the mushed pink 'goo' and gently rubbed it into the bites on Katie's feet.

Katie smiled with gratitude to the lady, primarily acknowledging her kindness, but very quickly she became aware of the soothing nature of this jungle paste.

Katie didn't meet up with Tim again until the evening. She enjoyed her day with the young girls of the village. They were kept busy with the chores. The heaviest work was fetching water. There was no running water like home, not that Katie had expected any, but she did think they might have a well in the village. But no, all the water had to be carried in plastic tubs from the river. Katie was surprised by the plastic pails; some had obviously been used for a long time, but how had they come to be found so deep in the jungle? The girls worked well together; there was a bucket for each house, with two for the bigger long house. This was the headman's hut where Tim and Katie had spent the night. The water was required for drinking and cooking, so Katie was quite concerned when she realised that the water buckets were being filled down by the logs where they had just washed themselves. Even at her young age, she knew that it was not safe to drink bath water! She was even more upset when she saw many of the villagers having a pee in the long grass beside the river. There didn't seem to be such a thing as a toilet, not even a hole in the ground!

Katie thought the local girls were really strong. The containers were as big as the bucket her Dad used to wash the car, when they lived in the UK, which held at least ten litres. He had a driver now who washed the car for him. Dad didn't have time for things like that. He was too busy, too important! After all, that was why he hardly ever took her riding anymore. Katie missed her father.

They filled these buckets to the brim, and carefully lifted them onto their heads. Then they climbed up the steep bank and carried them back to the hut. Katie had to help too, but because she was one of the smaller girls her bucket was only half filled. This exercise was repeated again before nightfall. Katie was shocked to see that the containers sat in the corner of the hut, near the cooking pot, completely uncovered. She promised herself that she would not drink anything without checking there were no beasties floating in it first!

Throughout the morning, Katie had seen the rest of the homes and noticed that many of them were damaged; some had roofs with bits blown off and one hut had collapsed sideways like a card house. The long house looked in the best condition as it had obviously had some work done on it. At least two of the others were not being used but having repairs done. There did look to be an area that had been recently cleared, and Katie wondered if they were going to build a new house there.

One of the old men came to find the children just before siesta time. Katie could see he was excited as he chatted away in the village tongue. He was pointing to the path that led into the jungle and signalled the children to follow him. About twenty of the children trotted behind Alfonso, as he was known, for about two hundred metres down the path. Then he told them to be very quiet as they crept along the next short distance. Finally, he looked up to the trees and there, with her cub, was a very large sloth just sitting quietly on a high branch munching leaves. Katie and her friends stayed for ages quietly watching the lovely creatures as both mother and cub ate their fill.

Late in the afternoon, the men and older boys began to arrive back in the village too. Some had been fishing; many had just been catching small fish but one successful young man was showing off his big catch. It looked to be about a metre long and had a very ugly mouth with long whisker like things coming from its jaw. One man returned to the village with a bird hanging from the end of his long blow pipe. It looked very familiar to Katie, coloured black, yellow, and red. When the man held up his prey to show the villagers she realised it was a beautiful toucan. How could they kill something so beautiful? She was really shocked!

Others returned laden with bananas and other fruits she didn't recognise. A group of young men and boys returned looking really tired. They had shovels and axes. It looked as if they had been farming the land.

The headman came back with the farmers. They had been hacking back the jungle to create a new field to plant yucca, the staple food of the villagers. The chief, whose name was Bruno, looked around forty years old, but it was hard to tell, as the villagers looked older than their years due to the excessive exposure to the sun. He wore a loose-fitting shirt, shorts and flip-flops like the other men. On his head, though, he had a ridiculous hat woven like a basket. Bruno was greeted by his wife, Illary. Katie discovered that the name Illary meant rainbow, and she certainly lived up to her name because she always dressed in baggy bright orange or pink tops with bright green or blue skirts or shorts. Katie thought Illary's clothes never matched, but the woman was always kind and gentle with both Tim and Katie. Katie noticed that there was something wrong with one of Illary's eyes. The right one seemed to have a white growth over the front of the eye, and Illary was often peering at small things. Katie wondered if the chief's wife was going blind.

Bruno took up his place on the matting by the side wall of the hut. Everyone who entered the long house acknowledged the chief by standing in front of him, bowing slightly and touching the side of their nose with their right index finger. Katie had been watching the mark of respect shown to the leader of the village, since he had arrived home. She had laughed when a little lad of about three had scrambled up the steps to the lodge, scurried passed the headman straight to his mother for a drink, without looking at the chief. A quick glance from the headman to the mother and the young boy was lifted and placed at the feet of the chief – his dad. The boy bowed, touched his nose in the prescribed way and was then picked up by his father and given a huge cuddle, much to the hilarity of everyone in the long house. Bruno was a very proud father, and his beaming, toothless, smile could be seen right across the long hut. Seeing this, four other young children aged from about two years to seven, ran over and leapt onto the big chief so as not to miss out on their embrace!

Tim came bounding up the steps of the house just after nightfall. 'Where have you been? I was worried about you,' Katie shouted anxiously to her brother. He was so excited there was obviously nothing wrong with him. Tim ran straight over to her to tell her all that had happened to him during the day.

Katie picked up the silence first, as looks passed between the adults in the lodge. Ronaldo whispered a few words to Tim in Spanish as he gently led Tim by the arm, over to the headman. Following Ronaldo's lead Tim respectfully bowed and touched his nose. The chief acknowledged Tim, and then to everyone's surprise he stood, greeted him in Spanish, and shook his hand. He then beckoned to Katie, who was sitting on the floor next to the girls. She quickly went over to the chief who shook her hand too.

A supper of fish and a gruel-like dish made from the yucca plant was had by all, washed down by water. Katie was a bit nervous about the water, but it was too dark to inspect the cup of liquid before she drank it. She was too thirsty and too tired to care. She didn't notice any 'bits'!

Tim wanted to tell Katie all about his adventures and the things he had learnt from Ronaldo, but after the meal he was invited to join Miguel, his brothers and the other men and boys, while Katie was expected to stay with the women folk. By the time he returned to speak with his little sister she was fast asleep between her new friends Mayu and Maria!

CHAPTER 14

Diplomatic Incident

The two boats sped silently downstream, the crew able to navigate by the moonlight. Capt. Pete was anxious as he knew that, if they could see easily, so too could the guerrillas. The team successfully negotiated the waterfall, the same one that, unknown to them, had caused Katie and Tim's canoe to capsize. The commandos carried their boats for several hundred metres along the bank, and so avoided the large boulders and steep drop.

'If the children came this way I don't know how they could possibly have coped with this fast flowing river and all theses boulders, not to mention the ten-metre drop,' Alex said, anxiously to Hugh.

'Maybe they've met up with someone to help them,' Hugh replied, trying to be positive.

The rest of the night was uneventful. However, tensions were raised as they joined the bigger river. The advance boat signalled trouble ahead followed by the command to keep close to the side. The sergeant in the first boat whispered over the radio that there was a village up ahead. Pete was quick to call the vessel back and both boats turned and headed upriver for a few hundred metres to find a safe landing area. The commandos went ashore some half a mile upstream from the village. Within ten minutes boats, equipment, and men had disappeared into the jungle.

'We need to check out the village to see if there are any militia there. Sergeant, take four volunteers and check it out,' Pete instructed his men. 'The rest lie low but I want weapons at the ready and lookouts as for code red.'

The sergeant and his men were gone about forty-five minutes before they reported back.

'Sir, the village has been abandoned, but I think the militia have paid the community a call. There are four men tied to posts on the bank of the river, each with a bullet in his head. It looks as if they were tortured first. They've been dead a few days. We found an old woman curled up in one of the huts; she's terrified. I've left O'Connor and Jenkins with her as I thought you would like to see for yourself.'

'Thanks Sarge. It'll be light in about ten minutes. Let's get ready to move out; we'll go by boat,' Pete replied.

The commandos entered the village and found everything as the sergeant had said. Hugh and Alex helped with the sweep of the houses. This was a relatively small village of eight huts, a school, and a small health post.

The young commandos who had been caring for the woman offered her some food. Private Jenkins was fluent in Spanish, which the woman understood, so he explained to her that they were searching for drug dealers. This helped her relax and by the time Capt. Pete, Alex and Hugh arrived, she was chatting happily to her young rescuers. Her name was Urpi. The woman told the commandos of how, about the time of the last full moon, twenty or more drug bandits arrived in three boats just before nightfall. The men folk were returning from the fields. The bandits ran through the village, firing their guns into the air and rounded up everyone. The people were told that they wanted them to grow coca plants and help with preparation of the narcotics. The headman, Bruno, said that they were a Christian village and that they would have nothing to do with this, as they knew it was wrong. Three of the bandits attacked him and beat him up badly; they knocked out all his front teeth. The guerrillas left but said that the villagers had no choice, that they would be back in a week with their boss and expected everyone to help, or face the consequences.

Everyone in the village was very frightened. The following morning, the men folk held a meeting. Bruno listened to the different opinions. The young men wanted to go to the town of Libertad and get rifles to protect the village, but that would take ten hours by powered canoe. Some wanted to go to Libertad to contact the government to ask for protection. A few others said that they should do as the militia wanted if they wished to stay alive. This group of villagers had heard of other villages where the drug crooks had killed anyone who refused to work for them. The government was not likely to send troops up here. They were too busy fighting on the Bolivian border against the remnants of the Shining Path group.

Bruno thought over all the options. He decided that it was useless to fight as the guerrillas had many weapons and were not frightened to use them. He didn't think that the government would work quickly enough to help them. As headman, it was he who made the final decision to move the whole village deep into the jungle. He knew of an abandoned village high up the Corentes River, the area where he had grown up. It was about ten hours by canoe. Many of the young men, including Miguel, one of Bruno's nephews, were unhappy with this plan. They were concerned about how they would survive in the long term. They would not be able to take their bananas down to Libertad on the weekly river boat or buy new supplies for the village. 'What about the health post?' they asked.

'The health worker wouldn't come to the village anymore from Libertad if someone had fever or our children needed vaccinations.' The village teacher said that if the village moved she would be returning to Libertad. She was not going deep into the jungle.

Bruno had called for a vote, to stay or go to the Corentes River. Most of the men folk crossed over to Bruno's side. It was agreed to pack up the following day, and leave at nightfall to avoid being seen.

The old woman went onto explain that four of the older men refused to go. They were not going to be hounded from their village. One was her husband. When he saw the guerrillas coming back he sent her into the jungle to hide. She heard the gun shots. She crept back into the village at night; only the bodies of her husband and his friends were left.

The old woman crumpled on the floor in tears as she reached the end of her story. Alex crouched down to comfort her.

Softly, in Spanish, he asked her if there had been any gringo children in the village in the last few weeks. She looked up with red dark eyes and shook her head. Alex pulled the broken woman close to himself, understanding something of her pain.

Pete and Hugh discussed the situation outside the hut where Urpi had been found. Alex sat on the bank of the river just staring at the water.

'I don't have permission to venture further into Peruvian territory, Hugh. My instructions were to escort you to the plane and see if there were any signs of survivors in the vicinity. We are already over forty kilometres into Peru; we must return to Columbia before dawn,' Pete said sadly.

'I know, you and your men have done more than we could have asked for. We know the children are alive, but they could be anywhere now. Perhaps the guerrillas have found them; we've seen enough evidence of their activities round this area! It's five days now since the accident; if they haven't been helped by someone who knows the jungle, I wouldn't give much for their chances, would you?' Hugh asked his young colleague.

'Children can be very resilient. Seems to me that they've had a miraculous escape from the plane; surely God didn't do such an amazing thing, just to wipe them out in the jungle. Do you believe in God?' Pete said, as he put an arm on Hugh's shoulder.

'Yes I do. Quite frankly, God is these kids' only hope. I'll go and speak to Alex and see what's going through his head. This is taking its toll on him; I've watched him age ten years in the last few days. His ginger hair is fast turning white,' Hugh replied, with a sigh.

Hugh and Alex talked at length while the soldiers made plans to move out back to Columbia. It was agreed that the old lady would go with them upriver to the neighbouring village. Hugh could see that Alex was physically and emotionally exhausted. He suggested that he and Alex return to Lima to be with Sarah. At least she would be ecstatic to know that the children had probably survived the plane crash. Looking for the children without the commandos would not only be too dangerous for them, but would be like looking for a needle in a haystack. Hugh suggested that Alex and Sarah fly up to Iquitos and hire fast boats to explore the rivers in this area as tourists.

'But surely we can ask for help from the Peruvian army and navy to search for the children?' Alex suggested.

'I doubt it. Remember, the Peruvians are insisting there are 'no survivors'. How can we convince them otherwise without blowing the cover off the commando unit. The Ministry of Defence in London will never agree to the presence of British troops on Peruvian soil being acknowledged. There would be an international incident over the affair involving Columbia as well as the UK; that would set back relationships twenty years.'

'Who cares about international relationships? These are our kids we're talking about!' Alex snapped.

'Steady on! I know how you feel, Alex, but the MoD has helped us enormously by allowing the 'boys' here to help search for the children. Without them, we would have had to accept that there were no survivors. At least now we have hope that the kids are alive. If we cause a diplomatic incident, the assistance that UK forces are giving to the Columbians in their war against drug runners will be withdrawn. If that were to happen, then the activities of the drug barons would go unchecked. Not only will these poor village folks continue to be terrorised, as we have just witnessed, but drugs will keep pouring onto the streets of Britain, destroying young lives and families.'

'I know, I know. And you'd be banged up in some military jail, back in the UK for breaching the Official Secrets Act, I suppose,' Alex grunted.

'Yeah, and that too! We have to think clearly. It would be best for the three of us to go to Iquitos, and then return to this area as tourists.'

Reluctantly, Alex agreed, although he knew he would have difficulty explaining all the 'diplomatic stuff' to Sarah. He missed her greatly, and more now than he could ever remember. He just wanted her to be near, to smell her sweet perfume and hold her in his arms. His heart ached for his wife.

* * *

Two days later, Alex and Hugh were on board the flight from Bogotá to Lima. The trip back to Columbia overnight had been tiring but uneventful. Number one boat had managed to slip quietly to the jetty of the neighbouring village and put Urpi ashore.

During the flight, Alex told Hugh of his Peruvian friend, Gilberto, who used to work in the Lima office. Gilberto was from Iquitos; he missed his family and the jungle very much when he was living in Lima, so when a post came up in the company office in Iquitos he was quick to apply. His local knowledge would be very helpful to them. Alex planned to contact him as soon as they returned to Lima.

As they flew over the jungle, Alex stared down at rivers that snaked round the vast forests below, hoping and praying that his children were alive. He promised himself there and then, that as long as he was able, he would never, never give up looking for them.

CHAPTER 15

Search Plans

Sarah was at the airport to meet Alex and Hugh. Alex had phoned from Bogotá, so she already knew that the children had most likely, and miraculously, survived the plane crash and was therefore 'on a high' with the news. Alex was overcome when he embraced his wife from the exhaustion of the previous few days; he sobbed on her shoulder. He didn't care who might see him crying like a baby as they stood in the middle of the airport.

Hugh escorted them back to the car and then on home through the Lima rush hour. Alex and Sarah, for once, were totally oblivious to the horns, sudden breaking and verbal exchanges between drivers at traffic halts which usually made them very anxious passengers. Even after three years in Lima, neither of them had grown accustomed to the lifestyle or the traffic. Today was different. Alex had his arm around Sarah, holding her close, telling her everything that had happened on their trip to the crash site.

Sarah was able to tell Alex about the news coverage, or rather the lack of it. The government had issued a statement the day Alex and Hugh had left for Columbia confirming that the search and rescue team reported no survivors. The team had, however, managed to retrieve the flight recorder. The aviation authority's initial assessment was that all one hundred and fifty passengers and crew had perished in the accident. The aircraft had most probably suffered an electrical fault due to the violent thunderstorm in the region and had burst into flames on impact. The authorities did not anticipate the recovery of bodies for some time due to the remote location of the wreckage. Sarah went on to say that, since the issuing of the statement, there had been no further information. She had tried phoning Señor De Silva, who was very polite and sympathetic, but he had added nothing to the original statement. Sarah had phoned both sets of grandparents while the brothers were away. Alex's father reported that the BBC had covered the loss of the Air Inca flight with all passengers and crew, on only two bulletins. Granddad had thought it was because the plane was on a relatively local flight and not an intercontinental plane likely to have many Europeans on board.

Once back at the house, Hugh left Alex and Sarah alone to catch up. It had been over a week since he left the UK. He knew he must contact HQ to see if he could extend his time in Peru; however, he wasn't too hopeful as he knew his regiment was for deployment to Afghanistan in two weeks. He was right. He had managed to speak directly to the brigadier who insisted on his immediate return to the regiment. For security reasons, the brigadier couldn't elaborate over unsecure communications. Hugh knew that it probably meant he would be going with a small unit in advance of the rest of his men, therefore he put up no resistance. He was, after all, a professional soldier at the pinnacle of his career, a senior officer in the SAS. Much as he wanted to stay and help his brother search for his darling children, he knew he couldn't.

After lunch, over coffee, Hugh broke the news to Alex and Sarah.

'I've been on to HQ. I have to return to the UK tonight. I'm sorry I cannot stay longer, but there is a big push on. I have to get back to the regiment,' Hugh said sadly.

'Hugh, you have done more than enough. If it hadn't been for you, we would have believed everything the authorities had put out. You have given us hope. Thanks to you, we have reason to believe the children have survived the crash. They are alive somewhere in the jungle!' Alex replied thankfully. 'It's just a shame that we can't find a way to convince the Peruvian authorities that there are some survivors. But I don't know how to do it without blowing the story about the commando unit. We understand the diplomatic situation, and realise we'll have to organise the search ourselves. Sarah and I are going up to Iquitos tomorrow. I'm going to phone Gilberto this afternoon, to enlist his help.'

'Yes, I think that is the best way forward. As we discussed on the flight down from Bogotá, you should hire a fast boat and go systematically up the tributaries of the Napo that drain the region of the crash site. You should visit each village in turn, and show photographs of the kids. I think that is your best hope. To go to the authorities and say you have been to the crash site with a British commando group is going to cause a political storm. Plus, it will cause the Peruvians too much embarrassment if you publically disagree with their story of 'no survivors'. They may well restrict your movements, which is the last thing you want. These countries never like to lose face, especially to a European country. There's been too much colonial history,' Hugh suggested.

'I do think the Peruvians really believe there have been no survivors. We have just been fortunate to have your skills and contacts, Hugh. It's a difficult time for the authorities;

the Peruvians never like to be on the international stage, and they don't have the financial resources that the UK or US have at their disposal,' Alex commented.

'I think, Alex, you should rest today. I'll book us on the first flight to Iquitos tomorrow,' Sarah piped in, gently stroking Alex's arm. 'When will you have to leave, Hugh?'

'I have managed to get a flight with American Airlines to Miami tonight. There's an RAF Hercules returning home tomorrow morning from a nearby US air force base, so if everything goes to plan, I'll be able to hitch a ride right back to the base. So I should find out within twenty-four hours where I'm about to be deployed.'

Hugh left as planned in the early evening. It was an emotional farewell. Hugh wanted desperately to stay and help with the search for the children, but he knew he couldn't. Alex piled off to bed soon afterwards leaving Sarah to pack for the Iquitos trip. Their flight was at six, just before dawn, which meant another early start.

Wearily, Alex sat in the departure lounge drinking strong coffee. It was seven in the morning; their flight had been delayed. Sarah went over to the gate to enquire.

Alex couldn't believe the answer.

'Vultures! You're kidding me!' Alex protested.

'That's what the young woman said,' Sarah confirmed.

An elderly Peruvian gentleman, who was sitting next to them, overheard their conversation. He volunteered that the early flight was often delayed because of vultures around the airstrip at Iquitos. The pilots were frightened of bird strike. He reminded them of an accident due to bird strike in Brazil the year before. Everyone on board had been killed. Alex thanked the man for his helpful comments, sat back in his chair and closed his eyes.

They stepped off the plane at Coronel Francisco Secoda Vigetta Airport in Iquitos four hours later. Sarah felt she had walked into a sauna. Unlike her husband, she had hardly ever been in the tropics as she didn't cope well with the heat. She wondered how she would cope travelling up and down the Amazon if it was this hot at ten thirty in the morning. How would the children cope with this heat? Thank goodness Alex had insisted that she and the children received all the immunisations necessary for a trip to the jungle shortly after they had arrived in Peru. He had planned to take the family on a jungle wildlife safari. They had even had yellow fever vaccinations, much against her will, but she was grateful now, knowing that the children were at least protected from that killer.

They were met by Gilberto, a jolly well-rounded man in his mid-forties. He was very sympathetic towards them, and promised to help in any way he could to find the children. He had a car waiting for them and took them to their hotel, the 'Victoria Regina', in the centre of the city.

Sarah had never experienced a city like it before. Alex had visited Thailand and the bustling cities of India, so it was not such a shock to him. It was incredibly noisy, with motorised rickshaws dodging everywhere. Luggage was strapped onto the platform at the back of the vehicle, while the owner's hand was draped over the backseat onto the baggage, to warn off any potential theft. There were scooters, overloaded with young children on the front and back, and not a safety helmet in sight!

Downtown Iquitos had some fascinating old façades, all invariably run down. Gilberto explained that, about a hundred years earlier, there had been huge rubber plantations all round the area. Iquitos was a bustling city, exporting the commodity along the Amazon River to Europe and America; that was until Malaysia started to produce rubber and the market declined. Ocean-going vessels used to come as far as Iquitos in their droves, but now only a few brought supplies to the city. Gilberto pointed out that tourism was one of the main sources of income;

visitors came from all over the world to see and experience the challenges and creatures of the jungle. Iquitos was only accessible by sea or by air, making the cost of buying a car well beyond the reach of most of the inhabitants, so there were very few cars in the city; hence, there were rickshaws and mopeds everywhere.

Alex and Sarah agreed to meet with Gilberto after lunch to plan the next stage of the search for the two children.

'I'll introduce you to young Carlos. He's my nephew; he has a fast boat,' Gilberto said as he left the couple. 'I'll come and collect you at two o'clock. You'll be able to have lunch here.'

Gilberto arrived around half an hour late. Alex and Sarah had lived in Peru for a while, so they were not upset by this as they knew Peruvians were invariably late. They squeezed into a rickshaw and sped out into the city traffic. The journey took them down to the river front. Alex signalled to Gilberto that he wanted to stop and look at the river.

The three clambered out of the rickshaw, and stood silently at first, taking in the magnificence of the river. At Iquitos, the Amazon is over two thousand miles from the Atlantic Ocean but is still several kilometres wide. It was hard to believe that ocean-going vessels could come so far inland. Along the bank of the river was evidence of what had been a majestic promenade at one time. However, in front, on slightly lower ground, with only the thatch roof tops showing, Gilberto pointed out the slum dwellings of some of the poor residents of Iquitos.

'There is another slum area known as Puerto Belen just over there,' Gilberto pointed away to the right of where they were standing. 'This is a real problem for the local government as the population of the shanty town is growing rapidly. Many villagers from the Amazonian jungle are leaving their homes in search of a new life in the city. They are driven off by fear of the drug militia along the Columbian border or, more recently, by the destruction of their way of life by mining or logging. The villagers cannot support their families in the city, as they have no skills, so they end up worse off. We have many 'piranhas' on our street, which is very sad.'

'We know all about them in Lima,' Alex said. 'They are street boys, kids that have been abandoned. They are just a nuisance! They hunt in packs; one of our young employees was robbed by them in downtown Lima only a couple of weeks ago. Anything that can be done to get them off the streets would help everyone.'

'Yes, that's right. They have a terrible existence on the streets. They eat from rubbish bins when they can, or steal to survive. Many of them die of pneumonia and food poisoning. Often, predatory tourists from the US and Europe abuse them. All very sad,' Gilberto said, gently trying to put over the other side of the argument.

'You seem to know a lot about the problem Gilberto,' Sarah commented.

'Our church runs a night shelter for about twenty boys, but it only reaches the tip of the iceberg,' he replied. 'We had better press on; Carlos will be waiting,' Gilberto said quickly, not wishing to dwell further on the sensitive subject of the street children. He knew that the work that Alex's organisation was involved in, oil exploration, was partly responsible for the migration of indigenous families to the shanty towns, and the worsening street boy problem in Iquitos. Gilberto also worked for Petro-Explore NMW. He had a well-paid job and a wife and three children to support. He enjoyed his work as an accountant for the Company, but didn't approve of the way his government gave licences to big international companies, without any thought for the impact on the local communities. Alex held a senior executive post with the company in Lima. Gilberto had worked in his department in Lima and had great respect for Alex as a person. But over the past three years, since he was relocated back to his Iquitos, he had become much more aware of the devastation the oil companies were causing the local Amazonian communities.

Carlos was very different from his uncle. He was tall for a Peruvian, at almost six feet, thin and athletic-looking with very dark eyes. He sat at the table in his small two-roomed house. His wife, Maribel, ushered away their two little children to the bedroom. After introductions Carlos cleared the debris from the family's earlier lunch, into a basin by the sink, and carefully wiped the table before laying out the maps. You could tell that he had a great respect for the geographers who had spent years mapping the Amazon and its tributaries, as he carefully unfolded the map which showed all the rivers from Iquitos to the Columbian border.

'Do you have the coordinates of the crash site?' he asked in well spoken English.

'Yes, here are the GPS coordinates,' Alex replied handing him the grid references on a piece of paper. Carlos carefully plotted the site on his map.

'About a hundred and fifty kilometres due north of Rumi Tumi on the Rio Napo,' he said thoughtfully. 'I take tourists up the Napo to San Ramon at least once a month so I know that part of the river quite well. I have many contacts up there. I have never been north of San Ramon but I know of someone who lives in the town who might be able to help.'

'When can we start?' Sarah said impatiently.

'You'll have to tell me what you want to do first. Stop at each village on the way north to see if they have seen any gringo kids, which will take some time or go as far up the river and as close to the crash site as possible and then work our way back slowly?

'We need to get as close to the crash site as fast as we can, and then start looking for the children,' Sarah interrupted Carlos.

'Yes, that's the only way that makes sense to me,' Alex agreed.

'I think that is the best way too. It will take us three days to reach San Ramon. Our first stop will be Mazan tomorrow night, then onto Bella Vista the next day. By late evening the following day, we will arrive in San Ramon,' Carlos pointed out the route as he spoke. He continued, 'At each of these villages we will be able to take on fuel. We will start at first light tomorrow. It doesn't look far as the bird flies but the Napo bends north again before it joins the Amazon so it will take us most of the day to reach Mazan.'

'Where will we sleep?' Alex asked, worried about Sarah.

'At the first three stops we will be able to find a roof over our heads in the small tourist places. But do not expect too much. Toilets are just a bucket on the floor, a jug of water to wash. Food's OK, if you like Peruvian food – fish, chicken, rice, yucca.'

'What's yucca?' Sarah asked.

'It's the villager's potato; they harvest it all over Amazonia. It's related to the yucca plant grown as an ornamental house-plant back home,' Alex responded knowingly.

'Will there be mosquito nets? I hate creepy crawlies,' Sarah added.

'We'll take our own, Sarah; it's safer that way. I don't want us to get dengue fever either, as I did when in the jungles of Borneo. They call it 'break-bone' fever, and I know why! The mosquitoes that cause the illness bite during the day so nets don't prevent it, but I've made sure that we've packed plenty of insect repellent. Do you know where we can buy nets and other supplies before we go? It was such a rush having only just returned from Columbia,' Alex asked.

'Sure I'll take you there once we've finished here,' Gilberto volunteered.

'Do you have life jackets on the boat?' Sarah piped up again, obviously rather anxious about the entire expedition. She knew she had to go. She wanted to go. She couldn't let Alex look for the children alone. She would just worry about all of them.

'Yes. I have some. It is the law in Peru we must have life jackets on board, but people very seldom wear them, too hot I suppose,' Carlos replied.

'Don't worry, Sarah; we'll sort everything out before we leave.' Alex gave Sarah one of those looks which said, "Trust me. I know what I'm doing".'

Sarah could see a change in her husband these last few days. He was much more affectionate towards her; he was really looking out for her. Since they had moved to Lima they had drifted apart, almost living separate lives. Alex was so busy with his work; in late, bringing paperwork home and sitting at his desk until one in the morning sometimes. The children hardly saw their father. Alex used to take Tim fishing and hill walking when they lived in the UK, but since coming to this country he had done very little with the children. At least once a month he had to go up country to Pucallpa to the drilling site there, and occasionally to Manus in Brazil for regional meetings. Petro-Explore NMW had several sites in Peru and Brazil and had huge expansion plans. Sarah believed that Alex was much happier when he was in the army; he had more belief in his work. He was away a lot then, but when he was home he spent all his time with the family. He had progressed very rapidly up through the company in the six years he had worked for them, but it didn't come naturally to him; he had to work very hard. His efforts had paid off because he was now one of their senior executives with overall responsibility for the work in Peru. He had hundreds of people working under him: in the offices in Lima, in Pucallpa and the new office in Iquitos, as well as the technical staff at the drilling sites. Sarah felt that their family life had suffered because of the huge stress on Alex. He was a much angrier man who would row with her over any small thing. Just sitting with him in the car in the Lima traffic could be embarrassing, with him swearing at other drivers from the back seat of the limo. She wondered how he would relate to the Amazonian villagers as she knew that he regarded the indigenous peoples as belonging to the 'Stone Age'. Ignorant tribesmen, who kept trying to halt the progress he and his company were trying to make as they explored for oil in the jungle. She, on the other hand, had sympathy for these ancient peoples; surely they mattered to God and it was wrong to chase them off the land their ancestors had lived on for thousands of years. But she had never quite gathered up the courage to tell Alex her views, and, that, she deeply regretted.

Alex's question interrupted her thoughts.

'Carlos, could we go down to the boat this afternoon, and have a look at her?' Alex asked. He was a little concerned that the 'fast' boat would be anything but fast. Would it be suitable for their purposes? What if they broke down up some remote river and had to spend the night on the boat. Would it be big enough? Alex's military training was beginning to kick in; be prepared for any eventuality. He knew he had to go and buy a rifle and a hand gun as he couldn't bring any weapons on the flight over. There was no way he was taking his wife into the jungle without a weapon.

'Sure, we could go right now, unless you want to look further at the maps,' Carlos replied.

Carlos shouted his goodbyes through to his family and soon the group were out in the street again. It was so hot

Sarah thought she was going to pass out; however, once back in the rickshaws, the welcome breeze cooled her down. The journey took about twenty minutes. The boat was tied up, down at the Nanay River, at the small bustling port. Gilberto explained that local villagers brought their produce in their small boats to take up to the Belen market, which was a very busy market and popular with tourists. Sarah saw another use for rickshaws. One country-looking woman was unloading chickens from the back of one of the 'motorcars'. There were hens tied together, in twos by the feet, stacked on top of each other in the space normally reserved for a suitcase. Sarah counted five couplets of chickens, ten in all.

'Look, Alex! That is so cruel; these hens must be terrified!' Sarah shouted above the noise.

'That's just the way life is here. It's the culture, the way they've always done things. We can't do anything about it. Those chickens will feed lots of hungry mouths,' Alex replied.

Carlos proudly took them down the muddy slope to his boat. He shouted above the noise of the harbour, 'This is Claudia!'

Alex looked the small vessel over, carefully noting the size and condition of the outboard motor. The roof looked as if had recently been replaced. Tucked up in the rails of the roof he retrieved a rather poor excuse for a life-jacket. He made a mental note to get new ones for Sarah and himself, but he didn't think it would be worth buying any for Carlos and the other lad, Pedro, who had now joined them, as he knew they would not wear them anyway. Carlos explained that Pedro would be going with them. He was Carlos's cousin; he slept on the boat all the time to prevent anyone stealing it.

While Alex was looking over the boat, Sarah was looking round the port. She noticed a vessel about the size of a small ferry, which had obviously been modified. It had a red cross painted on the side; she wondered if this was one of the medical ships she had heard about that took health care to the villagers on the Amazon. When the men returned, she asked Gilberto, 'Is that ship over there one of the medical ships we've heard about helping the peoples of the river?'

'Yes, there are several ships, mainly from the US but at least one from the UK. They're usually sponsored by churches from their home countries. The organizations employ Peruvians to man the ships and form the medical teams but, several times a year teams will fly in from the US or UK to join the trips,' Gilberto replied.

'Do you think they make a difference?' Sarah continued.

'The ones that work alongside the Peruvian authorities certainly do. They'll take Peruvian midwives and malaria teams to the remote villages. This makes childbirth safer for the women and the chances of reaching school age much greater for the children,' Gilberto replied.

'I suppose it must make a big impression on the visiting teams as well. Most of them will be well-paid doctors and nurses; the poverty must really shake them up,' Sarah continued.

'I bet it does,' Alex chipped in. 'I would think it makes them go home grateful for the health care in their own countries. Gilberto, the boat seems fine. Can you take us to somewhere we can buy supplies now?'

Carlos was happy to remain at the boat making final preparations for the early start, and it was agreed that Gilberto would bring Alex and Sarah at dawn. The three then returned to Iquitos to stock up for the trip. By the time they arrived back at the hotel they had mosquito nets, sleeping mats, water purification tablets, first aid kits, rucksacks – everything Alex thought necessary for a three-week expedition into the rainforest.

'Do we need all this equipment? And these guns! Do we really need them?' Sarah asked, as they checked through their purchases, and laid them carefully on the double bed.

'This is possibly going to be the toughest thing you've ever done, Sarah,' Alex replied as he took her in his arms. 'I don't want anything to happen to you. There are wild animals and dangerous drugs barons on this river. We have to take as many precautions as possible.' As Sarah snuggled into Alex's chest, he gently stroked her hair. She realised that he was now much more like the man she married. How sad, she thought, that it had taken such a disaster to bring them together again.

CHAPTER 16

Culture Shock

S arah was relieved to arrive in the regional town of Mazan. It had taken twelve hours, just as Carlos had predicted – a very noisy journey bouncing along the Amazon to start with, and then a sharp left up the Napo. It was a beautiful day with spectacular scenery unfolding as they sped along the magnificent river, but Sarah hardly noticed; she was preoccupied with thoughts of her children. Where had they slept the night? How were they coping with the heat and the insects? Would they find enough to eat? All these questions ran around her mind as they journeyed up the Rio Napo in the boat.

There had been much more river traffic than Alex had anticipated; everything from canoes to high-speed boats and launches. On one occasion, they had to manoeuvre out of the path of a large cargo vessel. Claudia bumped sickeningly over its wake, as the huge ship pushed on against the current towards Iquitos. Alex tried to imagine what these waters must have been like when Iquitos was the rubber capital of the world, with tall sailing ships heading downstream for the Atlantic, and then on to Europe with their cargo. They had stopped only twice on the journey for comfort stops and to allow Pedro and Carlos to change over the petrol tanks.

'I am so stiff,' Sarah said as she stretched on the jetty, 'and hungry! Where is the hotel?' she asked Carlos.

'Oh Señora, there is no hotel here, but there is a guest house where you will get a room. Pedro and I will stay with the boat. You should be able to get some food in one of the bars on the main street. Try 'Trick's', that's where my tourist passengers usually eat. Pedro will take your rucksack Señora and show you where to go,' Carlos instructed.

'Thanks, Carlos. What time are we leaving in the morning?' Alex asked, as he picked up his rucksack and rifle.

'Señor, you had better leave your rifle here, under the seats; the police will not be happy to see you with it in the town. There will always be one of us at the boat,' Carlos cautioned.

Alex agreed, emptied the magazine and stored the weapon under the back seat as instructed. He wasn't unduly concerned as his handgun was in his holster under his shirt and the rest of the ammunition was deep in his rucksack.

Pedro escorted the couple to a traditional house about two hundred metres from the river. They were greeted by a middle-aged woman, who showed them to a room at the back of the building. Sarah was shocked. There was a table in the corner with a jug and bowl for washing, and a rickety chair by the window. On the bare floorboards was a filthy looking mattress.

'We can't stay here Alex, it's awful!' Sarah pleaded.

'Sarah, we've no choice. There are no plush hotels this far out of Iquitos so I'm afraid you'll have to get used to it. This is why we brought hammocks and mosquito nets. One thing I learnt when in Borneo; be as self-sufficient as possible because there are no facilities,' Alex replied.

'I suppose you're right. Where's the loo? No you're kidding me! Not the bucket?!' Sarah exclaimed.

Alex smiled as he watched the look of horror on his wife's face.

'You could always use the family loo,' he said teasingly.

'Where is it?' Sarah asked.

'Look, it's out the back in that small shack, on the edge of the jungle. I don't think you would want to go out there in the middle of the night, would you?' he said as he peered out the window.

'No, I'll settle for the bucket,' Sarah conceded, reluctantly. 'Can we go and find a restaurant? I'm famished.'

'We'll go and find some food but I don't think it'll be a restaurant.'

The pair strung up their hammocks and nets from the cross-beams, removed their valuables to a smaller rucksack, and headed off to look for sustenance. They were quite surprised how busy this small jungle town was. It was big enough to support three or four motorised rickshaws, but most people were on foot. They found several bars that sold food but didn't like the look of any of them including the one recommended by Carlos. Alex decided on one that was very busy with locals; he believed that the villagers would only frequent a bar if the food was good.

Sarah was pleasantly surprised by the chicken and rice meal that was put before her. It was hot, tasty and plentiful. Both washed down the supper with Inca Cola, the national drink. At least they knew the cola had come from a factory that would be regulated by the government. Sarah didn't want to think about the kitchens, but consoled herself by the fact that the food was piping hot. She was always very strict with the children in the kitchen. She taught them the importance of washing their hands and to keep raw food away from cooked food. But for this trip, she told herself, "I'm going to stay calm". They had to eat or they wouldn't have the energy to find the children. In other words, she resigned herself to the fact that she would just have to get on with it, no matter what!

Within the hour they were back at their lodgings, relying on their head torches to find their way around the room. After fighting with the mosquito net and launching herself successfully into the hammock at the second attempt, Sarah fell quickly into a deep sleep. She was exhausted by the first day of their expedition to find the children. Alex found sleep much harder. He kept thinking about Tim and Katie, wondering if they were still alive. It was almost ten days now since the crash. How could young people of thirteen and ten years survive such jungle conditions? They may have been injured in the accident and died of their wounds. Perhaps one had been bitten by a snake? What if Tim had died and Katie was all alone? How could his little girl ever survive against such terrible odds? Maybe the militia had found them… The thoughts that followed were too much for him. He found himself praying 'Please God, help my dear, dear children; they are so innocent. What have they done to deserve this? I know I could have been a better father to them, a better husband. Don't punish them. I'm the guilty one; take me not them,' Alex sobbed quietly, before finally falling asleep.

Alex and Sarah rejoined Carlos at the boat, at dawn as arranged. Minutes later Pedro came running down the jetty clutching fresh bread. He climbed aboard to his seat among the petrol cans at the rear, and then they were off on the river again. The little port was busy with canoes heading out for a day's fishing, and there were at least two other tourist boats returning to Iquitos. Sarah wondered where these boats containing groups of men and women of different ages had been. She couldn't speak to Carlos above the noise of the engines which was a shame as she was sure he would know the answer. Alex read her thoughts.

'They're either from the States or Europe. They come to 'discover' themselves with the help of the witch doctors from the villages. There is a huge interest from westerners in the rituals of these tribal people, their forest medicines and the like. The local tribes have been quick to catch onto this type of tourism as it brings income to the village. Sadly, many of these westerners don't realise how dangerous it is to get into this sort of evil world. Gilberto was telling me all about it yesterday; his church is very worried about this sort of tourism as they believe it will bring a bad name to Iquitos ultimately.'

'Surely there are tourists who just want to experience the jungle and see the wildlife?' Sarah asked.

'Yes, but those fast boats are from the Native Secrets Company; Gilberto was specifically speaking about them. These people want to get high on drugs and have the 'ultimate' jungle experience; they are not really interested in the creatures of the forest. There are many good outfits in Iquitos who offer great ecological tours. Brian, in my office, had a wonderful time last vacation. He and his family couldn't praise the tour company enough. Their accommodation and food were first-class; no one fell ill. For him, the highlight was the bird watching. The family was taken by canoe, up small creeks, deep into the forest. So there was no engine noise to drown out the birdsong. He said it was a fantastic experience. Brian is a keen photographer and he took some wonderful shots. I've always meant to take Tim and Katie on a similar…'

Their conversation was interrupted. Sarah looked back towards Mazan and noticed that Pedro had suddenly disappeared.

'Where's Pedro? He must have fallen in the river!' Sarah shouted anxiously to Alex.

Alex grinned at his gullible wife and pointed above her head. There she recognised Pedro's silhouette as he clambered along the roof and jumped down in the bow to speak to Carlos!

'I thought it was 'man overboard.' She smiled sheepishly, as she snuggled into Alex's outstretched arm.

The journey up the river to Bella Vista was memorable. Sarah enjoyed the trip better this time, having become accustomed to the bouncing around and the continual deafening noise from the engine. At one time, they were 'buzzed' by a Peruvian Naval gunboat. Alex was a bit concerned but Carlos gave them a cheery wave and the sailors continued on their way. Alex left his seat and moved up front to talk with Carlos as he piloted the boat.

'What was that about?' Alex roared in Carlos's ear.

'They're from the naval base at Mazan. They patrol all the way to Bella Vista; they're looking for drug runners. The river Napo is used by the drug smugglers from Columbia. No need to worry, the captain of the speed boat recognised my boat. He was just checking it was me at the wheel and how many passengers I was carrying. He's more likely to stop and search us on the way back!' Carlos explained.

Lunch was a brief stop in a very small village of about six houses, called the 'Third of March'. The Peruvians often call their village after a special date or the day the village was founded. As usual, the children rushed to see the boat arrive and watched the passengers, especially the gringos.

Sarah observed how poor the children looked. Their clothes were dirty; some of the girls had matted-looking hair. The younger ones had obvious pot bellies, something she only remembered seeing in toddlers. She counted around thirty children standing watching them from the bank.

'These children look in a state,' Sarah commented to Alex. Carlos overheard Sarah's comments.

'This is a poor village. Over recent years many of the men have died, often at a young age. Life expectancy here for a boy is around thirty years.'

'What killed them?' Alex chipped in.

'There was an outbreak of yellow fever here five years ago. The women and children had been vaccinated as part of a government campaign the year before, but the story goes that, when the vaccinators came to the village, the men folk were out in the field working on the harvest, and so missed the vital yellow fever immunisation. The authorities knew this but they were so pressurised that they couldn't return. The men were supposed to go to the Mazan clinic but, like most men, they were frightened of the jab so never did. A costly mistake. Around twelve men and youths died needlessly,' Carlos explained. So they are a very poor village now with very few able men to harvest the fields or collect the fruit from the jungle.

'That's so sad, but why have the children such fat tummies?' Sarah asked.

'These kids' tummies are full of worms. They drink the river water. Look, there's a young girl fetching water for the house, straight out of the river. The water will be full of bacteria and worms. The worms cause anaemia and malnutrition; that's why they look so poorly,' Alex continued. 'And just to really sicken you Sarah, there are parasites called hook worms that bite into the toe spaces of bare-foot kids, and then get into the body that way.'

'Oh how disgusting! How do you know all this Mr Smarty Pants?' Sarah teased her husband.

'From Graham Drummond; he was the medic attached to our platoon in Borneo. Graham had a great interest in children's health in the developing world. He would chat all night about the causes of infant mortality and poor nutrition; it was all very interesting. I wonder what happened to Graham. He was on a short commission, so he's probably a consultant paediatrician somewhere now. Good chap,' Alex replied.

The headman of the village approached Carlos who explained they were only stopping for ten minutes to stretch their legs. They seemed to talk for a long while, and then Carlos returned.

'The headman is asking if we have any medicines. His ten month old son is very sick with diarrhoea; he's frightened the boy is going to die,' Carlos relayed.

'We've some rehydration powders in our First Aid kit, that would be of some help,' Sarah volunteered.

'But we might need them,' Alex complained.

'We have to do something! Could we go and see the little boy and speak to the mother to explain how to use the powders?' Sarah said, in a rash moment of bravery.

Alex nodded to Carlos who spoke with the chief again. A quick nod and Alex and Sarah were heading for the furthest hut.

Inside, a young woman was cradling an irritable infant on her knee, trying to console him. Sarah could see that the baby was ill, very dehydrated. His skin was wrinkly, and his eyes sunken, so she knew she had to help or the child would indeed die. Carlos explained to the mother who the gringos were. She smiled at Sarah who crouched down beside the baby, gently stroking his head.

'Ask the mother if she is giving the baby anything to drink?' Sarah suggested to Carlos.

'Only breast milk and some potion from the shaman, made from a plant extract,' Carlos replied. 'She wants to know if you have any gringo medicine. She has had good medicine from the boat that comes every few months. She wishes it would come, but it never seems to come when the family needs it.'

Sarah reached for the three rehydration sachets in her shirt pocket. The mother smiled broadly, suddenly feeling hopeful for her child. Sarah asked if they had any jugs or clean containers. The father produced two large Inca Cola bottles, presumably bought in Mazan or from the river boat.

'That'll do, but how can we make sure she uses clean water?' Sarah said, thoughtfully.

'I've heard Dr Drummond say that if a plastic bottle full of water is left in the sun for a few hours, most of the bacteria are killed off. There is plenty of sunshine here, perhaps that would work. Let's suggest they leave a bottle of water in the sun for four or five hours. That should do it,' Alex suggested.

'There is no other option. At least it's a litre bottle, so one sachet will be just right. We can spare enough for three days' treatment; the baby should be better by then or…' Sarah didn't like to think of the alternative outcome. 'Today we'll have to get them to boil some water in the pot and allow it to cool. Do they have a small spoon?' Sarah continued.

Carlos translated Sarah's instructions on how to prepare the drink and how to spoon the liquid into the sick child, a little amount every ten minutes. They said their goodbyes to the family and rejoined Pedro at the boat. As they sped off up the Napo, Alex embraced his wife shouting in her ear how proud he was of her.

They arrived in Bella Vista just as darkness was falling. The village paths were still lit, so as they approached they could see the community was much smaller than Mazan, with probably around fifty houses. The jetty was very busy as the river boat had just arrived. A few passengers from upstream were stepping off the gang plank, but a much bigger group was waiting to embark.

This vessel's ultimate destination was Iquitos. Sarah could see boxes of bananas sitting on the bank ready to be loaded. As she was peering towards the rickety vessel, she saw someone being carried on board on a stretcher.

'I wonder what's going on there?' she said to Carlos as he tied up their boat. Carlos turned and shouted to a group of young boys sitting on the bank; they were watching the activities on the river boat.

'Snake bite!' they shouted back to him.

'They'll be transporting the victim down to the Mazan clinic for anti-venom,' he turned and explained to Sarah. 'Mazan is the nearest clinic.'

'But it'll take ages for that boat to reach there. Don't they have a closer clinic?' she asked.

'There's a health care worker in most of the bigger villages who know how to treat malaria and how to do general first aid, but not much more. The nearest doctor is in Mazan. I only hope they have some anti-venom left. Last year, there were several snake bites, but they ran out of treatment at the clinic. It's because it is so expensive; the authorities can only supply a few doses to the outlying clinics,' Carlos continued.

'So what happens if they have no treatment?' Sarah asked.

'They die usually.'

Sarah gulped hard and immediately thought of the children.

'Come on,' Alex said quickly changing the subject. 'Let's find somewhere to eat. Carlos, where will we eat tonight?'

'Shouldn't we check the river boat, see if anyone has seen or heard anything about white children?' Sarah interrupted.

'You're right!' Alex said, mad at himself that he hadn't rushed over to the boat already. What was he thinking of? Was the heat getting to him too?

'You stay here with Pedro. Carlos and I will go and speak to the captain.' Before Sarah could protest, Alex and Carlos were off at full tilt to the riverboat.

The vessel looked a death trap to Alex, which didn't really surprise him. He remembered news reports reaching

Lima the year before; two river boats collided at night, somewhere in Amazonia, with great loss of life. The Napo Princess was jammed packed with people. Carlos quickly located the captain in the wheel house as he was shouting out instructions to his crew on the bank. Captain Dante had not heard anything of plane crashes or gringo children. He had been on this route for five years, up as far as Rumi Tumi then back to Iquitos each week.

'Go and speak to the passengers, they might be able to help,' he said to them in Spanish.

Carlos thanked the Captain then they descended the steps to the main deck. They had to fight their way past tethered chickens motionless with fear, and squealing pigs dancing about trying to escape. The passengers were crowded together. Many had put up hammocks, some holding mothers and two children. Alex was reminded that many of the dead in the river boat accident had been trapped by spinning hammocks; it sent a shiver down his spine.

The pair systematically passed through the busy deck questioning the passengers. Some refused to speak to Alex because he was a gringo. Carlos was treated a little more kindly. The only information they received was from one older man who reported seeing a plane flying low overhead about the time of the accident, but further questioning by Carlos ascertained that it must have been one of the search and rescue planes.

When they reached the back of the boat, Alex was overcome by the smell of the toilet buckets that stood behind a plastic screen. They were right next door to the kitchen area where a hot and busy cook was stirring a watery stew. Disgusting, Alex thought trying not to throw up.

The men rejoined Sarah, who was sitting on the bank surrounded by children. She had her small digital camera and was entertaining the kids, by showing pictures she had taken of them on the camera display screen.

Alex thought how attractive his wife looked with her blue safari shirt and light-coloured trousers, gently talking with the young children. He was amazed at how strong she was considering their terrible predicament.

'Any luck?' Sarah said as she disentangled herself from the youngsters.

'No, nothing doing,' Alex replied. 'About food… Carlos, what was it you were trying to tell us earlier?'

'My friend Eduardo has a wife and she will feed us. He will let you hang your hammocks in his house. This way,' Carlos answered as he handed Alex his rucksack.

Chicken and rice was the food of the day. 'Again!' thought Alex, but Eduardo and his wife were very hospitable. The hut was lit only by a small lamp, but even then the mosquitoes were very bad, attracted to the smallest light. Outside, they could see the street light was alive with insects too. There were thousands of mosquitoes, and other big winged creatures, frantically attacking the light. The big insects appeared so frightening, but they were apparently harmless – although it didn't look that way to the gringos.

'I didn't expect street lights or concrete paths this far from civilisation,' Sarah commented to Carlos.

'Most of the villages in this region have street lights; they run off a diesel generator… usually for two hours a night, but once the diesel is finished the villagers have to wait until they can afford some more,' Carlos answered. He then spoke quickly to Eduardo in his native dialect.

'The villagers can only manage to pay for diesel for two weeks out of four. The concrete paths were put in about three years ago by the government,' Carlos continued. 'These things often happen around election times. Everyone in Peru must vote, by law. So even in these remote parts, politicians try to encourage the people to vote for their party. So a little enticement never goes wrong!'

As usual, Sarah was exhausted and went off to her hammock straight after supper. She didn't sleep well, her mind thinking constantly about the children. Eventually, she did fall off to sleep, only to be wakened a short time later by a scratching noise above her head.

'Alex, are you awake?' she whispered.

'Yes, I hear it. I think there are some bats up in the thatch,' he said calmly.

'What kind of bats? Do they really have vampire bats around here?' Sarah asked rather anxiously.

'I don't think there is much fear of being sucked to death, but you don't want to be bitten by a bat, that's for sure. Only last month there were two people killed in the jungle from rabies and both developed it after a bite from a bat,' Alex cautioned.

'I didn't know bats carried rabies, but I know dogs can. That's why I stay well away from the dogs in the villages. I've never seen such awful-looking animals; they are thin, covered with sores and sometimes have huge growths, probably tumours, on their bodies. There's plenty work for vets around here.'

'Yeah, but I don't think the villagers would like to pay them. Time to sleep; it's going to be another busy day tomorrow,' Alex said, as he turned himself in his hammock.

'What about the bats, Alex?' Sarah asked, somewhat nervous about them still.

'Sarah, they'll not bother you; besides the mosquito net will keep them away. Now go to sleep!' Alex replied, impatiently, grumpy from lack of sleep.

Alex hadn't slept well since the crash and it was all beginning to catch up with him. But he realised that he must get some rest, as the real search was about to begin.

CHAPTER 17

Poor Reception

Late in the morning, two days later, the travellers arrived in the village of San Gorge. They had stopped overnight in Rumi Timi. Sarah was surprised that the river was still wide and fast. One of the most amazing events of the trip north had been watching clumps of six or seven large trees collapse into the river, due to undermining of the bank by the turbulent waters. Huge trees, fifteen metres high at least, if not more, sunk like tower blocks at demolition. It really brought home to Sarah the power of these Amazonian rivers. The rainy season meant that the rivers were very dangerous places for fast boats. The helmsman continually had to watch out for trees floating, just below the surface. Collision would certainly result in a boat capsizing. Now she understood why Carlos became more alert as the sun slipped below the horizon and how relieved he always was when they tied up for the night.

Alex had decided, in Iquitos, that San Gorge would be the furthest north they would venture. The crash site was to the south and east. If the children were alive and able to travel he knew that Tim would have enough geographical knowledge to head downstream in search of villages and rescue.

'How long are we going to stay here?' Sarah asked as she looked round the village.

'I think we should spend the next day here, asking the locals for any news, and then we should head back south calling at every village on the way,' Alex replied.

'But what about those tributaries we saw that join the Napo from the north east? We have passed several on the way up,' Sarah commented.

'I know, I've been thinking about those rivers. We may have to spend some days checking these as well,' Alex said thoughtfully.

'Is there a health post here? If so, maybe the clinic staff will travel into the jungle communities from here,' Sarah suggested.

'Yes, a good thought,' Alex continued. 'There's a health post, but there's no doctor. The nearest doctor is in Mazan, so Carlos told me. There's a health technician, or techno nurse as they are often known, who is trained to do baby jabs, first aid and the like. They'll probably know about the smaller villages nearby.'

The techno nurse was a young man of about twenty-five. They met up with him while he had his forceps in hand, just about to pull out a man's tooth. Carlos signalled him to continue; a grunt later and it was all over. The patient spat a mouthful of blood onto the floor, stood up and walked off patting the nurse on the back as a sign of thanks.

'Don't they have a dentist on this river either?' Sarah asked Carlos, as the young nurse put his forceps away in a small tray.

'The nearest dentist is in Mazan, so these techno nurses have had a little training in how to pull teeth,' Carlos replied.

'I don't want to have any dental trouble this trip, that's for sure! No local anaesthetic! How painful!' Sarah answered, wincing at the thought.

Carlos spoke with the nurse for some time, explaining why Alex and Sarah were here, so far up the Napo.

He discovered that the young man was responsible for a number of small villages within a fifty-kilometre radius of San Gorge. He had not heard anything of any gringo children but if he did he would contact Mazan clinic with any news. The nurse was due to go up one of the smaller rivers tomorrow, to a couple of outlying villages. He had to immunise the new babies and offer ante-natal advice to the mothers. He would keep a look out for the children.

Alex, Sarah and Carlos thanked the nurse and left to look round the village and speak to some other locals. Sarah had an uneasy feeling about the place. She felt that villagers were watching them, scurrying away when they saw them coming. She had noted that the young nurse had viewed them suspiciously. The children of this community were with their mothers; they had not come near the three of them as in other villages. There was none of the inquisitiveness of some of the previous places they had stopped.

Carlos realised that there was an atmosphere, something that he had not experienced here before. He decided to find the headman and find out what was going on.

Alex and Sarah sat on the riverbank watching the activity down by the boats. Surprisingly, they could see that many of the canoes were heading back to the village. They thought that was quite strange as it wasn't even mid-day. After about ten minutes Carlos came hurrying over to them. Alex saw quickly that there was a problem.

'What did you find out Carlos?' Sarah asked innocently.

'I'll tell you later, just head down to the boat as quick as you can. Don't ask any more questions just now; just do as I say, otherwise things could get quite nasty round here. Now go!' Carlos replied sternly. 'I'll go and pick up the fuel I've just bought from the chief. He wants us out of here fast!'

As Carlos headed off he shouted, 'Tell Pedro to start the engine!'

Alex and Sarah exchanged anxious glances. They'd never seen Carlos look so worried. Alex took his wife by the hand and helped her down the slope to the boat. Pedro was quick to follow instructions. It seemed to take forever, Alex thought, for Carlos to return. Several times he checked his holster to make sure his weapon was ready. As soon as Carlos was aboard they sped off down river. They travelled for about half an hour before Carlos found an area on the bank where he felt he could stop the fast boat.

'What was that all about?' Alex asked.

'Two weeks ago some gringos appeared at the village. They were given hospitality as is the custom round these waters. The next day two of the children disappeared. The headman thinks that the gringos sneaked in and kidnapped them,' Carlos explained.

'But why would anyone kidnap kids up here so far away from anywhere?' Sarah asked. 'No one would have the money to pay the ransom anyway.'

'Sarah, there have been reports of gangs coming to these remote parts and stealing young kids,' Alex explained.

'But why? What for?' Sarah persisted.

'They are taken to the cities and sold for their organs, for the transplant market,' Alex explained further. 'In Lima, there have been reports of children being kidnapped, and having their corneas removed and then being returned to their parents – blind! The police are getting much tougher in the cities now, but up here in the jungle it is impossible to protect these children, so the gangs have moved out into the jungle areas. I didn't want to tell you about it as

I knew how much it would upset you. It's happening all over the world. Street children are vulnerable as well as jungle kids. Sometimes parents have been known to sell a child unwittingly, thinking he or she is going to work for someone in the city. It's the usual story of the greedy preying on the poor and vulnerable.'

'Stop! That's disgusting! How can people do these things to children?' Sarah shouted, and then turned away and wept. Thinking of the cruelty to these children reminded her of their own predicament. What if her children ended up in the hands of such awful people?

'Surely doctors and nurses wouldn't take part in such awful acts?' Sarah asked, wiping her tears. 'They are highly skilled practitioners who would never knowingly do this sort of thing. Would they?'

'Money or threats can make some people do anything. You just need to think of the things that went on in the concentration camps during the Second World War,' Alex replied.

'I suppose so. Did the villagers think we were kidnappers?' Sarah asked, suddenly realising the danger they had been in.

'Yes, that is why the fishermen were coming back. Remember the drum beat we heard as we were talking to the nurse? That was the alarm call!'

'They might have killed us,' Sarah thought out loud.

'Yes!' Alex confirmed.

'Carlos, how are we for fuel? Did you get enough?' Alex continued.

'Yes, we should have enough to Santa Maria. We don't have much food though, as we didn't have time to pick up any from the village baker,' Carlos explained.

'Where to now?' Sarah asked. 'Will we get the same reception in all the villages round here?'

'It's hard to say. I think it would be best if you and Alex stay on the boat at the next community and I'll speak with the headman about your children,' Carlos suggested.

'If we do run into more problems, we'll have to sleep on the boat tonight, which might not be too comfortable for you.'

'If we have to, we have to; after all, the children will be living in worse conditions,' Sarah replied with resignation.

They stopped at each of the four villages on the way back down the river to Santa Maria. As planned Carlos spoke with the headman in each village while the gringos stayed in the boat.

While they were waiting for Carlos at the last village, Sarah watched as the women folk washed clothes, perched cross-legged on log platforms; she was suddenly grateful for her washing machine. Admittedly, they had generally only t-shirts and shorts to wash, but some of the men folk did wear jeans; certainly, there was no heavy bed linen or curtains. As usual, little children crouched on the bank and endlessly watched the visitors. Sarah was astonished to watch the little girls picking through their neighbour's hair; she supposed it was a form of grooming. Then horrified she watched the 'groomer' put something into her mouth. No, it couldn't be, Sarah wondered; they are not eating head lice? Sarah shivered with disgust.

Alex noticed her discomfort and commented, 'Yes that is what they do; I've seen it in the tribesmen of Borneo as well.'

'Hopefully, things will be alright in Santa Maria so we can stay in a house overnight,' Sarah commented completely changing the subject.

'Provided the jungle 'tom-toms' haven't reached there before us,' Alex cautioned.

'If that's the case, we won't even be safe to sleep in the boat, will we?' Sarah added.

'No we'll have to go upstream a bit and find somewhere to tie up for the night,' Alex advised.

Carlos returned in good spirits. The headman had been very friendly and had obviously not heard anything from San Gorge. Sadly, he had no news of the children either.

They arrived in Santa Maria by late afternoon. Carlos again visited the headman and found nothing of concern. No-one was in the least suspicious of them; in fact, the village children came round wanting to have their pictures taken.

Santa Maria was a village of about sixteen homes built in the usual rectangle. There were rickety goal posts at each end of the central common land, something they had seen in every community they had visited so far. This confirmed Alex's long held belief that football was a worldwide sport. From the richest clubs of Europe, to the lads in the slums of India or the Amazonian villages, most boys, and often girls, played football.

The visitors noticed that there was a new house being built. Several young men were working on the roof.

'I didn't think a village this small would have so many young men around,' Sarah commented to Carlos, as they walked round the village to their home for the night, a train of children following them like the rats of the Pied Piper fable.

'The headman told me they were from the neighbouring village up the Irky River. Usually, if there is a new house to be built, neighbours will come and help, and then they have a party afterwards!' Carlos replied. He pointed to the tributary, the Rio Irky, that joined the Napo only one hundred metres downstream from the village. He continued, 'There's going to be a football match and feast after they're finished. The chief said we were welcome to join in the celebrations.'

'What a change from San Gorge!' Sarah commented.

'We're going to go up the Irky River tomorrow. A hundred and fifty kilometres up that river is where we found the abandoned village,' Alex whispered to Sarah, out of earshot from Carlos.

'Maybe some of the 'visitors' will know something of the air crash,' Alex said to Carlos as he caught up with him along the path.

Alex and Sarah enjoyed the village life that evening. The football was a heated contest between the two village groups. Alex and Carlos were 'conscripted' into the away team to make up the numbers. Carlos proved to be an able striker scoring two goals which made him an instant hero. Alex found it all tough going as, despite being almost sundown, the temperature was in the upper thirties, Celsius. Sarah thought the fact that Alex was now over fifty, probably thirty years older than most of his team mates, was having a bigger effect on his performance than Alex would like to admit. His exhaustion was evident to the others in his team, so he was politely put in goals for the second half. The game ended in a respectable four all draw.

Alex was glad to sit down beside his wife for supper, grateful that he hadn't broken anything on the uneven surface. He admired the footballers who took part as all played barefoot, some sporting Brazilian football strips. One lad even had a Manchester United strip which amazed Alex.

'Where do they get the football strips from?' Alex asked Carlos.

'The men folk go down to the Belen Market in Iquitos at least once a year. Bananas, pineapples and other forest fruits are often bartered for football strips, much to the annoyance of the woman folk who, like all mothers, believe the money should be kept for the family.'

The food was cooked communally with all the households contributing. Fish caught earlier in the day were prepared over the open fires. Several of the scrawny, almost featherless, flea-ridden, chickens that Sarah had seen rushing around were caught by the older children. The birds were suitably dispatched, with much screeching, as the birds tried in vain to escape their executioners. For the first time in her life Sarah understood the term 'running around like a headless chicken', although she really wished she had not seen the spectacle. She realised she was quite a wimp; even the youngest children weren't perturbed.

At least the two gringos knew their food was fresh, as they sat down with all the villagers on the grass. Liquid refreshment was flowing too. The young men became progressively more inebriated. Alex was offered some of the masato and felt he had to accept. He knew it was the local alcoholic beverage distilled from the yucca plant but he had no real idea how it was made. Carlos was enjoying his first time of relaxation since they had left Iquitos so was swigging back the liquor rather freely. He noticed that Sarah had declined the drink and was sticking to water that she had sterilised with her tablets. He thought that was predictable, but he was surprised to see Alex imbibing. Carlos wondered if Alex knew how the drink was prepared. He decided not to enlighten him … at least not yet.

The mood of the village was becoming ever more relaxed. Someone brought a drum, and soon most of the young folk were involved in an energetic dance. Carlos was becoming less inhibited so sidled up to Alex to have the conversation about the masato. By this time he had noticed that Alex had had at least two beakers of the drink and he too was more relaxed than usual.

'Hi, Alex!' Carlos said above the drums. 'Are you enjoying yourself tonight?'

'A bit I suppose. Lots on my mind though, tomorrow and the kids for example,' Alex replied.

'Yeah, I understand,' Carlos said, but in reality he had misread Alex's frame of mind. The alcohol was sending Alex into a melancholic mood.

Completely tactlessly Carlos piped up again, 'Alex, are you enjoying the masato? Do you know how the villagers make it?'

'No, but I've a feeling you're going to tell me anyway.'

So Carlos began, 'The women of the community gather up the yucca roots. Then, one evening, they sit round a big pot and chew the plant to break down the fibres, finally spitting the mouthfuls into pot. The resultant mush is then left for a while to ferment into alcohol. Sometimes you can find bits of teeth in your drink. I remember …'

'Stop! I get the message! Thanks for the education,' Alex said as he 'accidentally' knocked over his beaker.

'What's wrong Alex?' Sarah asked suddenly, aware that her husband looked a bit green. After twenty years of marriage she knew, even by the light of a jungle fire, that her husband was about to be sick. Before he could answer her query, he was off behind the lodge uncontrollably emptying his stomach!

On his return, the couple made their excuses and retired to their hammocks. Alex was feeling better, but tired after the day's tension. So as not to worry Sarah and allow her to rest, he pretended to sleep, but he had no such intention. He had decided to stay awake each night from now on and try to sleep during the day on the boat. Their treatment at San Gorge had been a wake-up call. He wouldn't let anything happen to his lovely wife; she had suffered enough. Soon, she was gently snoring.

CHAPTER 18

Jungle Wasteland

Just after dawn they pulled away from the village of Santa Maria. They headed up the Irky River, one of the tributaries off the Napo. Pedro, who was perched in his usual seat at the back of the boat, started shouting. He was pointing to something in the river, in the turbulent waters where the two rivers met.

'What is it? What is wrong?' Sarah asked.

Alex looked to where Pedro was pointing. Suddenly three pink looking creatures broke the brown turbulent waters, disappearing again beneath the water.

'I think they're pink dolphins,' Alex shouted above the noise of the engines. Carlos turned round from his driving position and nodded in agreement.

'I didn't know there were such things as pink dolphins. We're so far from the sea. I thought dolphins were salt water creatures,' Sarah offered.

'Oh yeah, but they can be found all along the Amazon. They're related to the dolphin but survive well in these big rivers. You have to remember that the Amazon can be hundreds of feet deep. I remember watching a television programme with Tim last year. Marine biologists were diving into the depths of the river in Brazil. They were trying to discover some of the rare creatures that live at great depths. It was so deep they had to use mini subs with powerful lights to see down at the bottom of the river.'

'It's truly an amazing river system,' Sarah replied. 'I remember being shocked when I realised it was almost as far from the mouth of the Amazon to Iquitos, as it was across the Atlantic Ocean. No wonder it took early geographers years and years to map out the whole region.'

Carlos cut the engine for a few moments so they could enjoy the spectacle. The dolphins seemed to know they were being watched as they put on an impressive display. For a brief moment, Alex and Sarah were caught up in the beauty of nature, a little respite for their troubled minds.

Four hours later, the fast boat was well up the Irky River. Alex was using the GPS on his watch to pinpoint their position now. Carlos was most impressed by the technology. Alex wanted to check the villages as close to the crash site as possible, but the problem was, that this high up a small tributary was deep jungle country, and not all the communities were on the map. He planned to go to the village called 'March the Sixteenth', just south of the one he had entered with the commandos seven days earlier. He didn't want to take Sarah to see the abandoned village. He discussed with Carlos how far up the river he wanted him to take them, and realised it would take most of the afternoon.

Carlos was relieved; he didn't want to go any closer to the Columbian border. He knew all about the drug militias, even though he himself had never been this far off his usual Napo route. Before they had left Santa Maria he had spoken with Alex and explained his fears about the rest of the journey. He was frightened that Alex and Sarah would be kidnapped by Columbian guerrillas who might have strayed across the border. This troubled Alex too!

As they progressed up the river, the width decreased considerably to between forty and fifty metres. Sarah had noticed a white scum on the river and, every now and then, dead fish floating on the water. She realised that there were very few communities on the banks. An occasional dilapidated hut could be seen, but it looked as if the jungle had reclaimed the clearing. The river twisted back and forth, with tighter and tighter curves as the river continued to narrow and the jungle reached right down to the bank. Again, they came across another abandoned village and then another half an hour further upstream. There were more dead fish, and the water was covered with even more scum. As the river turned tightly to the left, the group were shocked by the view that greeted them; it was one of utter devastation.

On the right hand bank the trees had been cleared as far as Sarah could see. There were deep pits gouged out of the land which must have been dug by heavy machinery. It looked like the open cast mines she remembered from home, except this one was abandoned, with no sign of any restoration. She could see derelict huts and broken down rusted pieces of machinery. Oil drums were tipped over at the side of the river, having spewed out their toxic contents. Sarah was so shocked that she woke Alex, who had been asleep for about an hour.

'Look at this Alex!' she shouted to him. 'What a mess! Do you think it has been oil drilling or mining?'

'Not sure. I don't think it has been oil, probably precious metals. Gold perhaps. I don't know of any oil drilling up here,' Alex replied defensively.

Carlos stopped the engines to look as well. Sarah thought he looked visibly shocked at the wasteland.

'I have heard about the gold mining up here. It started five years ago but was abandoned last year. I didn't know it was on such a huge scale. It must stretch back about a couple of kilometres into the forest area and still continues round the next bend. Did you see the abandoned villages on the way up here?' Carlos sombrely asked his gringo friends.

'I did,' Sarah replied, 'but Alex was fast asleep. Why are they abandoned?'

'The Zuppo people lived on this river. The pollution from the mining was killing off the fish. You saw the dead fish as we came up. Much of the forest has been destroyed, driving away the wildlife. The Zuppo were hunters so they couldn't support themselves any more. The elders travelled to Iquitos to meet the regional government, but, even though the government had strict environmental controls, these were not adequately enforced. The mining company got away with murder.'

'Where have the people gone now?' Sarah asked.

'They finally left their villages because their women were having stillbirths or giving birth to children with deformities. I've heard it said that some have gone into the deep jungle to return to their traditional ways of life, as they do not trust their government anymore. Most have gone down to Puerto Belen, the shanty town of Iquitos, but they have become very poor as they cannot find work. It is so sad for my native peoples. They have lived here for hundreds of years, then suddenly they are robbed of their way of life. It is said that the tribes in Amazonia were decimated by viruses such as measles brought in by European explorers in the nineteenth century. Now their way of life is under attack again by the greed of the modern world. Why can't they be left alone?' Carlos said emotionally, turning away from his passengers. Sarah reached out a hand to comfort him.

'It's truly awful. I never imagined it would be this bad. How many people do you think have been affected in this area?' she asked gently.

'I don't know for sure, but probably three or four hundred,' he replied.

Alex said nothing but looked around taking in every detail of the scene.

Sarah knew that the last ten minutes had deeply affected him; she could tell by the expression on his face.

An hour later, they arrived at their destination. 'March the Sixteenth' was a sleepy little village of twelve huts. The canoes were returning from fishing just as Carlos was manoeuvring 'Claudia' into the bank and Pedro jumped ashore to tie up the boat.

Alex was uneasy. He picked up Carlos's tension. Climbing up the bank, Carlos was quickly surrounded by several of the village men folk, some with machetes hanging loosely by their sides. The conversation was brisk. Alex couldn't see everything that was going on, but he could hear voices being raised and he could see one or two other men coming running along the path. His hand began to rest on the holster of his side arm, his feet beginning to locate his rifle under the seat. He glanced at Sarah to warn her, but she was already fully alert. Alex passed her his hand gun and released the safety catch. She needed to be able to protect herself. He had shown her how to use the gun in the hotel room in Iquitos, just in case they ran into 'trouble.' Pedro was beginning to slither quietly down the bank, back to the boat, but was grabbed by two of the villagers. Things were not going well!

Fortunately the increasingly angry mob had not paid much attention to the passengers on the boat. Alex grabbed his rifle, told his wife to stay put, and then climbed the bank to help his new friends. The villagers shrank back when they saw the weapon, releasing both Carlos and Pedro who looked absolutely petrified.

'Tell them no one will get hurt, if they just drop their machetes and sit on the ground with their hands on their heads,' Alex barked to Carlos to communicate in the local dialect.

Carlos was quick to obey the command. The villagers didn't argue. Alex's presence was immense. He was no longer the hurting father. He was back in commando officer mode, all his military training coursing through his veins again.

'Tell them we are not militia, not drug barons, not child stealers!' Alex continued. 'We are looking for two lost gringo kids. Do they know anything?'

There was a visible relaxation of the village men. The headman spoke with much friendlier tones to Carlos. They had not seen any gringo kids.

'What happened in the community five kilometres up river from here?' Alex asked them. Carlos looked strangely at Alex who said, 'I'll explain later.'

The villagers knew all about the 'Paradise' hamlet. They knew the drug barons had visited them and terrorised them. They had been frightened that their village would be next.

Alex asked them if they knew where the villagers had gone. Somewhere into the deep jungle was the rumour, but no one knew for sure was the answer.

'Do you think we are safe to stay here tonight?' Alex asked Carlos.

Carlos shook his head. 'These people are traumatised. They're too frightened to offer us help. I think the druggies have been here and threatened them too. We should leave as soon as we can; we're no match for the drug lords; they have a lot more than machetes.'

'Right, let's get going downstream and find somewhere for the night before darkness,' Alex said with authority. 'You and Pedro get in the boat and start her up. I'll keep an eye on these guys. I don't trust them any more than they trust me.' Carlos and Pedro didn't need a second invitation.

Alex raised his weapon slightly, just to remind his captives not to move a muscle, as he backed slowly to the river bank. Once he heard the engines revving he slipped over the slope down to 'Claudia's deck. By the time they picked up their machetes and rushed to the bank, the boat was in the middle of the river well on its way. The abusive shouts and knife brandishing made Alex realise they had made the right decision.

'What now?' Sarah asked Alex, as she snuggled into his arm, trying to regain her composure. The whole incident had terrified her. She could see how close they were to being attacked again.

'We should find somewhere to tie up for the night, downstream a little,' Alex answered.

'Surely, we'll be eaten alive if we stay on the river overnight?' Sarah remarked.

'There's nowhere else to go. Carlos hates travelling in the dark; he's frightened we hit a half submerged log and capsize,' Alex explained.

'Yeah, but I don't want to be eaten alive by insects. Perhaps a snake will be able to slither on board if we tie up,' Sarah pointed out.

After about half an hour hurtling downstream at top speed, Alex signalled to Carlos to stop by the bank where there was a small clearing. Carlos was not happy, and neither was Pedro. Both men had a quick chat together before speaking with Alex.

'We can't stop here Señor Alex; it's not safe,' Carlos said. 'We must push on and get as far down the river as possible.'

'I thought you didn't want to travel at night?' Alex asked.

'That's right, Señor Alex, but we don't want to be shot by druggies or hacked to bits by frightened tribesmen who believe all gringos are bad and that those who work for them even worse!' Carlos replied, obviously fired up. 'Can you drive one of these boats? You are a military man aren't you? How did you know about the abandoned village?'

'OK, Carlos I'll come clean with you; after all, you're risking your life now,' Alex replied. Quickly, Alex brought Carlos up to speed about his previous military service and the excursion with the marines to the crash site. But he didn't fill him in on the fact that the British commando group had no business being in Peru. Carlos actually seemed much more relaxed once he had a fuller picture. He felt much safer when he discovered his passenger was a well-armed, highly trained ex-marine.

'Ok. Señor Alex, it is your turn to take the helm! There's a half moon so there'll be some light. I'll be your lookout. We'll do one hour on, one off. We should be back in Santa Maria before dawn. Maybe tomorrow afternoon we could visit the few villages at the south end of the River Irky,' Carlos suggested.

'That sounds good to me. Do we have enough petrol? Alex asked.

'Yes. There are two more drums in the rear beside Pedro. Enough to get us back, as long as you don't drive like a crazy man!' Carlos said teasingly.

With that, Alex pulled back the throttle; 'Claudia' rose up in the nose and was off, southward toward the Rio Napo.

Sarah managed to sleep across the seats most of the way to Santa Maria. The journey was uneventful; no one else was on the river. There were very few lights seen on the riverbank until they reached the villages just above the confluence of the two rivers. It reminded Alex of the drastic effect that the gold mining had had on this river community. In fact, it dawned on him that the entire Irky River, right up to the border with Ecuador, was depopulating because of western lifestyle choices. On the one hand, there was gold for the rich and, on the other, there were drugs for the hapless youth of developed cultures.

By the time Pedro had tied up 'Claudia' at Santa Maria's make-shift jetty, a hostile crowd had gathered on the bank. Some of the men folk were brandishing machetes. Word had reached the village from San Gorge. The headman shouted to Carlos threatening him with dire consequences, if they went ashore.

Alex signalled to Carlos to pull away from the bank so he turned the boat downstream towards Iquitos.

'What are we going to do now?' Sarah asked Alex. 'What about the villages just at the start of the Irky?'

'We risk being beaten up if we go there now because they are so close to Santa Maria. The villagers will have been well warned about us. If they've any gringo children staying with them, I think they would have brought them to us just to get us out of the area, and not put their own children at risk,' Alex replied.

Alex was becoming increasingly concerned about his wife's safety. He had lost his two children. He couldn't bear anything to happen to his Sarah.

'These tribesmen must be really frightened to be so suspicious of us. It does make me think that they have had children stolen by outsiders and ones that look European,' Sarah said thoughtfully.

'Between that and the way the people of the Irky have been treated by gold prospectors and drug barons, it's no surprise really,' Alex commented.

'I think we should continue down the Napo to the next village and start searching again. I must speak to Carlos and see how we are for water, food and fuel,' Alex said, going forward to speak to Carlos.

Five minutes later he returned to his seat next to Sarah.

'We need to find some fuel in the next fifty kilometres or we're in trouble. I don't know about you but I'm quite sick of stale bread and high cal bars. Carlos thinks we should stop briefly at the next two villages and then head to Libertad. If everyone is friendly then all will be well but if not we might have to 'help ourselves' to the petrol. We can't go further downstream than Libertad, that's for sure,' Alex tapped his rifle as he spoke.

'If we use force, then the headman will be on the radio to the authorities as soon as we leave and then we'll be faced by a gunboat before we reach Mazan,' Sarah pointed out.

'I know that's the problem. Maybe, then, you would like to pray that no one has heard anything about us,' Alex suggested.

'Yes, I think I shall,' Sarah agreed.

The 'Claudia' was able to stop at the two villages before Libertad. Not wanting to take any chances Carlos spoke briefly with the headman in each village while Alex and Sarah remained in the boat. Sadly there were no sightings or information about the children.

Libertad seemed to be a bigger community than most. Carlos received a warm welcome from the headman who remembered him from previous trips with tourists. The headman's brother Roger had worked with Carlos on a couple of trips out of Mazan the previous year, before Pedro was hired. Carlos had not realised that Roger had relatives in Libertad. This was indeed a stroke of luck. The chief, whose name was Orlando, welcomed Alex and Sarah with great dignity; he was very sympathetic to their story and promised to keep an eye open for any information from passing tribesmen, in the weeks ahead. Carlos was much more relaxed now; he felt he was among friends. He had no hesitation in recommending that the group spend the night in the village.

It was late afternoon by the time Alex and Sarah strung up their hammocks again. Alex said, 'I think your prayer has been answered Sarah. We seem to have found a place where the people don't hate us, at least not so far.'

'Yeah, so far. Let's go for a walk through the village as it's much cooler now,' Sarah suggested. 'But perhaps we should go and get Carlos so the villagers don't become suspicious of us gringos again.'

'That would be sensible after all the trouble we've had. I would quite like to sleep in the hammock tonight. Chicken and rice actually seems appealing,' Alex replied.

Carlos was keen to join them. He was enjoying celebrity status in Libertad having been a friend of the chief's brother. It was a beautiful evening as they walked along the bank of the river, towards the west; as the sun sunk lower in the sky, some children gathered round excitedly. One of the boys who had beautiful big brown eyes, and was probably about seven years old, came up to Sarah. He smiled revealing his rotten front teeth. He had something in between his fingers that he was holding out to Sarah. She shied away from him as she could see it was an insect. To her shock, the young man pulled back his hand and then put it to his mouth. He bit off the insect's head, spat that out onto the ground and then swallowed the rest of the body!

'Oh that's disgusting!' Sarah said, as she turned away trying not to vomit. The children giggled gleefully. When Sarah turned round again, she saw that three of the young boys had bundles of the little creatures folded in the front of their T-shirts. There were so many ants that she realised they must have been gathering them all afternoon. Once again the same little lad offered Sarah the delicacy, but this time he had a really mischievous glint in his eye. Sarah turned up her nose again but Carlos was not in the least perturbed as he reached into the lads T-shirt and pulled out a couple of wriggling ants, duly decapitated them with his teeth and munched.

'We used to catch these flying ants when I was little too. They are very sweet, just like honey,' he said. The kids were delighted.

The group continued to walk along the path towards the jungle. The families were sitting in their homes watching them as they passed, but there wasn't the suspicious glare they had witnessed in San Gorge. These were friendly faces. The mothers smiled as they looked out of the frameless windows, the fathers rocking back and forth in hammocks, just watching. The route took them past the school and the tiny health post. A little church was neatly decorated and the entrance path lined with stones. Thirty metres further on from the last hut was a clearing that had been cultivated.

'Yucca plants,' Carlos pointed out. 'They're the staple diet here in the jungle. It is used as you would use potato or rice. And of course masato! Remember Alex?' Carlos said teasingly.

'I remember, that disgusting drink,' Alex whined.

The trio walked on a little further. The view over the river was majestic. They could see an irrigated area to their right that had been planted out in rice. Only a couple of palm trees remained standing in this area as the jungle had been cleared for the fields.

Sarah and Alex wandered over to the bank of the river to take in the view as the sun was setting. Beautiful colours painted a wonderful picture. The sky, orange and fiery red, reflected on the river with the dark hues of the forest funnelling the landscape into the night. An occasional bat flew across the scene. The couple sat down on a fallen tree, Alex's arm lovingly draped over his wife's shoulder. They drank in the magnificent jungle vista. The noise of the creatures as they greeted the returning darkness was wonderful to hear. Carlos could see it was an intimate moment for the couple so kept a discreet distance but he was becoming increasingly nervous as the light had almost gone. He knew that the jungle was no place to be when it was dark, especially in the rainy season, as snakes were a very real threat at this time. Carlos had just cleared the vision of snakes from his mind when Sarah let out a blood curdling scream. He rushed to the couple to find Alex plunging his knife into a two metre snake, but it was all too late as Sarah was clutching her ankle. She had been bitten by the serpent.

'Am I going to die?' she screamed at Alex and Carlos.

Alex tried to reassure his wife but could tell by the look on Carlos's face this was a dangerous snake.

'Sarah don't move; we must keep you still,' Alex said as he stripped off his shirt. 'I am going to put a pad on the bite and tie it tight to keep the venom in one place. Carlos, hold my torch.'

'Should we not take her to the village and cut out the venom?' Carlos suggested.

'No. I remember from my army days, snake bites must be immobilised above and below the joint. We'll do that first before we move her, so find a couple of branches.'

The two men spent around ten minutes making the ankle immobile, and then they carried Sarah between them back to the headman's hut, remembering to pick up the dead snake.

The chief took one look at the snake and shook his head. All the men went outside to talk over the problem, while the women folk tried to make Sarah as comfortable as possible.

CHAPTER 19

Touch and Go

The chief called the snake the 'Green Dragon'. Five people had been bitten in his village by green dragons in the last ten years. Four died within a week of being bitten, but the fifth was lucky as there was anti-venom in the health post at the time.

Alex immediately inquired about anti-venom but the headman said that the health post was not in use just now. The last technical nurse returned to Iquitos six months ago and had not been replaced. Alex was becoming increasingly upset. What was happening to him? His world was falling apart. Everyone he loved was being taken away from him. But no! It was not going to happen to his lovely Sarah.

'Where will there be anti-venom?' he shouted at the chief.

'Maybe, in Mazan. Sometimes if they have had lots of snake bites the supply will be finished. They only have two or three doses given to them, every three months, by the health authority in Iquitos. They say it costs so much. We lost a young boy last year. He was only four years of age. When we took him to Mazan there was no anti-venom left. I think they don't put much value on a village boy's life. He was my sister's son, a beautiful boy. To her, he was everything,' the headman remembered sadly. His head bowed.

Alex put his hand on the chief's shoulder as he realised that he had been rude and insensitive to him. To these villagers, death from accidents, malaria, snake bite and the like, was a common occurrence, but it didn't mean they had no feelings.

'We can use the radio to see if there is any anti-venom in the clinic in Mazan,' the chief suggested, recovering his composure.

'That's a great idea. I'll go and speak to Sarah, while you do that. How long will it take for us to get back to Mazan?' Alex asked Carlos.

'From here with the current, about forty-eight hours. We can leave at dawn,' Carlos said.

'Sixty hours from now! We'll have to think of something else. You go and see what the chief finds out,' Alex instructed.

'Sarah, how do you feel?' Alex said softly as he crouched down beside his wife, gently holding her hand.

'My ankle is a bit sore and there is an itchy feeling creeping up my leg; it's about the middle of my shin now. Alex I'm frightened.'

'Don't worry. We'll get out of this OK. Trust me.'

Alex bowed his head and silently prayed for his wife. He knew he needed a miracle. Tears trickled from Sarah's eyes. She could see the look of love and desperation on her husband's face.

The couple were interrupted by the arrival of the village shaman dressed in all his fearsome regalia. Seeing him terrified Sarah. As a Christian, she considered his ways as evil and didn't want him anywhere near her. He tried to signal to Alex that he wanted to help but he didn't speak

Spanish, only the local dialect. He had a small pot with a black paste and was gently tugging at the dressing on Sarah's leg. Suddenly Alex understood he wanted to put paste on Sarah's bite. Alex was on his feet in a flash, gesticulating to the witch doctor that he must leave, but the witch doctor was getting upset and wildly danced round the couple shouting and screaming himself into a frenzy. Sarah was becoming agitated too, and tried to get up from the floor. The shaman was petrifying her. Alex was about to reach for his holster when Carlos and the chief returned. Carlos quickly assessed the situation, as did the headman.

A sharp exchange of words flew between the headman and the shaman who fell silent at first. Then, angrily, he turned to Sarah and shouted some angry words, spat in her direction and then spat at Alex before rushing from the hut.

'Phew! What was that all about?' Alex demanded of Carlos, his muscles taught ready to defend his wife.

'The shaman has just cast a spell on you both. It was because you would not accept his medicine and you have caused him to lose face in front of the villagers. Look the hut is emptying and the women folk will not attend us now,' Carlos replied.

'Never mind. I don't care! Look he has scared Sarah,' Alex said as he slipped onto the floor to calm his wife. 'What did you find out about the anti-venom?'

'Not good!' the headman replied. 'The last anti-venom was used yesterday.'

'Can the radio be used to reach Iquitos?' Alex asked, without a flicker of emotion. He was back in soldier mode again; the situation was becoming desperate. This was when he was at his best.

'Yes, I think so!' Carlos replied.

'Then try and get a message to Gilberto. Tell him to get a seaplane up here first thing tomorrow. If he cannot get a private one then try the military. Tell him to speak to Jarvis at the British Embassy in Lima if he needs some political muscle. Now go.'

'I'm on my way,' Carlos replied as he and the chief disappeared again into the darkness, leaving Alex cradling his wife in his arms.

'Has the shaman gone? He was so evil,' Sarah whispered to Alex.

'Yes, he's gone. Let's get you a drink, and then make you comfortable. We're going to fly you out of here in the morning, to Iquitos. Carlos and the headman are radioing Gilberto just now.'

Sarah only managed a few sips of water. She was very weak, dipping in and out of sleep. Alex kept bathing her head to keep her cool. It seemed like an eternity before Carlos returned, well over an hour at any rate.

'We reached Gilberto but it took some time. At first they couldn't locate him. He wasn't at home; he was out on the streets with his mission. He's going to do his best to get a sea plane here in the morning,' Carlos reported. 'I've to radio him again in two hours to find out what he has arranged.'

'Good. She is very weak already. I can't get her to drink more than a few sips,' Alex said. 'Let's hope Gilberto gets back with good news.'

Fortunately, Gilberto had the correct contacts in Iquitos. Petro-Explore NMW frequently used a small seaplane company to fly engineers to the drilling sites north-west of Iquitos. It was part of Gilberto's new job to organise these trips and sometimes accompany the Lima directors, so he knew the pilots. There were only two of them; both former Peruvian air force guys trying to make a living after being demobbed. Competition for contractual work with oil companies was very keen, so the aviators were very happy to oblige. Gilberto was going to come along to help in any way he could. Alex sent word back to Gilberto asking him to contact the doctor with the most experience in snake bites, in the best private hospital in the city. Gilberto had to ask the medic to send anti-venom up, with the plane, for Sarah. Alex was all too aware of how limited the facilities were in some of the state hospitals in remote Peru. He wanted only the best for his wife, no matter the cost.

The doctor refused to release any of the anti-venom to Gilberto as it should only be administered by someone with medical training. He advised that Sarah's best chance was to keep the limb with the bite immobilised, which of course Alex knew and had already done. He did agree, after further radio contact and information about Alex's first aid skills, to send up intravenous fluids for Sarah to have during the flight, as dehydration was a real danger for her.

By morning, Sarah was too weak to stand, so Alex and Carlos prepared a make shift stretcher, with the help of the headman. The rest of the villagers were too frightened of the witch doctor to provide any further help.

The seaplane arrived just about an hour after dawn. The pilot circled the village then dropped quickly down onto the river, gliding to a stop after only a short distance. Within minutes the plane had manoeuvred into the bank and Gilberto climbed out from the cockpit.

'Are we pleased to see you?' Alex shouted. 'How long did it take you?'

'Just under the hour. It's a lot quicker if you can fly like the bird!' Gilberto replied.

'Have you brought the intravenous fluids? Is there going to be an ambulance waiting at the airport?'

'Yes to both. Catch! How is Sarah?' Gilberto asked as he threw the rope to Carlos to secure the plane to the bank.

'Asleep and poorly. I hope I can put up this IV; it's a while since I've had to do this.'

'You'll   manage.   I'll   help   you,'   Gilberto   said

encouragingly. Then he jumped from the plane to dry land and was soon beside Alex, crouching over the patient.

Alex had lost none of his previous skills; within ten minutes, the IV was connected and Sarah was receiving urgent fluids. In the heat of the jungle she was dehydrating fast, so desperately needed the fluid.

The sea plane could only carry one passenger in the front, two in the back. Alex was determined to keep Sarah on the stretcher so the front seat had to come out. Alex took his seat in the back and the head end of the stretcher was lifted onto his lap with the other end resting on the floor just short of the co-pilot's pedals, a very tight fit.

Gilberto was in the back behind the pilot with as much of Alex's and Sarah's baggage as possible. The pilot was nervous as he was concerned the plane would be over-laden. He pumped some of the water from the plane's floats to redress the balance. Soon they were ready for take off. Alex thanked Carlos, Pedro and of course the headman.

The seaplane set off for the middle of the river. The pilot turned the aircraft into the wind, built up the revs and they sped downstream. Alex was so relieved to be flying out of the jungle, heading for the city, and the urgent medical care his wife needed. It appeared to take the aircraft ages to clear the river. Faster and faster they raced, but still they had not cleared the water. Maybe the plane was too heavy after all, Alex thought. He could see that the pilot was in deep concentration, beads of sweat on his forehead, his knuckles white on the joy stick. When it sounded as if the little engine was going to burst, the aviator pulled back on the stick and the nose of the aircraft began to lift. But Alex could still only see trees. Was there enough power to clear the tree line? The engine was still screaming as the plane pulled over the treetops with what looked like only centimetres to spare.

'That was a close call!' the pilot said to his passengers as the plane began to climb well above the jungle. I thought we were slightly overweight, but I didn't think it would be that exciting!'

Exciting! Is that what he called it? Alex thought. We could have all been killed. The end of two weeks of hell!

The landing was much better than the take off, with the ambulance waiting to receive them. Sarah was admitted to the resuscitation room of the Jesuit Mission Hospital, a private clinic in the only upmarket part of Iquitos, within an hour of touch down. Alex was dismissed by the clinical staff while they worked on Sarah.

Dr Antonio Gonzales came to speak to Alex about three quarters of an hour later.

'Your wife is very sick,' he said. We have given her the anti-venom but she has reacted very badly to it. Sometimes this happens because the anti-venom is prepared in the blood of horses which, of course, is foreign to humans, and patients can have a bad reaction.'

'You mean she has had an anaphylactic shock?' Alex said anxiously.

'Yes. How do you know about this reaction?' the doctor asked.

'From one of my colleagues; his son had a peanut allergy. The boy accidentally ate a sandwich that had been contaminated with peanut butter, at the school sports day. He was rushed to hospital; fortunately, the paramedics treated him on the way or he would have died.'

'The difference here is that, whenever we give anti-venom, we look out for these reactions, so your wife was treated very quickly with adrenaline and steroids. She's improving now, but she'll be in intensive care for several days.'

'Can I see her?' Alex asked.

'She's sleeping just now, but you may go in for a few minutes before we transfer her to the unit. You look exhausted. I think you should have some food and sleep before you come back.'

'Thank you, Doctor. I will.'

Alex was shown through to see Sarah.

He thought she looked awful. She was flushed and she had tubes everywhere. She was wired up to monitors and was wearing an oxygen mask. Sarah was asleep and Alex didn't want to waken her. His darling wife had been through so much he thought.

It was two weeks before Sarah was well enough to leave hospital. She had lost a lot of weight and was as weak and wobbly as a new born lamb. Sarah wanted to stay in Iquitos for as long as necessary in case there was any news of the children, but Alex over-ruled her. He knew she couldn't cope with the high temperatures. She was able to function in the air conditioning but was exhausted by the heat and so couldn't go out.

While Sarah had been recovering in hospital Alex had used his time well by organising a search for the children. He hired three groups of men to search different parts of the Rio Napo, and other rivers in the area of the crash site. Gilberto had helped him find suitable fast boat men for the work. Carlos who had returned safely, agreed to go back out in 'Claudia', once he had rested from his earlier adventures.

The couple remained in Iquitos only for a further week after Sarah's discharge from hospital. Gilberto agreed to supervise the search teams and promised to contact them if he heard any news. Alex and Sarah then flew back to Lima to allow Sarah to convalesce.

CHAPTER 20

Ruled by Fear

Tim and Katie settled into village life quickly, because they were young and very adaptable. They soon realised that, in a small jungle community everyone, except the infants and toddlers, had a role to play. The boys and men did the hunting, farming, fishing and building. The girls and womenfolk collected the water, washed the clothes, and did the cooking and the child rearing. From dawn until dusk everyone was busy, except in the middle of the day when it was too hot to work and a sleep in the shade was the usual custom.

Katie soon adjusted to the idea that she wouldn't see much of Tim because he was off with the older boys helping with the fishing or hunting. He loved it, especially when he went in the dugout canoe, away up the little tributaries far from the village. Tim couldn't get used to the noise of the jungle; it excited him immensely. The birds and the frogs seemed to make most of the noise, but sometimes they would hear the screeching of the monkeys high up in the canopy. Tim tried hard to see such creatures, but had to rely on the local boys' superior skills at spotting the primates.

Most of the time, Tim was with Ronaldo either fishing or hunting in the forest. Ronaldo taught Tim how to use a blow pipe to kill small animals. He showed the younger boy how to put poison on the tip of the dart, to paralyse the prey. The poison was taken from the moisture on the back of a particular frog. First they had to find the special frogs, but usually Ronaldo had a good idea where to look for them. These were beautiful black frogs with bright red colouring on their backs. When they found them, they had to handle them very carefully. If even a small amount of the poison rubbed onto a piece of broken skin, then the victim could die of paralysis. Tim knew he had to be very careful! He learnt how to make arrows by turning branches into well balanced feathered projectiles. These became lethal weapons with the added poison. They could be used with deadly accuracy to bring down small animals from high in the trees but Tim still had much to learn before he became a good shot. Tim didn't like killing anything, but he soon realised that the villagers had to eat or they would die. There was no supermarket down-town. He quickly understood that, unless all the men and boys worked together to hunt or farm, the community would starve.

Although there was no school building, the village children were gathered together each morning, after the chores were done. They met in the headman's lodge, as it was the biggest building in the community. There was no teacher in the village as the usual teacher had returned to Iquitos when the tribe headed for the deep jungle. Katie was shocked when Miguel arrived at the front of the group and took charge of the children. He was very strict with everyone but knew how to keep the children's attention. He had a blackboard which he had insisted the men brought from the other village. He taught the children elementary arithmetic and how to read and write in Spanish. Katie was amazed at how good he was as a teacher. She enjoyed the school times as it helped her Spanish, and the more the village children understood Spanish the more she could communicate with them. Miguel often used Katie to help the younger children, which pleased her enormously.

One day after school, Tim told Katie that he had been talking with Miguel about his life here in the jungle. Miguel explained to him that when he lived with his family in Bella Vista he had gone right through elementary school from age five to eleven years old. He loved school and was usually best in his class. He enjoyed hearing about other regions of Peru, about the government in Iquitos and the capital city Lima. Miguel said he would like to go there some day. For the next three years he had travelled by river boat to Mazan to attend the senior school. He would go to the school on a Monday and return to his own village on the Friday. He stayed in the school hostel with about thirty other boys. His father gathered many more bananas than the other men of his village to pay for the schooling. His father wanted Miguel to study; he knew he was a bright boy. Miguel wanted to go to university in Iquitos but he couldn't. After his father died, there was no money for his education. Miguel wanted to be a teacher, but he had to return to his village and work with the other young men. He still wanted to go and live in Iquitos. There, he planned to make his fortune and pay himself through university. He would teach at first but when he was older and had more experience he would be a politician, really changing things and making life better for his people. For now, he believed he must be with his tribe through this difficult time. He didn't agree with the headman's decision to come into the deep jungle. Miguel thought that they should have gone to the government for help and not run away from the drug criminals. Miguel believed his tribe had gone back fifty years by coming to this village with no education, no health care and no government support. But he was loyal to his uncle, the chief, and obeyed his wishes as is the tradition of his tribe.

'How long do you think we have been in the village now?' Katie asked her big brother. 'Why has no one found us yet?'

'I think we have been here about three months now; at least I counted three new moons,' Tim replied. 'I don't know why no one has found us. Dad will never give up looking for us. Uncle Hugh will help him, I know he will,' Tim replied with an emotional waver in his voice.

'But what if they think we are dead? They are not going to look for us then are they?' Katie said very matter of fact. 'Why doesn't the headman arrange for us to be taken out of here?'

'Miguel has said that the chief has forbidden anyone to leave the village in case the drugs militia find this hidden place. He believes that they'll come and kill everyone in revenge for not helping them. The chief had heard of such horrible things happening when the Shining Path were in control of this region, ten years ago,' Tim explained.

'What was Shining Path?' Katie asked.

'They were a guerrilla movement who fought against the government and terrorised the people. Many of the poor people who lived in the country left their homes to get away from them. They moved to the cities, but ended up in the slums,' Tim replied.

'How do you know so much about them? Are they still in the jungle today?' Katie said, looking a bit worried.

'We studied 'The Shining Path' in modern history last term. Their leader was caught and put into prison where he'll stay for the rest of his life,' Tim said knowledgeably.

'Thank goodness!' Katie said with a little shudder. 'He must have been a horrible man. How long do you think it will be before the chief will feel safe?'

'Don't know but we can't leave here ourselves. We would never survive. We have to be patient. At least everyone likes us and we're looked after,' Tim said trying to encourage Katie.

'I suppose you're right,' Katie conceded.

The following morning, there was great excitement in the village. The men folk had headed off early as usual. Katie had noticed some of the older women going to the hut of Nicky, the young pregnant girl. Katie thought she seemed very young to be married. The girl looked about fifteen and her husband Cesar looked only a little older. Recently, Katie had seen that the girl was looking very tired and even she had thought that Nicky's baby must be due soon. Katie ran to find her friend Maria. Her new friend was a bit more confident with her Spanish so the two girls could chat to each other; if they didn't know the word they used sign language. Often they were in fits of laughter as they tried to understand one another. They had become good friends.

The chat among the young girls of the village was all about Nicky. How long had she been trying to give birth? Did the baby start to come last night or was it just this morning? Would it be a boy or a girl? The young girls were sitting cross-legged on the river bank near to Nicky's hut waiting for news. They could easily hear the groans coming from Nicky as the birth pangs wracked her young body. The mothers of the community had to call the girls to do their chores, which they did reluctantly, but as soon as the water fetching was finished, they were back waiting by the river bank. The men folk returned and there was still no word of the baby. The groans from Nicky's hut were growing louder and more frequent. When darkness fell, the yells took on an eerie character. The girls continued to sit on the bank despite the insects biting badly that evening. The moon was high in the sky. Katie watched the bats dart across in the moonlight. She wondered if they really would suck her blood dry as she had heard from the comic books. The children were ushered to bed at the usual time, still no word of Nicky's baby. Katie could tell that the women of the village were very anxious about the mother-to-be. Maria, her friend, whispered to her that the witch doctor had been summoned to Nicky's hut, which meant that there was a big problem. Katie was sad because she thought that Nicky was so young and, from her grunting, was obviously in great pain.

In the morning, when the girls woke up there was a great commotion around the hut of the pregnant girl. Women folk were weeping and the men were huddled together talking, but obviously sad. Katie thought that the baby must have died. She was shocked to discover that the young mother had died as well as her baby. Nicky's baby had been the wrong way round, coming feet first. It had been a long birth and the baby's head had become stuck. The baby died because of lack of air and Nicky died from exhaustion. When Katie heard the full story she wept with the other girls. Nicky had been very kind to her, and she had been looking forward to being a mother very much. Katie had never heard of anyone dying while having a baby back home. But that was probably because they went into hospital and the doctors and nurses looked after them, she thought.

Tim and Katie were together the next day, along with the whole village, for the funeral of Nicky and her newborn baby. The gringo children had never been to a funeral before. Katie was relieved that her big brother was there as she was really frightened and upset. They found it a very sad occasion, but also very strange. The headman took charge and read some verses from a Spanish bible, which Tim and Katie managed to understand. But then the witch doctor appeared in his ceremonial dress and danced menacingly round the crowd of mourners. Katie was scared by him, especially when he jumped up to her and Tim. The wild man shook two animal skulls in their faces, and then he spat and stamped his feet at them. He continued this for some time until the chief shouted at him. Miguel signalled to Tim and Katie to leave the group and return to the village. They didn't stay to watch the burial of Nicky and her baby.

'What was that all about?' Katie asked Tim.

'I don't know, I'll ask Miguel later. He seems upset just now,' Tim replied.

Katie noticed that her new friends stayed away from her the rest of that awful day, which really upset her. She couldn't wait for Tim to get back from the yucca field. She spent the day on her own sitting under the big banana tree by the bank of the river.

Tim found his sister asleep. He gently woke her to make sure she was alright.

'Are you Ok?' he asked.

'Yeah. I was just sad. No one has spoken to me all day. I guess I just nodded off. What have I done? What's wrong with everyone?'

'Miguel said that the witch doctor was trying to blame us for Nicky's death,' Tim explained.

'Us? What did we have to do with it?'

'According to Miguel, this old witch doctor is very frightened of gringos and especially their medicine. I suppose he's concerned he could lose his position and power within the tribe,' Tim replied. 'He doesn't like you because he heard from Ronaldo how you saved my life. Remember that time when I nearly drowned? He thinks you have special powers and that makes you his rival. So he cast a spell on us at the funeral, hoping to get rid of us. The witch doctor gave Nicky some potion from the jungle last night and it was just after taking it that she died. So the medicine man was frightened that the villagers blamed him for the young woman's death. It was very convenient that two gringos were in the village and he could blame them!

'Miguel is furious! He doesn't believe in all the witch doctor's spells and treatments. The rest of the villagers aren't as well educated as Miguel and so they believe if the witch doctor casts a spell on you, then you must be a bad person. He told me the other day that he's a Christian,' Tim continued.

'What do you mean?' Katie asked.

'Every few months, a visiting medical boat used to visit Paradise village, you know the one that was attacked by the drug barons. He became a Christian after hearing about Jesus. The doctors and dentists on board were missionaries from the United States. They treated Pablo when he was ill with malaria, and saved his life. Miguel wanted to know why these doctors came all the way from America to help his people. One of the young doctors explained to him that they came because they loved God and that God loved Miguel and his people. Miguel was so shocked by the answer that he had to find out more about God.'

'So that's why Miguel was angry and why no one will speak to me today! It'll be awful staying here if no one will speak to us. But how can we get away? We don't know where we are. I want to go home, Tim. I want to be with Mum and Dad again!' Katie said as she burst into tears. Tim put his arm round his little sister's shoulder to comfort her.

'We'll get home. Dad will find us. I know he will. Don't cry. Miguel is going to speak to the chief tonight; he thinks the chief will tell the villagers that it was not our fault and that we are to be treated as guests.'

Miguel managed to persuade the headman to overrule the witch doctor. After supper the chief spoke to the whole community and told them that the gringo children had nothing to do with Nicky's death. They had nothing to do with the other young mother and baby who died six months before or the two children who died of fever last year. These things just happened in the jungle; no-one was to blame.

When the witch doctor heard this he rushed from the long hut and went off into the jungle; he was not seen again for the rest of the month.

Katie was delighted, as were her new friends. Once the chief had finished speaking, Maria and the other girls rushed across to Katie, grabbed her by the hand and took her outside with them to talk about everything that had happened.

Over the next couple of weeks, village life continued much as normal. However, one afternoon, just before sunset, two large canoes arrived from upstream. Katie had never seen so many people crammed into two small boats. The women were sitting on the rims of the canoes with their backsides just centimetres off the water. She wondered how the boats had not sunk. The chief went to speak to the leaders, with his young men surrounding him in case of trouble. Katie was anxiously looking for Tim but she relaxed when she saw he was standing with Ronaldo; the two had become good friends. The visitors, who were mainly women, children and a few old men, were found to be friendly. They were allowed to rest for the night in the village. The women-folk of the village were instructed to lay on a feast for the guests. The group were the last of a village community two hour's canoe trip upstream. They had wanted to remain in their village, which they founded twenty years earlier. But they had nowhere to hunt anymore and had so many sick people. Their leaders decided that they had to abandon the village.

Katie was sitting quietly in the back of the long house with the other girls, as the visitors' leaders described how many of their young men had died before their time. They didn't know for sure why this was happening but they blamed the oil drilling company.

Katie's friends tried to explain to her, with the little Spanish they shared, everything that was being discussed by the elders, but she only managed to get half the story. She watched while the men folk became more and more drunk with the masato. She was worried that Tim would have to drink this as he was one of the older boys. Fortunately, he managed to avoid the brew. He had heard Ronaldo proudly tell stories of how it was made and its effects. His mother's warning about the dangers of alcohol rang only slightly in his ears, but when he heard how the women folk chewed up the yucca plant and then spat it into a tank he decided that nothing would make him drink it anyway.

Later in the evening Tim joined his sister and filled her in on some of the gaps in the story about the visitors. They were from the Matsi tribe, a group who had survived in the jungle for hundreds of years. They lived near the Ecuador border in a community called San Carlos.

Two years ago, an oil company started exploration. Government officials came to the village right at the start and assured the Matsi that the drilling would have no effect on the village community. The officials said that strict environmental rules would have to be followed as part of international agreements. So the oil men set up camp half an hour upstream from San Carlos. About a hundred workers lived there. At first, it was good as there was some work for the tribesmen. They were allowed to buy goods from the company store. The new neighbours respected the villagers' right to exist in peace. But the drilling didn't go well, and they moved closer to the river, ripping up huge areas of the forest. This meant that the hunters had to travel deeper into the jungle, far from their usual hunting tracks. They were often away for days. Then the villagers noticed that the river water tasted differently. Then disaster struck! The fish in the river died and there were hundreds of fish floating on the water. To make matters worse, the young men often visited the camp and drank heavily with the oil men.

The village leaders went to the camp to speak to the bosses. The oilmen denied that they were polluting the river but they did admit that some of their workers had been jaundiced and had to be evacuated to Iquitos. The Matsi asked them not to destroy anymore of the jungle in the area. The oilmen refused and chased off the tribal leaders. The village chief responded by banning his people from working or visiting the drilling camp but still another two of the young men died.

After a year, four of the families from the village left to start a new community downstream, but this visiting group tried to stay longer. Sadly, things only became worse. The chief's first grandson died the week before the Matsi abandoned their village. The boy was only two days old. The chief knew then that there was no future for the Matsi in San Carlos, so they had to leave.

'That is so sad!' Katie said to Tim. 'The poor little boy; his mother must have been so upset.'

'Yes, she's the one who always walks at the back of the group and has been sitting on her own,' Tim commented.

'I've heard about pollution from oil fields in geography, but I thought they had to follow government guidelines. I bet Dad made sure his company kept to the rules. I suppose up here, far away from the authorities and with only a few tribes affected, nobody bothers; especially when there is so much money to make from the oil,' Tim continued.

'I remember watching a programme on the television, about large areas of forest being destroyed in Brazil. The loggers were clearing the trees to make huge fields to grow soya and wheat. The local Amazon Indians were fighting the government to keep their lands so they could continue to hunt and support their families. I didn't really understand the problem then, but I think I do now. Are they going to destroy the rain forest in Peru to make big farms as well?' Katie asked her big brother.

'Mum said that there was some logging going on near the Brazilian border last year, but it was stopped by the Peruvian government after pressure from other countries. I think it was to do with global warming,' Tim replied.

Katie and Tim joined the rest of the village as they waved off the visitors the next morning. Shortly afterwards, Tim and Miguel headed out to fish and Katie and the girls went about their daily chores.

CHAPTER 21

Too Much to Bear

There was a great commotion around noon. The old lady, called Nan, had fallen down the two steps to her hut. She was the woman who had helped Katie, when she first arrived at the village, with her wonderful herbal remedy for ant bites. But now she was rolling in agony clutching her right hip. The women folk rushed to her aid to try and help her up, but she was in severe pain. Eventually, two of the women managed to get Nan onto her feet and helped her to her mat on the floor, but she was crying in terrible pain. She couldn't put any weight on her right leg. Katie had grown very fond of Nan, collecting her water and fire wood every day, and Nan loved Katie too, often spending time brushing her dark brown hair or repairing her torn shorts. Nan's husband, Marco, died of a snake bite about ten years earlier, which made her very lonely. But the worst thing that happened to her was when her five children died in a canoeing accident. The other girls told Katie all about it that afternoon after Nan's fall.

About twenty years before, Nan and her husband and their five children had to go to Mazan to register for the elections. They had to register in the town of birth of the father of the family, which in Marco's case was Mazan.

It was in the rainy season, so the river Napo was in full flood. Nan was holding the little baby girl, and the other children who were three, five, seven and ten years old, were seated in the middle of the boat. Marco was in the back of the canoe controlling the pecky-pecky, a small motorised propeller. It was raining heavily, and the journey was taking longer than expected because, on two separate occasions, weed had wrapped itself round the propeller shaft of the pecky-pecky, so they had to stop to clear it. By the time darkness fell, they were still two hours from Mazan.

They could have stopped and sheltered in a village for the night, something that Marco and Nan would regret not having done for the rest of their lives, but they didn't. Marco just didn't see the half submerged tree trunk, otherwise he would have swerved, as he had on several occasions throughout the long journey. The canoe, with everyone in it, was catapulted into the air as it hit the log. The baby girl was ripped from Nan's arms like a rag doll and disappeared into the night. Nan never saw the little one again. The children had been asleep, dozing off to the drone of the engine. They didn't stand a chance, thrown like twigs in a gale. Nan was a good swimmer but when she surfaced and realised what had happened, she frantically called for her children. Only the oldest child Theo cried out 'Mama, Mama'. Then silence! Marco grabbed Nan's arm and pulled her to the up-turned boat. Both clung to the hull crying out for their children and trying to locate them. But nothing! They had all been dragged away by the fearsome current. The pair started to kick towards the river bank, eventually managing to push the capsized boat into the bank. All they could do in the dark was wait for dawn.

Marco righted his canoe in the morning and made an improvised paddle as the pecky-pecky had been lost. He paddled slowly downstream, searching the bank as they went, to the nearest village. Nan sat weeping.

The villagers in the next community immediately organised searches of both banks of the river Napo, but nothing. Marco and Nan's children were gone forever.

The couple didn't have any more children. They had to leave their own village of Tampra because the witch doctor put it about the community that they had been given the 'evil eye' and that was why disaster had struck their family; so others in the community shunned them. They moved further up river to live in Nan's father's home in Paradise village.

Katie was really sad to hear the awful things that had happened to her elderly friend.

'How can so many terrible things happen to one person?' she asked Tim when he returned that night.

'Out here, anything can happen. There is no hospital nearby when someone has an accident. Ronaldo told me what happened to his father Juan, four years ago. He was helping to thatch a new roof when he lost his footing; he fell off and broke his back. He was bundled into a canoe and taken to the health post several hours away, but there was no doctor, only a health care worker who gave him some paracetamol. He could do nothing for him. So he was taken back to his village where the villagers plied him with masato to help kill the pain. Juan never got off the floor again. He died three weeks later; he was only thirty. Ronaldo and Pablo were still young and, as their mother died giving birth to Pablo, they were all alone. That is why they have been looked after by the chief as Juan was his brother,' Tim replied.

'So the boys have been orphans for four years. That's awful! I wonder if Nan will get better,' Katie asked.

'Ronaldo said that the women folk thought she had broken her hip,' Tim commented.

'Didn't Granny Mitchell break her hip last year?' Katie remembered.

'Yes, she fell off steps while cleaning her cupboards. Remember, Mum was furious that she was up the steps at her age. She ended up in hospital for three weeks. She had a big operation and a new hip,' Tim recollected.

'So will Nan go to hospital?' Katie asked.

'There was no mention of hospital from Ronaldo,' Tim answered. 'Even if there was a hospital close by, Nan would have to pay for the operation. It's not like back home where everything is paid for on the Health Service. So I don't know what's going to happen. I'll try and find out from Ronaldo.'

The next day, Katie was allowed to go and see Nan; she took her some water. Mayu's mum was looking after her. Nan looked really old, lying on the floor covered only by a thin blanket. She refused the water, and she wasn't eating either. Katie sat with her for a little while, holding her hand. This old lady meant a lot to her. She didn't want her to die, but even at her young age she could see that Nan had given up and lost the will to live.

Katie realised why Nan had given up when she next spoke with Tim. He explained that there was not going to be any hospital. In the first place, the chief had refused to let anyone leave the village. Secondly, it would take four days to get Nan to Iquitos, and she wouldn't cope with such a journey while in so much pain. And, thirdly, there was no money in the village to pay for an operation anyway.

'That's horrible!' Katie said to her brother. 'Can't we do something to help her?'

'No, I don't think so. The chief has made his decision,' Tim replied.

Four days later, Nan was dead. Katie was very upset. She had seen so much death in the last few months. All the passengers on the plane, Aunt Susie, Nicky and her baby and now a lovely old lady who had been so kind to her – all dead. When would this nightmare end? When would they get back to Lima and Mum and Dad?

Katie couldn't hold back the tears anymore; she wept and wept. Mayu and Maria tried their best but they couldn't get through to Katie. She was upset for days after Nan's death.

Miguel realised that Katie was not her usual self, as he was taking school. She wouldn't take part and seemed to be distracted, not paying any attention. He spoke to Tim about his sister and found that her big brother was worried about her too. Katie had started sitting on her own, sometimes for hours, by the riverbank just watching the water. After a few days, she stopped eating. Tim tried to talk to his sister but she just clammed up. The chief's wife, Illary, tried to coax her to eat as well. It was as if the trauma of the last three months had finally caught up with Katie.

A couple of days later, she was ill with a high fever. She awoke in the night shouting for her mother, delirious with the high temperature. Katie was vomiting and was shivering – symptoms of malaria. Illary realised this, so took Katie into the long house. There was no health post in the village and no medicines to treat her. The chief ordered that she be treated by traditional methods, the way generations of Amazonian Indians had cared for their sick. Tim was anxious about the decision but he knew there was no alternative. He had heard his chemistry teacher explain that some western scientists were desperate to analyse at least some of the hundred of compounds used by the tribes' folk. Each hoped that their company would find a wonder drug for Aids or cancer treatment, based on the herbal remedies of the Indians. Tim prayed that the substance given to his sister was one of those treatments that worked. He was relieved to see that it was no magic potion given out by the witch doctor but a remedy that the chief trusted himself.

Mayu and Maria were sent into the jungle to bring back the leaves of the mungo tree to make the special tea. Miguel was angry again! He had grown very fond of Katie and Tim. He knew that Katie needed to be taken to a health post for proper treatment. He asked the chief to let him take her and Tim to the health post at San Marino on the Napo. The headman refused. He was still frightened that the drug barons would find out where they were hiding. Miguel had a huge row with his uncle the headman, but still the chief refused to give his permission for them to leave. He would not risk the entire community for a gringo child.

Miguel decided that it was time to act. The chief was doing the wrong thing; he was living in the past. Miguel was not just a member of the Hati tribe, he was also a Peruvian and very proud of the fact. He didn't want to defy the chief, and he knew he could never return if he went against his authority, but he didn't want to live the rest of his life in fear. Ever since his father died, his uncle had looked after Miguel and his two brothers as his own. Miguel had always respected him as the leader of the tribe, but this time he was so wrong. This young girl would die if she stayed here, just like his sister Marie had died. He knew that he must try to get treatment for Katie and get her and Tim to Iquitos and back to their family. They had been here too long already. Maybe it was too late to save Katie, but he knew he had to try.

Later that day, Miguel met with Tim and explained his plan to him.

'We'll leave tonight after everyone is asleep. It's a full moon so we'll be able to go safely by canoe,' Miguel explained to Tim.

'How long will it take to get to the health post?' Tim asked.

'It'll take half the night to reach the Napo River and then the rest of the night to reach San Gorge,' Miguel replied.

'I hope Katie will be alright; she's very weak. What about Ronaldo and Pablo? Are they coming too?' Tim asked.

'I have to speak with them first, because, if they leave the tribe, they cannot come back. They must decide. It'll come as a shock to them as I've never spoken to them about my disagreements with the chief. Because we owed him so much, we had to be loyal. He has been like a father to us; Pablo, in particular, is very fond of his Uncle,' Miguel said. 'I'll get the canoe ready and come for you and Katie later tonight. Make some excuse to sleep quite close to Katie so you can get away easily.'

'That should be easy to do; these last two nights she has been so hot that she has sat by the door of the hut where it's cooler, so tonight I'll sit with her and at your signal we'll slip away.'

'Good, see you later.'

'Thank you Miguel, you're a good friend. You're risking a lot for us,' Tim said thankfully, as he watched the young man walk back to his hut. Miguel wasn't very tall, probably average for a Peruvian Tim thought, but strong and muscular. His biceps were huge compared to Tim's, and his legs were like tree trunks with powerful calf and thigh muscles. Tim realised it was from years of working hard in the fields. He thought all the young men in the village looked very strong; even Pablo, who was smaller than Tim, looked to be really tough for his age.

Katie's vomiting had stopped now. She was taking some fluid but she still had a fever. Tim went to the hut to visit her and spend time with her. He told her of Miguel's plan. Despite feeling awful, Katie managed a smile and whispered to her brother, 'Take me home Tim, it's time to see Mum and Dad again.'

'Let's move you to the doorway so Miguel can pick you up and take you to the canoe.'

Katie groaned as her brother helped her to her feet and over to the door. Tim said to Illary that he would stay with Katie for a while and take care of her so Illary could go to bed.

It was a beautiful night. The moon was high in the sky, the stars as bright as could be. It wasn't long before the family in the hut were fast asleep and the chief was snoring in his hammock.

Katie fell asleep resting on her brother's lap. She had been sleeping for about an hour when Miguel signalled to Tim from the bushes. Miguel crept over and lifted Katie from Tim's knee and then carried her, still asleep, to the canoe. Tim couldn't believe it when he arrived at the water side. Ronaldo and Pablo were waiting there, with huge broad grins on their faces, their white teeth glinting in the moonlight.

'My brothers want to come too,' Miguel said proudly.

'They didn't think I could manage myself!' Smiling, he helped the boys make Katie as comfortable as possible.

'But there is no way back for any of you! You can't come back here,' Tim whispered to the brothers.

'We know, but we must do the right thing. You're our friends. Our uncle has made the wrong decisions about you and the future of our tribe, and we brothers want to stay together,' Ronaldo replied.

'Ssh! Let's get out of here before anyone realises we're away,' Miguel said. Pablo pushed off quietly from the bank.

CHAPTER 22

Saved by Love

The group were very relieved to have escaped without being noticed. It could have been pretty messy if they had been confronted by the chief. There would have been a big fight and the boys would have been expelled from the village in disgrace.

'What about the canoe? Did you steal it?' Tim asked the boys.

'No, this canoe belonged to our father. He made it the year before he died. We have used it since then. The pecky-pecky is ours too, so we haven't stolen anything. We know it's wrong to steal. The fuel was our allocation for next month, to fish with. We'll have to sell the boat though, to help pay for the river boat tickets,' Miguel replied.

'But you'll need the boat to survive when you settle in your new village,' Tim said.

'We've decided that we're all going with you to Iquitos, to start a new life there. We're not going to separate; Pablo is too young to be on his own anyway,' Ronaldo answered.

'That's fantastic! First you save our lives and now you're going to go where you've never been to take us home. You are 'Good Samaritans!'

'What's a Samaritan?' Pablo asked.

'Someone who helps a stranger in difficulty; it's a name that comes from a story in the Bible. I'll read it to you sometime,' Tim said, grinning at the thought of going home.

'When we get to Iquitos and then you go home to Lima, do you think we will still keep in contact with you? Will we still be friends?' Ronaldo said thoughtfully.

'Yes, we must. We will keep in touch! I promise!' said Katie.

'You have done so much for us. We owe our lives to you. So I promise you, we will always keep in contact with you,' echoed Tim.

Pablo and Miguel quickly agreed as well. The five shook hands and the promise was sealed.

The river current was strong, so even after twenty minutes paddling they were far away from the village. It was safe enough for Miguel to start up the pecky-pecky. But he couldn't get it to fire up. After several attempts he signalled to the boys to paddle for the river bank. Once there they manoeuvred the little boat so Miguel could inspect the little outboard motor. As Miguel worked, Pablo steadied the canoe, standing up to his knees in the water. It was difficult for the boys to see the problem as the moonlight was just not quite bright enough. Finally Miguel realised that weed had become entangled in the motor. He took his jungle knife and freed the blades. Suddenly Pablo screamed, and then disappeared from the side of the canoe; he was wildly splashing and thrashing about in the water. Miguel quickly understood the problem. Pablo had been grabbed by a crocodile.

'Camen!' he shouted and dived into the river with his knife clenched between his teeth.

The river became a boiling cauldron of water, the canoe tossing almost to the point of capsize. Occasionally, Tim caught a glint from Miguel's knife as he wrestled with the croc trying to force it to release Pablo. Miguel managed to get on top of the croc, and jabbed his knife into one eye then the other. The reptile now mortally wounded released Pablo. Miguel dragged his brother to the bank where Ronaldo was waiting to help him. Pablo had a large gash in his right lower leg, but he was alive. Tim quickly removed his shirt and tied it round Pablo's wound to stop the bleeding. He made Pablo lie flat on the ground and lifted his leg high in the air, just as he had been taught in the scouts. Pablo was very tearful after his ordeal. He knew he had been minutes from death. Had it not been for Miguel's bravery and quick thinking, the camen would have dragged him off to a deep pool, where he would have drowned and become supper for a hungry crocodile!

It took the group several minutes to take in all that had just happened. Tim and Ronaldo comforted Pablo and praised Miguel for his actions. Miguel was having none of it. 'He's my little brother. It was my job to save him. Just as well that wasn't a full grown camen. It was still a juvenile. Pablo would have lost his leg and probably his life, if it had been his "Mama." We'll get him stitched up at the health post,' he said to the others.

Once Pablo's leg had stopped bleeding, they helped him into the canoe. The other boys made him sit with his leg up over the side of the canoe to stop any further bleeding. This time the pecky-pecky started with one pull of the cord and they were on their way again. Katie was asleep, curled up in the bottom of the canoe.

As Miguel had anticipated, they arrived at the Napo River halfway through the night. The water became very choppy with turbulence as their little tributary joined the massive Napo. Frantically, the boys had to scoop the water out of the canoe. Tim was frightened they were going to sink. Water splashed on Katie's face, waking her up with a jump. Tim had to restrain his sister. She didn't know where she was so tried to get up, making the canoe even more unstable.

Miraculously, after five minutes, the canoe settled. It had passed over the worst of the turbulence and all was well. Miguel was still tense. He knew that if a large speed boat passed, the wash could threaten them again. He opted to stay close to the river bank in case he had to take refuge. The difficulty with this was that, in the half light, he might hit a submerged tree. Tim knew all about this danger so he took turns with the others at the bow of the canoe to act as look out.

Katie seemed a bit brighter now; the cool of the journey had brought down her temperature. Ronaldo encouraged her to take some water before she slipped back to sleep. Pablo was resting quietly in the bottom of the canoe in deep thought.

The last leg of their journey to San Gorge passed off without any problems. No speed boats passed as it was very early in the morning. They tied up their canoe at the jetty area and were met by an inquisitive dawn fisherman. Miguel chatted to him and found him really helpful. He directed Miguel to the health post but he wasn't sure if the health care worker was still in his hut or out hunting already. Miguel knew that the health worker in the village was usually a farmer but trained by the authorities to identify and treat malaria and do any necessary first aid. He hoped that having arrived so early he might be able to catch the health man before he left for his work.

'I'll run and try to find him; you stay in the boat till I come back,' Miguel said to the group.

Miguel was back in about ten minutes with Amaro the health worker. He was a young, strapping man in his late twenties, wearing a navy blue baseball cap and Brazil football strip. Amaro was a happy character who willingly went down the steep bank to the canoe and helped the boys carry Katie and Pablo to the health post. This was a small designated, brick structure in a corner of the village. It had been built to the usual government design with whitewashed walls and light blue woodwork; by the look of the paintwork, it had been built several years earlier.

By the time they arrived at the post, the sun had fully risen. Amaro then discovered that two of the group were gringos! He hadn't realised at first because they were dressed in the usual sort of clothes that village children wear, their own clothes having been ripped and destroyed weeks before. He was shocked, and wondered why two gringo children would be in the jungle, but after discussion with Miguel he relaxed a bit and started to assess Katie. He had only limited skills, but he knew malaria when he saw it and soon agreed that Katie probably had the disease. He thought it was falciparum malaria, the most serious type, but he needed to check. Amaro explained to the boys that he had been given a new kit by the health department only six months ago and he could use this to check which type of malaria Katie had. The only problem was that he had no medicine left to treat falciparum as he used the last dose the day before. Amaro told them that the government only gave a fixed allocation per village and they had a lot of malaria this last month. He would look at Pablo once he finished with Katie.

Miguel passed Tim a worrying glance. The oldest of the brothers had picked up something wasn't quite right. Amaro went to the cupboard and came out with the testing kit. Katie was looking a bit anxious now but calmed when she discovered it was only a pinprick of blood he required to put on the end of a chemical strip.

Five minutes later Amaro had the answer – it was falciparum, but reiterated that he had no treatment for this kind of malaria. He was very apologetic and suggested that they return to their canoe and travel on downstream to the next village. Maybe there the health care worker would have the correct drugs.

Miguel didn't buy into Amaro's story. When he met him in his house he had been confident that he would be able to help Miguel's group but since he discovered Katie and Tim were gringos his whole attitude had changed; eye contact was only fleeting, his face tense. But Miguel said nothing until Amaro had dealt with Pablo's wound.

Pablo had been very lucky. The croc had grabbed his leg just mid calf. There were two deep wounds into the muscle which required to be stitched. He was very brave, as the health worker stitched up his leg without any local anaesthetic. Tim couldn't believe his eyes; surely there would be something to kill the pain? The local boys didn't even know what Tim was talking about! After the bandages were on Pablo's leg, Miguel asked Amaro to check again that he didn't have any of the correct medicine for Katie. But again Amaro said he had none.

Ronaldo and Tim could sense the tension rising in the room. Suddenly Miguel grabbed the health worker by the throat and pinned him to the wall. Tim shut the door of the health post in case anyone could see what was going on.

'Why will you not give us treatment for the girl?' Miguel demanded of the nurse.

'I don't treat gringos!' he replied bitterly, through clenched teeth.

'Why not? What have they done to you?' Miguel asked without releasing his grip.

'They took my sister and another child from the village. We've never seen her again.'

'What happened?' Miguel pressed further.

'A group of gringos, men and women came to the village about four months ago; the chief treated them as guests. They came back in the night and stole our children.

I'll never do anything for any gringo again. The chief has forbidden us to even speak to gringos,' Amaro continued.

'OK, calm down. That was a terrible thing to do, but it was nothing to do with these two. I told you they were in a big plane that crashed in the jungle. They were the only survivors; they've suffered enough. We're trying to take them back to Iquitos to find their parents. Now will you help us?' Miguel asked again.

'I can't. The chief has spoken.'

'If we tie you to this chair and make it look as if you were robbed, would that make it easier for you or do I have to beat it out of you? We are not leaving till we have the right treatment for Katie. The choice is yours.' Miguel pushed the man hard against the wall to make his point.

'OK! OK!' The 'nurse' gave in. 'But you must leave as soon as I give you the treatment. The gringo children must not be seen here! We scared off some gringos two months ago. They admitted they were looking for children so the men folk got together and chased them away with machetes. The gringo kids might be killed; there is so much bad feeling. The witch doctor has stirred up the village.'

Ten minutes later they were all back in the canoe heading downstream. Katie had swallowed the first dose of her tablets. The health worker was left securely tied to the chair. They kept going for at least an hour, and then Miguel pulled the canoe into the bank.

'We need to plan our next move,' Miguel said rather anxiously. We have only half a can of petrol left. We need to get as far away from San Gorge as possible because they'll radio ahead to the local villages and tell them about us. We need to find a friendly tribe where we can stay for a few weeks. This would give time for Katie to rest, and for Pablo's leg to heal. We'll need time to gather bananas to pay for our boat trip to Iquitos.'

'If we could make it to Villa Luisa, our cousin Rosa married a boy from there. I'm sure she would help us. She only went to live there last year,' Ronaldo suggested.

'I had forgotten about her. She was clever in junior school but her parents wouldn't let her go to senior school in Mazan. She wanted to be a nurse but her father wouldn't hear of it. We've enough fuel for about twenty kilometres then we'll have to paddle. But I think it's a good idea. We need somewhere for Katie and Pablo to recover and grow strong before we travel the long distance to Iquitos,' Miguel mused. 'It'll take us two days to get there but we'll make it. Tim what do you think?'

'Why are we waiting? Sounds good to me! Let's get away from these villages that hate gringos. The story Amaro told about the children disappearing was awful. No wonder they hate us!' Tim replied.

'Pablo, are you OK?' Miguel asked his little brother.

'Yes. I'm fed up sitting with my leg up in the air all the time though,' he complained.

'Don't worry. Once we're out of fuel you'll be paddling with the rest of us. Katie, how are you feeling?' Miguel asked.

'Hungry,' she replied.

'That's a good sign; these tablets really work fast! Your fever is better now; that's good,' Miguel replied. 'Right let's get going again.'

Miguel kept the canoe close to the shore, but this time they were not so lucky with speed boats. Several boats shot past them, some heading down river towards Mazan, others travelling a little slower against the current up to the Ecuador border region. Some of the fast boats were carrying oil men, others tourists. On one occasion an oil barge, which must have been carrying tons of fuel, crept past producing a huge tidal wave. Miguel saw it coming so crept closer to the river bank for safety.

The fuel was pretty low so when they came upon what looked like an abandoned village, Miguel decided to stop. They needed to find somewhere to spend the night. He and Ronaldo wandered through the tumbled down shacks finding no one. They thought it would be ideal. There was about one hour of light left so the group set to finding a reasonable hut to call home. Pablo was still in the canoe trying to catch some fish while Ronaldo disappeared into the jungle in search of food. Tim remained in the shade of the hut with his sister.

'Tim, do you think we're going to make it?' Katie asked.

'I think the boys are determined to get us to Iquitos. Once we're there, we'll be able to phone home,' Tim said optimistically.

'What a surprise it'll be for Mum and Dad. How long is it since the plane crash?' Katie wondered.

'I think it will be about three months. There hasn't been much rain recently, so I think we are heading into the dry season. Look how the water level has dropped. The river banks are so steep. Some of them must be at least two to three metres high now.'

'Three months? Do you think they'll have given up and decided we're dead,' Katie asked.

'No, Mum and Dad will never give up on us. That reminds me of something the health worker said back in San Gorge,' Tim recalled.

'What?'

'He said that two months ago they chased away gringos who said "they were looking for children." Do you think if you were going to kidnap kids that you would tell villagers "that you were looking for children?" I don't think so,' Tim said.

'No, I wouldn't. Do you think they're looking for us? Do you think it was Mum and Dad? Could it have been?' Katie cried out with excitement.

Tim grabbed his little sister and gave her a huge cuddle.

'I think it could have been!' he said gleefully. 'I told you, they'll never give up!'

Ronaldo came back with bananas and other fruit that Tim had not seen before. The new fruit tasted delicious; everyone was more cheerful after scoffing their way through the improvised meal. Even Katie managed to eat some banana.

'There are loads of bananas back in the jungle, untouched just waiting to be harvested. Do you think we should spend some time here and gather some? We could use the bananas to barter for petrol at the next village,' Ronaldo asked his big brother.

'It's a good idea but the only problem is that we aren't far enough away from San Gorge. I think they'll have radioed ahead to other villages to warn them to watch out for us,' Miguel replied.

'I forgot about that; you're probably right,' Ronaldo replied.

'However, we do have room in the canoe for some fruit; it could be useful up ahead if we need to buy anything. Even if we took some to Rosa she might look more kindly on us and put us up for awhile, at least till we have gathered enough to pay for the river boat. Yes, I think we should spend the morning gathering bananas. We'll still have enough time to get to Villa Luisa by night fall,' Miguel explained.

'What about the fuel? We may have to paddle the last bit. Remember?' Tim commented.

'I checked the fuel level. It's not as bad as I thought. I don't think there will be too much paddling as the river current has been strong, so we haven't pushed the engine at full power. If we have to paddle we'll still arrive in the early evening. But we need to rise at dawn and gather the fruit as quickly as possible,' said Miguel. We need to have a watchman overnight just in case the villagers of San Gorge come looking for us. Let's get the canoe out of the water. We'll use the hut that backs onto the jungle, so if anyone comes looking for us we can slip into the forest out of sight. Pablo, you can take the first watch sitting over by that log, while we get everything settled in the hut. Come on, I'll help you to the tree,' Miguel said, as he piggy-backed his little brother over to the log. 'Remember the bird call we used as kids? Use it if there are any problems. Right, let's get going.'

Tim helped Katie to the hut at the rear of the village; it was in quite a good state, which surprised Tim. There was nothing left in it, but the roof and walls were intact. He settled Katie, leaning her against the wall of the house and went to look to see if he could help the others. It was quite dark now, but he could just make out his friends, coming towards him with the canoe hoisted on their shoulders. Suddenly there was a shrill bird call. It stopped Miguel dead in his tracks.

'That's Pablo; someone must be coming. Get Katie! We must take off into the jungle. We'll meet you at the back of the hut. Go!' Miguel barked at Tim.

Tim knew he had to act fast as Miguel looked very worried. Maybe it was the village men from San Gorge trying to chase them down. Katie was almost asleep again but with Tim's' help she stumbled out of the hut and round to where Ronaldo and Miguel were waiting for them. Together they headed off into the forest. They struggled on together for about a hundred metres then put down the canoe and hid it in the undergrowth. Miguel found a good spot for Katie and Tim to sit.

'Don't move from here until we come for you. We must go and find Pablo and find out what's going on.' Miguel dictated the action again. 'Ronaldo, you'll have to come with me. I might need your help.'

Miguel and Ronaldo crept back to the river bank just below the village. The few clouds in the sky had cleared so they could see by the moonlight two fast boats tied up at the water's edge. In the village they saw an armed sentry by the river guarding the boats. It looked as if there were fifteen men scattered around the place. One was beginning to set a fire in the middle of the village so they were probably planning to spend the night here. Miguel couldn't see any sign of Pablo but hopefully he was hiding somewhere. It looked to Miguel that these guys were druggies. The army wouldn't have boats like these and they would be flying the Peruvian flag. There were no flags on the boats. They would most likely move on in the morning.

'We must not let them find us. If they find the gringos they may try to ransom them and most likely kill us,' Ronaldo whispered to his brother. 'Do you think this is the same group that attacked our village and killed the old men?'

'It is hard to know if they are the same lot, but you are right, we must go deeper into the jungle tonight. Leave the canoe where it is and hope they don't find it. You go back to Katie and Tim and wait for me while I go and look for Pablo,' Miguel instructed.

The brothers parted. It took Ronaldo only a few minutes to find Katie and Tim, both of whom were frightened and miserable. They were being eaten alive by insects from the forest floor and on the wing.

Miguel crept past the guard to reach the tree where he had left Pablo but he was not there. Miguel used his bird call to try and raise him but… nothing. He searched around for a few minutes but he had to get back to the others. Pablo could look after himself; he knew how to disappear in the forest. Even with a bandaged leg, Miguel was confident that his little brother would be able to take care of himself. He had done so many times before when fooling with his brothers; in fact, Pablo was an expert at it.

Once Miguel had rejoined the others, they set off deeper into the jungle following a path, probably a route the hunters from the village used regularly. It wasn't very overgrown, indicating that it probably wasn't long since the village had been abandoned. Katie was still very weak, but the boys carried her along, first Ronaldo took her on his back then Miguel. Tim was amazed at the brothers' love for them, foreigners in their lives, yet they always put the gringos before themselves. Tim was very touched by their care. They carried her for at least a quarter of a mile, and then set her down beside a big tree trunk.

'We'll stay here for the night,' Miguel said. There's a stream over there so we can get some water. We'll have to watch out for the big cats though; I saw tracks as we came along the path. It would be best if we climbed up into the tree, then we would be away from snakes and any jaguars,' Miguel said

'I can't get into the tree,' Katie moaned.

'Don't worry; we'll help you and I'll tie you on so you won't fall off!' Ronaldo offered.

'How will you tie her on; we've no ropes,' Tim noted.

'Oh yes we have. Look!' Miguel answered as he grabbed a handful of large creepers hanging down from a neighbouring tree. 'Never say "never" in the jungle. If you know how, you can get everything you need to survive in the forest.'

Within ten minutes, Katie was securely straddled on a branch, with her back to the trunk, about two metres off the forest floor. Tim was on a slightly higher branch looking down on his sister. Miguel and Ronaldo took turns guarding the group.

Katie was very nervous perched on the tree but she realised there was no alternative. She certainly didn't want to be on the forest floor being eaten alive by ants or at risk from hungry snakes. No, this was much safer, but still scary. She had had two doses of her treatment now, and she was feeling slightly better. She was still very hot but not shivery, and her headache was gone. Maybe it was just that her temperature was down at the moment so she felt a bit better, or just possibly the medicines were starting to work, she thought. Katie dozed off.

Just before dawn as Katie began to rouse she felt something moving round her leg. Now it was coming up to her knee, onto her waist moving round her waist. Was she dreaming? No it was moving quickly now, beginning to tighten its grip. Katie put her hand down instinctively to feel what it was in the dark. It was cold, rippling, moving …it was a snake! Katie screamed and screamed at the top of her voice. Ronaldo was on watch and he responded first.

'What is it? What is it?' he cried to her. What's wrong?'

But Katie was hysterical; she couldn't answer him. Ronaldo grabbed his machete and bounded up the tree to a branch just below where Katie was perched. In the moonlight he could see the slithering monster that had wrapped itself round Katie. He knew he didn't have much time before the snake squeezed the life out of the young girl. But where was the head? He knew the only way to kill a snake was to cut off its head, but it was coiling so fast in the half light, he couldn't see where the head was.

Tim was fully alert and looking down on the scene from the higher branch. 'Ronaldo the head is behind her left shoulder coming round to you, now!' Tim shouted at the top of his voice so he could be heard above Katie's screams.

Ronaldo kept his cool. He snatched the head with his left hand, just as it was about to disappear round Katie's right arm to complete another coil. He sliced it clean off with his machete and dropped the head to the forest floor. Katie was still screaming, too terrified to realise that the vice grip that was round her chest was starting to relax. Now Ronaldo was up on the branch with her. He uncoiled the dead snake. Tim was trying to calm his sister down. Ronaldo was using his machete again but this time to cut through the creepers that were keeping Katie securely tied to the branch. He knew she would never be quietened until she was down on the ground. Miguel rushed to help as he too wanted Katie quietened as quickly as possible; the druggies just might have heard her screaming and come to investigate. They needed to move on just in case.

Once on the ground, Tim was able to get through to his hysterical sister. 'It's alright Katie. The snake is dead, it can't hurt you! Ronaldo killed it,' Tim said, as he hugged his sister.

As the sun rose, the group were astonished to see that the snake lying at their feet was a four metre anaconda! Ronaldo was looking at the creature in disbelief.

'I've never killed an anaconda before,' he said proudly, still not sure it had really happened.

Miguel congratulated Ronaldo. 'You did well little brother. Katie would have been dead with one more coil and squeeze. She wouldn't have been able to breathe,' Miguel confirmed.

'We have to move on. All that noise might have attracted the militia,' Miguel said anxiously. 'Ssh, someone's coming!'

Miguel signalled to the others to hide in the undergrowth. They could hear crashing as somebody came slowly and laboriously along the path. Miguel thought they were about fifty metres away. He signalled to Ronaldo that he was going to go to the right of the path so he could get behind the unwelcome visitor and 'jump' him if he found the group. The rest hid quietly in the undergrowth.

A couple of minutes later Miguel was in place. Katie was still being held by Tim to try and keep her calm. Her heart was thumping in her chest so loudly that Tim could hear it above all the jungle noise. At least he assumed it was Katie's. Maybe it was his own! After all, he was very scared. If it was a druggie they were as good as dead.

The crashing grew louder and louder; any minute now Tim expected to see one or two men in military fatigues carrying machine guns and machetes. He could see brave Miguel ready to pounce, but what chance would he have against heavily armed men?

'Shh,' he whispered in Katie's ear.

Suddenly the 'intruder' stumbled into view.

Miguel jumped out on him and pinned him to the ground.

'It's Pablo!' Ronaldo shouted.

Miguel released his grip and allowed his victim to sit up before giving him a mighty hug!

'Pablo, we thought you were one of the militia!' Ronaldo said to him.

'You guys were making such a noise it's just as well I'm not. They left the village just before dawn, about half an hour ago. I've been watching them all night. They did a lot of eating and drinking; most of them were drunk out of their minds. What was all that noise? I found you so easily. I could hear you from the village,' Pablo answered.

'It was all to do with Katie not liking snakes!' Tim said, as he pointed to the dead anaconda lying at the foot of the tree.

'Wow! He's a big one, isn't he? Are you alright Katie?' Pablo asked.

'Yes, thanks. I'm much better now, but it was such a nightmare. Thank you, Ronaldo. You saved my life,' Katie said.

'Pablo you shouldn't have walked all that way without help. You'll make your leg bleed again,' Miguel cautioned.

'I used this stick. Look no blood on my bandage. It's fine! Besides, I had to come and find you guys,' Pablo replied, with a huge grin.

'Hey, enough of this! Let's get back to the village and find something to eat and then get down to Villa Luis. Far too much excitement for one day, and it's just after sunrise!' Miguel said gleefully.

CHAPTER 23

Nimrod II

Miguel and his group of travellers paddled into Villa Luisa, about an hour after nightfall. The fuel had taken them to within three hours' paddling time, so with the strong current it wasn't too difficult to reach their destination. They decided it would be best if he and Ronaldo went to find Rosa and check that it was safe. With all the excitement in the jungle earlier, the plan to harvest some bananas had not materialised. Miguel was hoping his cousin would still give them somewhere to stay for a week or so, until they had enough money for the river boat.

Rosa was a kind and thoughtful girl. Miguel explained everything about the gringo children. As far as she and her husband, Rico, were concerned, the boys and Katie would be welcome to stay for as long as necessary, until they had gathered enough bananas. There had been no trouble from gringos in Villa Luisa, so Rico and Rosa didn't think anyone would be hostile to Katie and Tim. Rico and Miguel would have to take them to the headman in the morning to explain the situation. Rosa and Rico were so good to Tim and Katie. They made a special meal for everyone, and even found two hammocks for the 'softie' gringos. As planned next morning, Katie and Tim were introduced to the headman and their story told. He was most sympathetic and assured Miguel that some of his young men would help them gather the bananas. With the extra help they would be ready to catch the next river boat to Iquitos, which was due in five day's time.

Rosa took charge of Katie's convalescence, making sure she took the medicines at the right time and that she was given extra food to build up her strength. Rosa and Rico had a baby girl called Tina, who was ten months old. As Katie improved she had more energy to help with Tina which was good, as they both enjoyed each other's company. Working with Tina not only helped Rosa get on with her chores, but it really lifted Katie's spirits. It helped her forget some of the awful things that had happened to her in the last few months.

Tim went out with the boys and collected the fruit. It took three full days of hard work, even with the help of five other young men. The headman had suggested that the boys gather more than necessary for the tickets so that they would have some fruit to sell when they arrived in Iquitos.

The days passed quickly. The villagers here were so kind to them and they treated them as favoured guests. They had been taken all round the village. The gringo guests were taken to the school which was run by two teachers, sent up from Iquitos. It was a very basic building with a thatch roof, mud on the floor and a blackboard on one wall. The children were seated at small wooden desks. Tim and Katie were invited to tell the children where they were from and what had happened to them. The village children's knowledge surprised Tim. There was a map of the world on the wall so he was able to show the boys and girls where he was born. He saw that, in one classroom, the teacher had been teaching biology. The children were keen to learn and happy to show Tim and Katie their knowledge of Spanish. Like most of the villagers on the Peruvian Amazon, the tribe spoke their own dialect so had to learn the national language of Spanish. The village had a small chapel. Tim and Katie were told that it was built by a priest a long time ago, but he left and never returned. The headman insisted, however, that the chapel be kept in good condition because occasionally a pastor came up from Mazan.

Tim asked Rosa about the broken-down well in the middle of the village. Rosa said that she had been told by the village elders it had been put there ten years ago by American missionaries. They had arrived in a boat and helped their sick people and fixed their teeth. The missionaries came three or four times, and on one occasion they built the well. Nobody knows why they dug the well because it was easy enough to get the water from the river. The villagers didn't like the taste of the water, so didn't use it anyway. Tim tried to explain to Rosa that the river water was not clean and could make people sick. He wondered if the missionaries had explained to the community why they needed a well. Perhaps if they had, the well would have been used. Maybe we don't give these people enough respect he thought.

Rosa took Tim to meet a young physically disabled boy, called Rafael, who lived in one of the houses. She told Tim that Rafael was about seventeen but he couldn't walk; he could only crawl about the floor. He couldn't talk either but communicated by pointing. His mother, a friend of Rosa, loved her son very much, but she had to do everything for him. Rafael had been like this since he was a little child. He used to be able to toddle about and feed himself like other youngsters until he was ill with a very high fever. Afterwards, he couldn't walk anymore. His parents thought that he had malaria then and that this had damaged his brain.

Tim was shocked at what he saw. A thin young man writhed around the floor, wearing a grubby shirt and shorts.

There were ants crawling on his legs. He was smiling up at Tim, trying to reach him. With a trembling, outstretched arm, he tried to catch the gringo boy's hand. Rafael was drooling as he smiled. Unable to control his saliva, the skin on his chin was red raw from the constant moisture. Rosa encouraged Tim to kneel down beside the young man and take his hand. Rafael always liked visitors. His mother came over and welcomed Tim with some food, but at the same time made a fuss of her lovely boy. Rafael's young brother came into the house with his friend and the pair bounded over to Rafael and sat down beside him, much to his delight. Tim could feel the tears well up in him. Here was a boy only a few years older than himself who was condemned to a life on the floor. No wheelchair to allow his mother to take him outside, no hospital nearby to help him, yet still he seemed happy with his lot. How did the family cope with such a damaged boy? At least, Tim thought, despite everything he was loved by his family and friends.

Already it was the night before they were due to catch the river boat and Tim and Katie were excited about the next leg of the journey. In less than a week they should be back in civilisation and then be able to contact their parents. The community of Villa Luis held a celebration football match and communal supper in honour of their guests. Tim, Miguel, and Ronaldo, plus a few new friends, made up one team and played against the rest of the village. Reluctantly, Pablo had to cheer from the sidelines as he was still limping after his narrow escape. He did love the extra attention he received from the young girls of the community. They were amazed that he had survived an encounter with a camen.

The whole village turned out to watch. Tim couldn't believe his eyes. There was Rafael, dressed in a yellow Brazilian football strip, propped up beside his mother, waving and smiling at the footballers. The home team won five to the 'visitors' three, much to the delight of the community.

By now Katie was much improved; her fever all gone thanks to the medicine. She tucked into the feast that had been prepared of fish, chicken, rice and yucca washed down with squashed fruit juices and masato. It was an incredible experience for Katie and Tim. Miguel and his brothers enjoyed the festivities as well and were equally excited about the new chapter of their lives that was waiting for them in Iquitos.

The river boat arrived just after dawn. It was crowded with people and animals. Katie had never seen a boat quite like it. It was named the Nimrod II, and was about thirty metres long with two decks. The hull had not seen any paint in a long time. The passengers were all crammed onto the main deck. The bow area housed the livestock, hens in crates, and pigs tied to railings – the noise was deafening! The bananas were stored in the bow as well. The captain separated off, rather generously Tim thought, several bunches of fruit as payment for the fares of his five new passengers.

The villagers came to the riverbank to send them off. Just as they were about to board Rosa gave Katie the hammock she had been using. 'This will make your journey more pleasant,' she said with a smile.

'Thank you very much Rosa. Thank you for getting me better and fit to travel home. I'll never forget your kindness,' Katie whispered as she embraced Rosa.

'Come and visit us with your family some day,' Rosa shouted as the river boat reversed away from the log jetty, large puffs of black diesel coming from the stern.

'We will!' shouted Tim.

So Nimrod II, set off down the Rio Napo, stopping at every village on the way. The gringo children drew many strange looks from their fellow passengers. Miguel was concerned for Katie's safety as most people had not seen a foreign girl before. Katie was dressed in a typical village girl's clothes of a loose, bright coloured, pink top and dark blue baggy shorts, and her hair had been cut by Maria's mother, so she no longer wore a western hairstyle. However, even though Katie had deep dark eyes, brown hair and was now well tanned, it was still obvious to all she was a gringo. Ronaldo helped hang Katie's hammock on the main deck beside all the others. He too, was anxious about some of the looks Katie was attracting. He spoke to Miguel about it; together they decided to sell some more of their bananas to buy two hammocks. The captain was a ruthless man who agreed, but it cost the travellers the rest of their fruit. It meant that the boys could hang a hammock one on either side of Katie and so keep watch over her. It was agreed among the four boys that two of them would be with Katie at all times, until she was safely returned to her parents. Miguel had heard of young Amazonian girls disappearing into the hands of men who wanted to exploit them. He had a suspicion that a gringo girl would be an extra special prize. He shivered with disgust at the thought. He vowed there and then that, he and his brothers would look after Katie and Tim and get them back to their family.

Katie couldn't help notice the smell on the boat. It was disgusting – all these hot and sweaty bodies in such a small space. Some had been on the boat for five days, Miguel explained, having travelled all the way from Ecuador. Then, of course, there was the bucket that passed as a toilet. Katie had learned to cope in the villages by nipping into the jungle with the other girls, but this was a stinking excuse for a toilet. She tried very hard not to go!

The ticket price included the food. This was cooked at the back of the boat next to the toilet. This didn't seem to bother anyone on board except the gringos. The cook was a big, greasy man who wore a filthy apron. He had two huge cauldrons, one with rice and the other some meat and vegetable concoction. Tim took one look at him and thought 'stomach bug,' and *he* was a thirteen-year-old who never helped in the kitchen if he could get away with it. But he had heard his mother harp on and on about hand washing and putting food in the fridge. Where was the fridge when you needed one he thought? How on earth was he going to force himself to eat any food on this five-day 'cruise'?

Despite all, Tim and Katie did enjoy travelling downstream. They could relax a bit more now and take in the beauty of Amazonia. They watched the pink dolphins who were sometimes swimming at the bow, other times diving and playing together in the middle of the river. The sunsets were like nothing they had ever seen, beautiful mixtures of colours of orange and red that filled the horizon as far as they could see. One night, they watched a magnificent thunderstorm light up the sky, away to the left of the ship. It seemed to last for hours. Fortunately, it didn't come close to them, much to Katie's huge relief. She didn't like thunder! The dawn was always different, sometimes clear blue skies, and other times the river was covered with an eerie mist, like something out of a ghost story. This caused the captain to slow down in case he collided with canoes or other early morning river traffic.

Katie was amazed the first time she saw the huge barges of logs floating gently down the river. They were destined for the saw mills in the cities. She thought there must have been several hundred logs all tethered together, and there in the middle a little plastic shelter for the 'logsman' and his family to take refuge. It would be a long 'float' to market relying on the river current to take them, followed by a slow journey back home by the river boat.

The children really loved leaning over the rail as Nimrod II manoeuvred herself into one little village after another. They surveyed the activities in each community. Much depended on the time of day the vessel arrived. If it was early in the morning, the villagers would be down at the river collecting water or washing pots and pans, and the men folk would be climbing into their canoes for a day's fishing. If it was at the end of the day, the scene would be different, with mothers sitting on the tethered logs washing their children, or sometimes an elderly woman would be seated all alone on a log float washing her hair. Older children would be playing in the water. They would dive fearlessly off the logs into the deep river, with all the attendant laughter infectiously causing smiles from the onlookers on the boat. The children enjoyed having fun in the mighty Napo River.

Tim would have loved to join them, but was too frightened of the strong currents that whirled at the stern of the ship. He was also concerned that the boat went without him. Miguel and his brothers had no such fear, so whenever the Nimrod tied up, they were off the back of the boat with the other young men, cooling off in the river.

Katie and Tim were content to watch the feverish activity that always occurred with the arrival of the river boat. The riverside was piled high with fruits, mainly bananas but others that the youngsters still didn't recognise. In the smaller communities, the whole village turned out to watch, their children squatting for ages on the river bank, just watching everything that was going on. Usually, passengers joined the boat heading down river.

Mazan was the biggest town the Nimrod called at, but even here the stop was under an hour. A considerable number of passengers left the ship at this town. Katie and Tim thought the conditions would be less cramped on the ship, but they were quickly disappointed when many people joined the vessel at the last minute.

The final leg of the river boat journey was even more exciting for the young survivors and their new friends. When the Napo joined the River Amazon, they were all amazed by the width and power of the mighty river. On one occasion, the Nimrod had to give way to an oil tanker heading for Iquitos. It was such a huge vessel, Miguel and his brothers stared in disbelief.

Tim was beginning to think of what would happen when they arrived in Iquitos. How quickly would they be able to contact their parents? How would they phone them if they had no money? They could go to the police and tell them the whole story; they would surely help them he thought. He spoke with Miguel to find out what he was thinking they would do when they arrived in the city. They knew from the captain that they would dock at about eleven o'clock at night and that the port was three miles from the city centre. Would it be safe to walk into the city at night? Miguel was not confident about anything now. He was a jungle man, and he knew nothing of city life. Tim was worried too as everyone in the group looked scruffy with torn T-shirts and shorts. Like Katie, his own clothes had been ripped and discarded, so he too was dressed just like a village youth.

Tim was thinking about all these problems when an amazing coincidence occurred; Miguel spotted one of his old school friends from Mazan, Eduardo. He had joined the river boat in his home village and was heading down to Iquitos. Miguel rushed over to his old classmate. Miguel told Eduardo of his plans and also his concerns – no money, nowhere to stay and no job. Eduardo was keen to help as he and Miguel had been good friends during their schooldays. He turned out to be a useful contact too. Eduardo had a cousin who lived in Puerto Belen and he knew that if Miguel explained who he was, then his cousin would help him. Eduardo took a small piece of paper from his note book and drew a diagram showing Miguel how to find his cousin's house.

Eduardo explained, 'There is a row of houses between the school and the River Nanay; my cousin's house is the third one in the row. He will help you; he and his wife are good people. Good luck my friend, I hope you get your young friends safely home.'

CHAPTER 24

Brutal Encounter

The children had been standing at the bow of the riverboat since darkness had fallen. They were all waiting and wondering what lay ahead of them. They peered into the darkness for the first signs of the city. As the Nimrod II rounded the bend, Tim and Katie caught their first glimpse of the lights of Iquitos. It seemed to be a huge place, with lights twinkling for as far as they could see. They shouted and yelled with delight. Tim grabbed his little sister and cuddled her in his excitement. Miguel, Pablo and Ronaldo rushed over and joined in the group hug; their fellow passengers wondering what on earth was going on.

It took another hour before the riverboat turned into the mouth of the Rio Nanay, heading for the port where they would finally end their river journey. Even at eleven o'clock at night the young people could see that the quayside was busy with hundreds of people, all out and about enjoying themselves. They passed floating fuel stations where men were filling up small boats with gasoline. Tim and his sister couldn't think of an equivalent system back home. As they drew closer they could hear the loud music coming from the bars. Tim and Katie were really excited now. They would soon be home with their Mum and Dad! Tim wondered if his parents would recognise them as they were dressed so scruffily!

While the vessel was manoeuvring to dock, the five youngsters discussed the plan for the rest of the night. They had no money, so the quick phone call home was not going to happen straight off. Miguel took charge, but not with his usual confidence. He decided the best thing to do was to walk to Puerto Belen and see if they could find Eduardo's cousin in the morning.

'Where will we sleep tonight?' Katie asked the older boys.

'We'll have to sleep rough till we can get some help in the morning,' Tim replied. 'Puerto Belen is about a three mile walk, so that'll take a bit of time anyway.'

'Maybe we'll find a policeman who will help us,' Katie suggested.

The five friends were glad to be off the boat. They set off immediately for the city to find the district of Belen. As they walked along the streets heading out of the port they were all shocked, especially Miguel and his brothers. They couldn't believe their eyes! There were so many shops, bars and restaurants, each with bright lights and loud music. Ronaldo and Pablo were mesmerised. The busiest village they had ever visited was Mazan. But they hadn't had the time to leave the riverboat to walk round the provincial town. At least they saw the shops and bars from the quayside. Here they jostled passed the many locals who were out and about enjoying the night. Many appeared as if they were drunk or high on drugs. Once again, the boys could see the strange looks that the gringo children were attracting, especially Katie. The boys kept the young girl safely between them.

After about a half-hour walk, they were out of the port area and heading along a quieter street. A police pick-up drove passed and then stopped in front of them. Two police men jumped out and came towards the group. Katie thought this was just what they needed, some help from the police. Tim knew differently. He had noticed they had their batons drawn. Even in the poor light he could see the menacing look on their faces, as they approached!

'Hey, piranha, what are you doing here?' one of the officers called. 'We've told you before we don't want any street boys around here. The mayor doesn't want you frightening off tourists by stealing from them. We're going to teach you a lesson!'

Without any warning the officers laid into the children with their sticks. Immediately, Pablo was knocked to the ground, stunned by a blow to the head.

'Run!' Miguel shouted as he grabbed one of the officers round his waist and dragged him into the road. Ronaldo helped his brother by tripping up the policeman. The other officer immediately turned from Tim and Katie to help his colleague.

'Run, Tim, run!' Miguel shouted again as he fought with the policeman. Tim grabbed his sister's hand and they ran as fast as they could up an alley-way into the darkness. They ran and ran, past derelict warehouses, scattering rats and other creatures of the night before them. Suddenly they heard a shot ring out, and then another. This was followed by sirens, two or three different ones, all in the area of the city from where they'd come. Exhausted they huddled in the doorway of an empty house. Katie was so winded she vomited. Tim couldn't speak at first.

'Did you hear those shots?' Katie asked.

'Yes, I think the boys have been shot,' Tim said, his voice quivering with fear and emotion.

'But they were police! They were supposed to help us not harm us,' Katie replied, her idea of the normal world shattered again. When she realised that the boys might be dead she started to cry. 'Why? Why?' she sobbed.

'The police thought we were street kids. Our torn shirts and scruffy state, I suppose,' Tim answered.

'What do you mean, 'street kids'? Katie whispered.

'They're children who have been tossed out on the street by their parents. The authorities don't like them around tourist spots because visitors are put off. They feel threatened by the wild boys,' Tim explained.

'But why would any parent put their child out on the street?' Katie asked innocently.

'The poor often have big families, and sometimes they can't feed everyone. When a new baby comes along they take the oldest boy somewhere he hasn't been before and 'lose' him. Mr Fernandez, my maths teacher, explained it one day at school. This was after he had been mugged by a gang of them in Lima. Stripped naked he was, left with nothing, not even his socks! Our class thought it was quite funny really, but it's not at all. Several street boys were killed by the police in Lima last summer. I remember Mum and Dad talking about it. Mum was shocked by Dad's attitude; he seemed to sympathise with the police!'

'What are we going to do now?' Katie asked.

'Find somewhere to hide until morning, and then try and find Eduardo's cousin as planned. We'll have to keep well away from the police though. They might shoot first and ask questions later!' Tim said, as he put his arm round his little sister.

'We'll be alright. We just need to find an adult we can trust to help us contact Mum and Dad. We'll be back in Lima in two days,' Tim said reassuringly.

'I hope so.'

'Let's keep moving till we find a safer place. The police might still be looking for us.'

'What about Miguel and the others? Maybe one of them is alive and badly hurt. We need to go and find out what happened and help them,' Katie pleaded, as she tugged at Tim's sleeve to go back towards the port.

'No! Katie we must not; it's too dangerous! We'll be killed! Miguel said to run. You know how much he wants us to get back home. He has risked his life so often for us.'

'I know, that's the whole point. The boys have done so much for us we have to go and help them!' Katie started to cry again.

'Think about it. They are either dead or in a police cell by now. We can do nothing to help them. We'll only get ourselves killed! Now come on! We're wasting time!' Tim said very sternly. 'Look there are car lights coming this way! It could be the police, we must hide!'

Tim grabbed Katie, and the pair ran across the dusty track to behind a shed that Tim had spotted. The scared youngsters peered out as two police pick-ups drove slowly by. Armed officers, standing on the back, peered out into the darkness. Katie could hear Tim's heart pounding in his chest as the two cowered together.

'They're going,' Katie whispered. She had just finished saying that, when a third pick-up appeared. This time instead of gunmen, two big police dogs barked ferociously from the back of the truck. The vehicle stopped about thirty metres from the kids. The dogs were quickly offloaded.

'We have to go!' Tim whispered, 'or we're dead!'

The kids left their hiding place as quietly as possible, but the dogs' acute hearing picked them up. Soon the children were racing for their lives down a steep bank towards the Rio Amazon. The moonlight was a God-send. They could see the river only a hundred metres in front of them, at the bottom of a slope. Tim realised that if they could make it to the water the dogs would lose the scent. But, Tim tripped over some old wire and rolled over several times. Katie scrambled down to help her brother back to his feet. The dogs were at the top of the incline now. They were huge Alsatians, baying like blood hounds, desperate for a kill. They looked ferocious silhouetted against the clear sky.

'Get up, Tim. Get up!' Katie screamed. Tim staggered to his feet badly dazed. He had knocked his head and seemed not to know what was going on.

'Come on, Tim. We have to go!' Katie yelled at him. She took his arm and they stumbled towards an old ramshackle building only a few metres to their right. As they approached it, a door opened and two children in rags shouted to them, 'Over here, come over!'

Katie decided in an instant that she had no choice but to trust the children. The dogs were tearing down the hill after them and she could hear the shouts of the policemen.

Once Tim and Katie were inside the two boys slammed the door behind them. The building was stinking and frightening but at least the dogs couldn't get at them – just now! But then Katie had a horrible thought *'they were trapped!'* The dogs were already baying at the door and the policemen would be here in thirty seconds!

Tim was less dazed, but now terrified! The smell, the darkness, and the growling of the dogs were too much for him. He was trembling, tears rolling down his cheeks.

The smaller of the two street lads, who was probably about ten or eleven years old, seemed to understand his fear so he gently took his hand but led him swiftly over to a hole in the floor. There a ladder descended deep underground. The bigger boy led the way and scampered down first, followed by Katie, Tim and then the smaller boy, who closed the man-hole cover behind them. As she climbed down in the darkness, Katie could hear children's voices and see lights coming from below. The stench was almost too much to bear; Katie thought she was going to vomit. It was a long way down, but the noise of those below soon grew loud enough to drown out the noise of the dogs!

Once on the ground, the smaller boy chased everyone away from the bottom of the ladder and made them crouch against the walls of the tunnel. The whole group fell silent

… then there was a terrific noise! Several rounds of gunfire were shot down the manhole, ricocheting off the walls for what seemed a very long time. Katie and Tim huddled into each other, hands over their ears trying to block out some of the tremendous din. It was over as fast as it started. Everyone lay silently for a further five minutes then one of the boys crept to the bottom of the ladder to check that the police had gone.

The smaller boy who had helped them took some stale bread and water to Katie and Tim to welcome them to the group. He spoke Spanish and told Katie and Tim that they were safe now. He explained that the police never come down here to the sewer; it is too smelly for them and they don't like rats! He introduced himself as Rico. He was the leader of the street gang. There were twenty of them living here.

Rico went onto explain that he and Andres, the other boy, had been up in the streets looking for food when they heard the dogs. They realised that some kids were in trouble, so they knew they had to help. Rico and Andres had been friends for a long time. They had met on the 'street' and were rescued by this gang. Street boys have always looked out for other boys, especially when the police were after them.

Tim had regained his composure but Katie started to cry. The smell was overpowering; that plus the poor light made the sewer a very frightening place to be. She could hardly see the others; the only light came from the top of the tunnel wall where the boys had somehow dug away a few bricks at street level, just beneath a street light. Tim tried to comfort his sister. Rico was quick to realise the problem and spoke with the other members of the gang. Within minutes the entire group was on the move. Andres took Katie by the arm and Tim followed close behind. 'Where are we going'? Tim asked Rico.

'The tunnel is wider and lighter where the sewers empty into the river. We'll go there till morning; sometimes the police send the dogs there so we'll have to post a look-out. I don't think they'll come tonight though as they raided the area by the river only two nights ago. It'll take us half an hour to get there,' Rico added.

Sure enough, the light improved as they approached the river. Tim jumped a few times as rats scurried away in front of him.

'Don't worry about the rats,' Andres said as he saw his new friend jump. 'They live here with us, they don't harm us. They're our friends!'

'Rats bring disease that can kill people,' Tim cautioned, remembering about his history lesson on the Black Death; the disease spread by rats that killed millions of people in England in the fourteenth century.

'What's a disease?' Rico chipped in.

'Something, that makes you sick,' Tim replied.

'We get sick but it's not the rats. We just die of hunger or are beaten up by adults. The grown-ups are the worst. They hurt us, abuse us, whenever they can,' Andres replied, nonchalantly.

'Why would grown-ups want to hurt you? Why did the police chase us and beat up Ronaldo and the others?' Katie asked innocently.

'To survive here, we have to steal or let men do horrible things to us. Then they give us some money for food or a bag of glue. But you're too young to understand,' Rico answered.

Tim whispered, 'Sex!' to his sister who was stunned.

'But they're just children!' she shouted, unable to fully comprehend what had been said to her.

'Keep your voices down. There's a café above us, they might hear us. They know we come here, so they may call the police,' Rico warned.

The tunnel was now about three metres wide, the opening to the river about twenty-five metres from where they stood. The sewage waste was now in a concrete conduit with hard mud banking, wide enough for them to sit. Carved out in the walls were little nooks where the boys stored small bits and pieces.

'We must get some sleep now. Andres, you sort out the lookouts for the night,' Rico instructed. 'Tomorrow, we'll try and get some more food,' he added.

Katie lay down beside her brother. 'I hope we can get out of here tomorrow,' she whispered. 'But if we can't get help from the police, who will help us?'

'Maybe we can get to Miguel's friend's house?' Tim replied.

'You can't leave here looking and smelling like you do. The police will have you, if not them, the "snatchers!"' Rico cautioned.

'Who are the "snatchers"?' Tim asked.

'They kidnap the "new boys" on the street and sell them to gringos. The new boys are not so sick when they first come to live rough, so the snatchers lift them while they are still healthy. They sell them onto the gringos, who kill them for their kidneys or parts of their eyes – all to make money out of some rich person who is sick or blind,' Rico explained.

'That's disgusting!' Tim replied. 'How do you know?'

'One day, before I ended up on the streets, my four-year old cousin, Isabel, was snatched. She lived in Belen with her mother. My aunt and Isabel were down at the river Nanay waiting for the evening river boat to arrive. A gringo and two others in a fast boat grabbed Isabel off the jetty. My aunt could do nothing. They roared away into the darkness. One week later, Isabel was found at the same spot, this time lying on the jetty. She was blind in her left eye because they had removed her eye and sewn up her eyelids. Isabel had a huge scar as well, and she was in a lot of pain. The wound went all the way from her tummy button round to her spine. The snatchers had removed part of her insides, her kidney I think.'

'Rico, that is awful!' Katie said. 'How is she now?'

'She died two weeks later. Her wound was dirty and started to leak horrible yellow stuff. She vomited all the time as well. She was really ill. My aunt took her to the local hospital; they gave her some tablets for two days but she didn't get better,' Rico said, his voice quivering.

'So the snatchers were to blame for Isabel's death,' Tim acknowledged. 'But some horrible surgeon must have done the operations. I thought doctors were supposed to always help their patients. But I suppose some people will do anything for money! That's just awful!' Tim said holding his head in his hands. He felt sick at the thought of what he had just heard and very worried. How were they ever going to get back home, he wondered?

'Come on, Tim, we need to sleep,' Katie said softly to her brother who was still staring into space, trying to sort out in his young mind the ugliness of all he had heard.

The pair slept surprisingly soundly, considering their surroundings. Tim came to as the sunlight streamed in through the mouth of the sewer. From his position lying on his side, he could see a small speed boat pass by on the river. Rico and the other lads were awake too, but Tim noted that some of them seemed rather quiet. Several of the boys were sniffing into small bags, looking very dopey.

'What are they doing?' Tim shouted across to Rico.

'There's no food. No breakfast. The boys are killing their hunger pains by sniffing glue. Would you like some?' Rico asked.

'Not likely! No food at all?'

'No, the boys went out last night to the bridge at the Rango River, but no one came.'

'What do you mean?' Tim enquired.

'Three or four times a week, a man and his wife come down to the bridge with soup and bread for the boys. But not last night,' Rico replied. 'Maybe the police have frightened them off.'

Tim sat bolt upright. There were some adults helping the boys. Maybe they would be able to help him and Katie.

'Who are these people? Is it a trick? Are they connected to the police?' Tim asked suspiciously. He had become as distrustful as the street boys.

'They feed us and are kind to us. If one of us is sick they hand out some medicine as well. They talk to us about God and how much He loves us. I think they belong to a church group. We don't believe all that God stuff though. If God loved us, why did he take us from our homes, our families? I guess, I must have done something really bad, but I can't remember what it was. My mother would never hurt me. So it must have been God's fault,' Rico explained, his voice tailing off to a mumble.

Regaining his self-control he continued,

'Sometimes young men come with Mama and Papa – that's what we call them – to help hand out the food and just talk to us. They've been coming to the bridge for over a year now and never with the police.'

'Mama and Papa must be good people, if they've been coming out late at night for so long, to help the boys,' Tim supposed.

'Yes, you're right. We've wondered why they do it,' Rico pondered.

'Maybe it is because they love God. And that is why they love you guys. That's what my Mum would say at any rate. There must be some reason though,' Tim suggested.

'I don't know! But they are good to us,' Rico admitted.

'Papa has tried to persuade some of us to go and stay in a hostel. I'm not so sure. It could be a trap. We'll wait a bit longer and see how things go.'

'Do you think they'll come tonight?' Tim asked nervously.

'Yeah. If they weren't there last night, they'll probably come tonight.'

'Can you take Katie and me? They might help us get back to our parents.'

'That was my plan,' Rico said with a great big grin.

Tim was so excited. He woke his sister and told her all about the possible rendezvous that night.

CHAPTER 25

Black Hole

Sarah's recovery was very slow. Physically, she could manage to walk round their flat, but she refused to go out, except to the hospital clinics. Initially, Alex thought she was still feeling weak from her illness, but her appetite was very poor and she hardly slept. The best doctors in Lima were consulted. Sarah had recovered from the snake bite but had now dipped into a depression. A psychiatrist was called in but despite his recommendations Sarah refused his medication. She just withdrew into herself. Things became so bad that she spoke to Alex but would see no one else. She spent ours hugging a photograph of the children. When she did sleep for short times, she would snuggle into Katie's favourite jumper and Tim's T-shirt; she seemed to get comfort from the faint scent of her children. Alex watched helplessly as Sarah continued to lose weight and age in front of his eyes.

Alex was faring slightly better. He had to look after his lovely wife. The last few months had taught him just how much she meant to him. He had been back up to Iquitos four times since the first search and kept in regular contact with Gilberto. He and Gilberto had become good friends. Alex had changed. Away from his high-pressure work as an oil executive he was becoming more like his old self, caring and compassionate. Gilberto saw a completely different side to his old boss. Soon Gilberto was confident enough to take Alex to the night shelter to show him the work with the street children. Alex was shocked. Some of the boys were in a poor state, thin, dirty and hungry. Whenever he could, Alex would go with Gilberto to the shelter to help out.

Alex really came to understand the meaning of poverty when Gilberto took him to the municipal dump, on the outskirts of Iquitos. There, a community of around a hundred families lived, mostly migrants from the Amazonian villages. From morning to night these people picked over the heaps of stinking rubbish. Men, women and children pulled at the disgusting waste to find anything of value. Even children as young as five chased off the vultures to fight for scraps of food. Bad as all that was, what really upset Alex was hearing from Gilberto that these families were Christians so would not work on Sundays. But they allowed other poor people from outwith their community to come and work the site, while they rested on the Lord's Day. Alex then understood that there were human beings in the world who were poorer than the rubbish pickers. He walked off the tip and wept!

Before he returned to Lima, he donated several hundred dollars to Gilberto's church for their street boys' shelter and their work among the rubbish tip people.

The men Alex had recruited to search for the children in Napo river area failed to find any trace of them. Two groups were employed to go to the Peruvian–Columbian border area to investigate there; the third worked around the Mazan area as it was an important regional town. Sadly, no new information was found. After two months, Alex called off the search. It had been a long shot anyway. Gilberto assured his friend that he would continue to be vigilant and would keep reminding his friends and acquaintances about the children.

It was almost three months now since the aircraft had crashed. The official Peruvian line was that the plane had suffered an electrical fault in a severe tropical storm. There were no survivors. The remains of the passengers had been recovered and removed to Lima. Many were unrecognisable and would require long involved forensic analysis for accurate identification. So far, the children's remains had not been identified. However, the authorities maintained that they were unlikely to positively identify anyone who had been seated in the first section of the aircraft, as it had been extensively destroyed in the fireball. As the Baxter children's allocated seats were in the front, they were formally declared deceased.

When the official from the Accident Investigation Department visited Sarah and Alex with their findings, it was deeply distressing for the parents. But the report didn't destroy their hope that just possibly, their precious children had survived and were still alive in the jungle. Sarah and Alex felt this deeply in their hearts and would not give up hope.

Aunt Susie's remains had been identified six weeks after the crash. Her body was flown back home to Scotland for burial. Sarah and Alex didn't make the journey to Edinburgh as Sarah was deemed too unwell to travel, and Alex refused to leave his wife in Peru all alone.

Alex had to go back to work. The company had been very understanding, but he knew that with the official report now in the public domain he had to return to work or return home to the UK. Sarah refused to leave Peru; she was convinced her children were still alive. The psychiatrist said she was suffering an abnormal grief reaction. Alex was deeply concerned about his wife; Sarah looked so awful, he was frightened he was going to lose her too.

Sarah had resisted the idea of her parents coming out to Peru as they were getting on in years and Granny didn't like flying. However, Alex decided that Sarah might improve if she was surrounded by family, rather than Peruvian servants, especially when he went back to work.

Granny and Papa were 'young' seventy-five year olds. Looking after their small holding, in retirement, had kept them fit. When the couple had agreed to go to Peru they decided to sell all the animals, but their neighbours wouldn't hear of it and agreed to look after the farm while they were gone. Sarah did seem to pick up for a while with the arrival of her parents. She put on a little weight each week. Granny and Papa had a strong faith and they prayed daily with their daughter, asking God to return the children safely.

After a couple of weeks Sarah announced to Alex that she wanted to go to Iquitos to organise another search for the children. But he wouldn't hear of it, concerned the trip would further damage her health. Sarah withdrew into herself again.

CHAPTER 26

Street Life

The children didn't move all day. Rico had advised them it would be safer to stay in the sewer until after dark. Andres had disappeared shortly after sunrise and returned halfway through the day with some cold pasta he had retrieved from the back of an Italian restaurant, in downtown Iquitos. Katie was disgusted and wouldn't eat any of it but Tim was ravenous; he tucked in with the other boys. It tasted surprisingly good he thought and didn't look too dirty either. Katie was very thirsty now but again refused to drink from the can of river water that the boys produced.

'You have to drink Katie,' Tim reminded her. 'If you don't you'll be too weak to go out tonight to the 'soup' man. This could be our big chance to find someone to help us.'

Katie agreed and reluctantly took the water.

Throughout the day Tim and Rico talked about their lives. Tim relived the nightmare of the plane crash and how they had survived in the jungle, thanks to Miguel and his brothers.

Rico told of how he and his family had come to Iquitos from a small village near Nauta. His father had died of jaundice so his mother decided to come to the city to join her sister, who was living in Puerto Belen. She thought the family would be better off. But Rico spoke of the overcrowding in his aunt's house, and about strange men that used to come to the house at night. He heard them when he was lying trying to sleep. Different men came every night. He asked his mother about it but she would start to cry. He was only five at the time and didn't understand that she was selling herself to buy food for him and his two young sisters. He loved his mother very much and missed her.

About a year after they arrived in Belen, a new man, called Alfonso, came to live with them. Shortly afterwards, his Mum had a baby, a little boy. Alfonso was always horrible to Rico. Sometimes he would throw Rico across the room for no reason. One day, about four months after the man arrived, Rico went shopping with his mother to a new market place, one he had never been to before. They travelled in this man's canoe for about half an hour to the other side of Iquitos. He and his mother went into the market place, and then a strange thing happened. His mother sat him on a wall underneath a big clock. She gave him a kiss and a cuddle and told him to wait till she came back. Rico's Mum never did come back. He waited all day. That night he fell asleep at the foot of the wall. The next day he waited and the next, but still she didn't come. He didn't know how to get home. He was miserable. He thought he must have done something really bad for his mother to leave him all alone. He hung around that market for days just hoping his mother would appear at any time.

At the end of that first week, he met Andres. He had been left in the market by his big sister, around the same time. The boys were very hungry and so started to steal apples and bread from the market stalls, just to stay alive.

Rico knew it was wrong to steal, but they would have died otherwise. One afternoon, Andres stole an apple and the man behind the stall ran after them. Other people joined in and very quickly there was a mob of traders running after them, screaming at the top of their voices. Some were armed with sticks. Rico was sure they were going to be killed. As they ran into an alleyway behind a hotel three youths grabbed them and bundled them over a dusty banking – just in time! They could hear the mob running past. The older lads took Rico and Andres in the opposite direction, into the main cemetery of Iquitos. They pelted down the paths between the head stones until they came to a dark, grey and frightening looking mausoleum. The youths took Rico and Carlos round the back of the structure and squeezed through a hole, entering the tomb. There they all flopped down exhausted. Rico explained that the older boys were some of the first members of this gang. They had saved his and Andres' life.

'That must've been really scary in the cemetery,' Katie said.

'No, not really. You see, the dead don't hurt street kids; it's only the living,' Rico replied.

'How long ago was that?' Tim asked.

'About seven years ago!' Rico replied.

'You mean you have lived like this for seven years,' Katie said with astonishment. 'Where are the older boys who saved your lives? You seem to be the oldest here now,' she continued.

'They're all dead. Two of them, Bruno and Pedro, fell off a roof when they were being chased by security guards. They were very badly injured, but no one helped them. They just died in the street where they lay. The city dust cart picked up their bodies. The other one, Cesar, our leader for three years, died last year, down here in the sewer. He was sick for days, coughing all the time; he could hardly breathe.

One morning we found him dead. He was my friend,' Rico continued. 'Lots of boys have died down here; some get sick. If we can't find enough food, some die of hunger. Others just give up and sniff the glue bags, all the while moaning for their mothers. I suppose they're the lucky ones, getting away from this hell.'

'Does nobody help you? Doesn't anybody care?' Katie asked.

'Nobody wants to know street boys. We're seen as rats, something to be stood on and killed. That's why we live with the rats; they're our friends. That's not completely true. Sometimes some of the police officers are kind to us. They catch us and give us a warning to stay away from an area. One day, one young officer actually gave me some money, out of his own pocket, to go and buy some food. You should have seen the look his mate gave him! But that is very rare; most want to get rid of us. They see it as their duty to the city. Of course, there is also the man we are going to meet tonight. He has been good to us, bringing us food. He cares about us, I know he does,' Rico explained, allowing himself a soft smile as he spoke.

'When will we go to meet him? Katie asked.

'Not until it's really late and most people are in their beds – around midnight. He knows we'll not come until then, in case the police come after us. So you must take some more water or you'll not be able to come with us. It's about half an hour's walk from here,' Rico answered.

'Ok, I suppose you're right. What if he doesn't come tonight?' Katie continued.

'He'll come. He never leaves us more than two nights, and he wasn't there last night,' Andres assured her. 'I'll go and try and find you some food. You haven't eaten anything.'

Andres disappeared for over an hour while the rest of the group continued to sniff their glue bags and snooze.

Tim and Katie just stayed where they were, thinking about home.

Suddenly, there was a commotion from behind them, from further up the sewer. They could see someone coming out of the gloom, staggering from side to side as he came along the tunnel. Two or three of the boys were alert now wondering what was happening. Two faint whistles were heard, and then they all relaxed. It was Andres, but he looked hurt. He was bleeding from his nose and face. His T-shirt was badly ripped. He had been in a fight.

'What happened? Are you alright?' Katie said as she and the others rushed over to him. Andres lay on his back, eyes closed, and panting heavily. He was holding his chest. Each breath was causing him great pain.

'This is for you Katie,' he gasped, as he handed her a bar of chocolate.'

'Did you go to the tourist mall?' Rico shouted at him. 'You know it's too dangerous to go there! Look what has happened to you!'

'I thought I'd got away. But a big security guard caught me as I ran up the ally, at the side of the shops. He was waiting for me. He has beaten me about a bit, hasn't he?' Andres winced in pain. 'At least he didn't call the police. He told me the next time I came back he would use his gun. I believe him. I think he has broken a couple of my ribs,' Andres winced again.

'Andres, are you OK?' Katie asked.

'I just need some sleep and I'll be fine,' Andres groaned.

'Have some of the chocolate; it'll give you some strength,' Katie suggested. But just at that the injured boy started to vomit, horrible dark stuff. Tim had never seen anybody throw up black mess like that before. As Andres lay back down, Tim could see a trickle of red blood running from his mouth and over his chin. Andres was writhing in pain now. Rico tried to comfort his friend. He brought over a glue bag and let him sniff the fumes.

'Don't do that!' Tim yelled at him. 'He's sick enough without that poison! Tim knew that glue sniffing was really dangerous. Some kid back home had died from inhaling glue vapours. It was all over the local paper, back in Chester, where they used to live. It happened just before they left to live in Peru.

'Can't you see he's in terrible pain? The glue will dull the pain?' Rico insisted.

'We need to get him to a hospital,' Tim suggested. The other boys merely laughed! They gathered round their friend pushing Tim and Katie away.

'No hospital would let us in the building, let alone help the likes of us,' said Mateo, one of the older boys.

Andres was quiet, and he wasn't panting anymore. The boys tried to speak to him but he was sleeping. He was very pale. His arm had fallen from his chest and lay limply at his side. Blood continued to trickle slowly from his mouth.

'He's peaceful now,' Rico said. 'Let's leave him to rest for a while.'

The group settled back into their usual places, to while away another few hours before it was time to go to the 'soup' man.

After about half an hour Tim noticed Rico crept across the tunnel to check on his friend. Tim thought that Andres hadn't moved at all since they left him. Rico was now leaning across his friend. The other boys sensed something was wrong and had gathered as well. Rico stood up and announced in a shaky voice, 'Andres is dead!'

Each of the boys froze to the spot for at least a minute just looking at Andres's body. Silently, they each filed passed Andres and made the sign of the cross, something they had seen adults do when someone died. Each then returned to his own area of the tunnel and his own thoughts.

Katie started to cry. 'He died because of me! He lost his life because I wouldn't eat that filthy pasta. Andres risked his life to get food for me and yet he hardly knew me! It's as if I killed him!' Tim comforted his sister, as she wept into his shoulder.

Rico continued to sit by the body of his friend, head bowed. He was a twelve-year-old who had lost so much of his childhood and seen so many ghastly things. The death of his closest friend seemed too much to bear. But he was the leader of this gang and he must look out for the younger boys. After a while, Rico instructed three of the stronger boys to help him move Andres' body.

'Where are you taking him?' Tim asked softly.

'We'll take him to the mouth of the tunnel. We'll throw him in the river, after the sun goes down,' Rico said.

'If the soup man's God does love us, then Andres will be with Him in heaven. He'll be at peace and out of this hell that we live in!' Rico continued thoughtfully.

'God does love us. Let me help,' Tim volunteered.

'No! The gang will deal with its dead, alone,' Rico replied firmly.

The boys were at the mouth of the tunnel for ages. It was now really dark and Katie could hardly see Tim. She had stopped crying now, but had not spoken since the boys left.

'Do you think we'll still go to meet the soup man tonight, Tim?'

'I don't know. Rico and the boys might be too upset to leave the tunnel. We can't insist.'

'Tim, I can't stay here any longer. If we do, I think we'll die like Andres – maybe even in the next couple of days,' Katie continued.

'You mustn't think like that Katie. I know what you are saying, but you must not give up! We haven't come through so much to die in this stinking sewer. Surely God wouldn't let us survive the plane crash and the jungle, only to die here. We must not give up now! We mustn't give up… we mustn't!' Tim said trying to reassure Katie and himself.

Just then the boys came back along the tunnel. Rico came over to Tim and Katie and said, 'We'll leave for the Rango Bridge in an hour. Andres was my best friend here, and he liked you two very much. He spoke to me last night and said that we must get you back to your parents as soon as possible, or you'll end up worthless like us. You're not like us, you're gringos. This doesn't happen to gringos!'

Katie and Tim were extremely relieved to finally emerge from the sewer. They didn't have much time to celebrate their escape. They had to run to keep up with the boys, as they dodged along alleyways, and crawled along dried up ditches to reach the River Rango district of Iquitos. Every precaution was taken to keep out of the way of police and security men. At last, they were within sight of the bridge where the 'soup' man would be. The group hid behind a low wall where they could see under the arches of the bridge and the surrounding area.

'The soup van is on the bridge, parked in the usual place,' Mateo cheerfully reported to Rico. Mateo had acted as scout, making sure nothing suspicious was happening.

'What about that other van parked beside the tree, just twenty metres from the arches? It looks like security from here. I can just make out the lights on the top. We'd better check before we go any closer. It just might be a trap, the authorities trying to get rid of another dozen or so piranhas. I'll go and have a look. If I don't return take them all back to the sewer. It's the only safe place!' Rico instructed Mateo.

'No, no! I'm not going back to the sewer!' Katie screamed.

'Shh! You'll bring all the police in the area down on our heads!' Mateo cautioned.

Tim held tight to his sister, not only to reassure her, but also to keep himself calm. The man under the bridge could be their only hope now, but Tim knew they couldn't put the gang at risk after all they have done for them.

Rico was back in ten minutes with a big grin on his face. 'It's a security van alright but it's all smashed up. It has been in an accident. The wheels are missing, mirrors, anything of value, so it must have happened a while ago. The soup man is there and he is waiting for us, so let's go. Mateo, you keep watch first, and blow your whistle if you see anything unusual. I'll come back and swap with you in a while,' Rico said, with authority. Mateo was proud of his new role of second in command, since Andres' death.

Tim and Katie were instructed by Rico to hang back slightly until he and the others had spoken with the soup man. Tim could see that the man was a Peruvian of about forty years old, a little overweight, beginning to grey. He had two younger men with him, probably both in their early twenties. The young guys were handing out soup and bread to the street boys who sat quietly on their haunches, filling their hungry bellies.

Rico chatted with the soup man for a few minutes and then waved the gringo children over. The kind man approached them gently and spoke with them in English.

'Are you Katie and Tim Baxter?' he asked.

'Yes!' the children answered in unison.

'My name is Gilberto; I'm a friend of your mother and father. We've been searching for you in the jungle since your plane crashed.' The soup man crouched down and gathered the children in his arms.

The children sobbed in his grasp, knowing at last they were safe. Gilberto wept. He was overcome by the realisation that the children he and his wife had been praying for everyday, these last few months, had been delivered into his hands by a loving God.

'I think we have a phone call to make. What do you think?' he said in a very emotional voice to Tim and Katie. But before he had time to get his phone from his pocket, a sharp whistle was heard.

'We've to leave; there's trouble! Please don't forget about us, gringo kids. Pray for us!' Rico shouted.

The street kids took off before Tim and Katie could reply. They were left standing beside Gilberto as they watched a police car scream after a truck. A false alarm, but the street kids had fled.

'Come on you two! Let's get you out of here and up to the truck,' Gilberto said, as they set off up the slope.

CHAPTER 27

Miracle

It was just after two in the morning when the phone rang in Lima. Alex and Sarah were in bed. Sarah was awake but Alex was fast asleep, exhausted after a hard day back at the office. Sarah nudged Alex. The phone was at his side of the bed. It was probably someone phoning from one of the company's offshore drilling sites, she thought. The 'offshore' people always forgot the time difference which used to greatly irritate Sarah, but these days it didn't seem important.

'Hi, Baxter speaking. Oh! It's you Gilberto… What! Say that again! …'

Sarah was upright in bed now fully alert, as was Alex.

'The children? You've found the children! Of thank God! Thank you, God. Where? … Are they alright? … Of course we want to speak to them!' Sarah grabbed the phone from Alex just as Tim began to speak. Tears of joy ran down their cheeks as they spoke first with Tim then Katie. The conversations lasted for half an hour. Alex and Sarah promised to be on the next plane to Iquitos.

The children were looked after by Gilberto and his wife, Antonella. Showers, hot food and warm beds were made ready for them. For the first night in months the children slept comfortably and soundly until dawn. Then they were up, dressed in clean shorts and T-shirts and rushed off to the airport to meet the first flight from Lima.

Sarah and Alex walked through the arrivals hall, this time oblivious of the heat, humidity and bustle of this tourist place. As they impatiently stood in line to exit the airport they tried to peer outside to catch a glimpse of their beloved children. The youngsters were standing at the front of the noisy, waiting multitude. Shouts of joy greeted them!

'Mum, Dad! We're over here!' Tim and Katie shouted and waved with excitement. 'We're here. Over here!' The children jumped up and down to attract the attention of their parents. Alex and Sarah were trying to push through the crowd to reach the barrier that separated them from their children. Taxi drivers and bus drivers were vying for business from travellers who had arrived off the Lima flight, all oblivious of the delightful reunion that was about to take place. The police tried half heartedly to keep the crowd under control, but they knew that in ten minutes all would be on their way into the city. Alex reached Katie first and with outstretched hands he leaned over the fence and lifted his daughter into his arms, smothering her with a father's hugs and kisses. Tim pushed past some unsuspecting, heavily laden eco-tourists to grab hold of his Mum in an embrace neither would ever forget. The tears flowed and flowed, but this time they were tears of joy.

Gilberto and his wife watched the scene with tears in their own eyes. 'God must be smiling today, when he sees this wonderful reunion. Thank you God,' Gilberto said, with deep gratitude to His Father in heaven, who had answered all their prayers.

Gilberto and Antonella allowed the family as much space as possible over the next few days to give the children the chance to tell their parents all about their experiences.

Alex couldn't believe the way the villagers had cared for his children, but what shocked him most was how the street kids had rescued his kids. He was moved to tears by the story of Andres' death. 'How could anyone beat up a young child like that?' he said. Then he remembered how much he had despised the 'piranha' who had crossed his path in Lima. 'Human beings are capable of such cruelty,' he added.

Sarah wanted to organise the flights home to Lima as soon as the children felt able to fly. But the children refused to go without finding Miguel and his brothers.

'We have to find out what has happened to them. Without them we would still be in the jungle, probably dead by now!' Katie pleaded with her father.

'At least let us go to Belen to Eduardo's cousin's house and see if they know anything about them. Or Dad you could come with us to the police station to ask if they have been arrested. They'll speak to you when they know you are a director of Petro-Explore NMW,' Tim insisted.

Gilberto joined in the discussions, 'I could take you to Belen. I know where the school is so it should be quite easy to find the house. I don't hold out much hope of getting any help from the police. They'll be polite but they'll not admit to having any street boys in custody. I've tried to find boys before.'

'OK! OK! I see how much it means to you both. Your Mum just wants to get you back home as quickly as possible,' Alex agreed. Sarah smiled acknowledging that, as it was really important to the children, she knew it had to be done. Katie hugged her Dad and Mum in turn.

'When should we go Gilberto? Katie asked.

'I didn't say you could go young lady,' Alex interrupted. 'We've just got you safely back. We aren't taking you anywhere that is the least bit risky! Nor you Tim!'

'Dad, we have to go, they're our dearest friends now.

We're not going home till we know they're safe! Are we, Tim?' Katie shouted, and then she burst into tears. Sarah rushed to comfort her daughter. Katie cried and cried. 'We can't let anything happen to them. They've become like family to us,' Katie continued to weep. She just wouldn't be comforted.

'It's alright Katie we'll all go together, this afternoon,' Alex confirmed.

Still, Katie cried. She cuddled her mother for half an hour, sobbing quietly into her chest.

'It's OK little one. Let it all come. You've been through so much. But you're safe now,' Sarah whispered softly as she rocked her daughter gently in her arms.

'Andres died because of me. It's all my fault. It's as if I killed him myself,' Katie wailed.

'No! No! It's not your fault. His mother and father abandoned him, probably because they were too poor to feed him. But it was the security guard who kicked him so badly. Never forget that!' Alex explained. As he stroked the head of his little girl, his eyes filled with tears.

Later that afternoon, Katie, Tim and their parents set off for Belen. Gilberto enlisted the help of one of his teenage volunteers, Juan, who was well known in Belen and wouldn't be viewed with suspicion. Gilberto explained to the group that the way into the school would be wet and muddy. Puerto Belen lies on the banks of the Itaya River and, in the rainy season, the river floods the shanty town. The inhabitants need to travel by canoe when the water is at its highest. At this time of year, the waters are falling, so it's possible to walk in, but it would still be sludgy. He reminded them that the sewer from Iquitos overflowed into the Itaya River, so the area would be contaminated with sewage.

As they walked gingerly through the sticky mud, Sarah was shocked at the poverty that surrounded her. Children played in muddy pools she knew were contaminated with sewage, watched by many, big, black, ugly vultures. Some of the vultures were scavenging through piles of waste. Sarah shuddered at the sight. She felt sick at what she saw. No wonder so many young children die before they reach five years old in places like this.

As they progressed further into the shanty town, the ground was wetter, so the locals had put long logs or planks down to walk on, but these were very slippery. Alex took Sarah by the hand to help her. She noted how much Alex had changed these last few months. He looked older with extra wrinkles, and his hair was much whiter, yet he was much more attentive to her. Sarah felt guilty that she had been such a burden to him lately, as if he hadn't had enough to worry about without her being difficult. She supposed that they had all changed over the past three months. Katie was coping very well with the logs and she had no need of her mother's hand, as she would have done previously. No doubt as everyone became reacquainted more changes would be evident. None of them would ever be the same again.

Sarah noticed the large number of children watching the group as they approached the centre of the township. Toddlers stood high up on open floors on platforms that passed as their homes, looking down on the group three metres below. Some of the houses were on stilts but others were built on logs. The logs, which enabled the homes to float in the high water of the rainy season, were now resting in the mud. The local children wore scruffy T-shirts and had little pot bellies hanging over shorts. Worms, she thought, and no wonder with the filthy water round here. Surely they didn't drink it! There must be a clean source of water somewhere! But, as they walked through the streets, she was aghast to see boys and old men fishing from logs and girls fetching water from the filthy river, confirming her worst fears.

Gilberto's young friend was talking to an old woman who was sitting on the steps of the school, pleating her long grey hair. The conversation was becoming quite animated as she pointed this way and that, hopefully the directions to the cousin's house, Alex thought.

Round a couple of corners and across a very unsteady and unsafe walkway, they arrived at the foot of a ladder. The steps led to the trap door of the house above.

'Juan and I will go first,' Gilberto insisted.

The children nodded in agreement and waited patiently as Gilberto and Juan knocked and were admitted to the humble dwelling. Within five minutes the rest of the group were invited to climb up into the hut. To the delight of Tim and Katie there were Ronaldo and Pablo sitting together on a hammock. The two young native boys jumped up and embraced their gringo friends.

'What about Miguel, where is he?' Tim asked anxiously.

The young woman who lived in the house beckoned to the children to go to the back of the dwelling. Tim and Katie could tell by the look on Ronaldo and Pablo's faces that this was not good. Tim followed the girl and peered behind an old piece of curtain that separated off a sleeping area. Lying huddled on the floor was a wretched looking figure.

'Miguel, Miguel, wake up! You have visitors,' she said tenderly.

The shape moved and turned slowly round.

Tim gasped at what he saw. Katie heard him and ran to see. Miguel's face was unrecognisable. His eyes were so swollen he could hardly see; his nose was badly twisted. Miguel held his left arm with his right hand to steady it, obviously in great pain.

'Miguel, don't die! No! Not you too. You saved us from the police that night; you mustn't die. Dad, dad help! We must help him,' Katie screamed, stamping her feet as if in a two-year-old tantrum. The memory of what happened to Andres was fresh in her mind.

'I'm here Katie; it's alright,' Alex said as he rushed round to see behind the screen.

'Someone has made a right mess of you son. We need to get you to a doctor. You've a few broken bones by the looks of things,' Alex said as he calmed the situation, his military training kicking in without him even being aware of it. 'Let's pull back this curtain so we can get a better look at you.'

'Is that you Tim and Katie? Are you both OK?' Miguel said in a soft voice.

'Yes, we're fine. This is our father and mother and their friend Gilberto. You and your brothers will be safe now. It's our turn to look after you,' Tim answered assuredly.

Alex was assessing Miguel's injuries. 'I think you have broken some bones in your face. Your left arm is probably broken, and by the pain in your chest, I would say a few ribs. Can you see?'

'I can't see anything with my left eye but each day my right eye is a little better, as the swelling goes down,' Miguel replied.

Ronaldo explained what had happened to the boys. 'Miguel was knocked unconscious by the police and left for dead. Pablo and I managed to escape and then they all turned on Miguel. We hid and watched; we couldn't do anything to help. It was horrible! They kicked him and hit him with their sticks. We thought they had killed him. Once the police had left after you two, and all was quiet, we went to Miguel. We dragged him over a bank into some bushes. After about an hour he woke up but he was very drowsy and badly hurt.'

'We heard shots, at least three,' Tim said. 'We thought they had shot at least one of you.'

'There was a policewoman with them. She fired her gun into the air. I think they wanted to scare us off. They could have killed us if they had wanted to,' Pablo piped up. 'But they have made a mess of Miguel.'

'Don't worry boys. We'll get Miguel to the best private hospital in Iquitos. He'll soon be well again,' Alex said.

'But, we have no money to pay,' Pablo said.

'After all you boys have done for Tim and Katie, you don't have to worry about hospital bills. We'll take care of those,' Sarah assured them.

Gilberto thanked the young woman for looking after the boys. Miguel was lifted to his feet by Alex and Juan and gently helped down the steep ladder to the ground below.

It took some time to retrace their steps through Belen. However, by nightfall, Miguel had been assessed by the medical staff at the Nazarene mission hospital. The fact that he, a native boy, had been brought to the hospital by gringos caused a few eyebrows to be raised. But as soon as Alex identified himself as one of the directors of Petro-Explore NMW, Miguel was given first-class attention.

The doctor broke the news gently to Miguel that he had permanent damage to the back of his left eye due to the assault and that he would not see again in that eye. His right cheek bone was broken and as this had caused his good eye to slip slightly this would require an operation in the next few days. The doctor also confirmed that Miguel had a fracture of his left arm which needed manipulated and plastered. His ribs were broken in four places but would heal themselves.

It was late in the evening before Miguel was allowed visitors. By this time he was sitting up on the trolley, all cleaned up, and much more comfortable.

'My church runs a boys' home,' Gilberto explained. 'It's in a village just a few kilometres outside Iquitos, on the road to Nauta. I think you will prefer to be in the country till you get used to your new life in the town. We have cleared a room for you, so the three of you can sleep there. You can call the place home till you are better Miguel. I will take you there and introduce you to the house parents, Philip and Maria, who will look after you.'

Gilberto realised that it was a huge culture shock for the village boys to arrive in a city like Iquitos. They weren't accustomed to the buzz of the streets, the noise, the crowds and generally the pace of life. Even the motorised rickshaws were new to them. The concept of telephones, televisions, and computers would all be unfamiliar to them, so a gradual introduction to city life was needed or the boys would be totally overwhelmed. The house parents would introduce them, in a controlled way, to their new life.

It didn't take the boys long to make up their minds. A quick exchange of glances and almost in unison the brothers said,

'Yes please! Thank you.'

Tim and Katie returned with their parents to Gilberto's house. They visited Miguel and the brothers regularly in their new home to check they were settling into their surroundings. They asked Gilberto if he thought they would be able to see Rico again.

'I've been back four times in the last week and still no sign of any of them. Boys from the other gangs know nothing of Rico either,' Gilberto reported.

'Why is Rico not bringing the boys to you for food?' Katie asked. We want to help him. He could come to the hostel, get off the streets. He hates it; he told us.'

'It's not easy for boys to come off the streets. To sleep in a bed, and eat regular meals is more than they can cope with. That's why, at the start, we feed them with soup and bread two or three times a week and try to get to know them. But they are very suspicious. Too many adults have harmed them. Some of them think we are a trap set by the police. Rico might come back yet. He will be upset by the death of his friend Andres. Perhaps he has put his head in a glue bag to ease his pain; if so, he will sleep for many days before he surfaces again. If he does come back, I will try and persuade him to come to our hostel down by the cemetery. There, the boys can come and go as they please. There are some mattresses on the floor and some food for them. This hostel is run by former street boys who relate much better to the street kids than we can. I'll let you know if I find him again,' Gilberto promised.

The Baxter family stayed in Iquitos for a further week, long enough to see Miguel successfully through his operation. Alex and Gilberto organised a permanent home for the three brothers, in a supported hostel in Iquitos. Hopefully, the boys would be ready to move there in a further three months, in time for the new academic year. But it would all depend how quickly they adjusted to their new way of life. The two younger brothers would be admitted to a senior school to complete their secondary education. Miguel was too old for school, but Gilberto found a place for him in a college, where he could study for the qualifications he needed to gain entry to the university. He was determined to be a teacher. The boys were totally funded by Alex and Sarah, who were delighted to be able to repay the boys for all they had done for Tim and Katie. The Baxter's returned to Iquitos regularly to meet up with Miguel, Ronaldo and Pablo, who had all become a part of their family.

Epilogue

Despite everything that happened to them, the Baxters did not return to Britain for a further five years. As a family, they decided to stay on in Peru. Tim and Katie didn't want to leave and abandon Miguel and his brothers in Iquitos, and Alex and Sarah were determined to find a way to help the street children of Lima.

They founded a small charity called 'Help a Street Kid,' or HASK as it came to be known. This was set up to care for at least some of the street boys that lived near the city centre. Sarah didn't return to her editorial job but became heavily involved with promoting the work of HASK and fundraising. She worked with her pastor, Jim, and several local churches in Lima to increase awareness of the 'piranha' problem and the desperation of these children. Sarah was successful in finding young Peruvian volunteers to help her set up some night feeding stations for the boys.

The Baxters became a very close family, never taking each other for granted. Alex and Sarah renewed their marriage vows, in their church, in front of their children, family and friends. It was a special day of thanksgiving. Alex made sure that he was free at weekends to be with his family, and that he took all of his generous holiday allocation. He continued with his high-powered executive job, but he learnt to delegate more responsibility to his juniors. It was an extremely well-paid position and the family needed the income, not only to support their own children but the boys in Iquitos, and of course Sarah's work at HASK. But Alex was a different man. All who knew him realised he had changed.

He became the Regional Director for Petro-Explore NMW, but his attitude to the Amazonian people had altered completely. No longer did he regard them as being stuck in the Stone Age. No longer did he bully his way through meetings or soften agents with 'little brown' envelopes of cash. As often as he could, he held negotiations with the local leaders himself. Oil wells were only dug after thorough and fair consultation with the villagers, and pollution kept strictly under control. However, Alex was not at peace with himself even with these compromises. He could see that oil exploration in Amazonia, together with deforestation by the loggers, was causing huge problems for the indigenous population. Collectively, these operations were fuelling the street child problem.

His friendship with Gilberto flourished. When he was in Iquitos on business, he made time to visit Gilberto, and helped him with his street boy work. He always visited Miguel and his brothers, making sure they were well looked after and that they were adjusting to city life. Alex knew he could never fully repay the boys for all they had done for Tim and Katie, but he was determined he was going to try. Sadly, however, no contact was ever made with Rico again.

Alex's bosses in Switzerland, however, were pressurising him for faster progress in South America, but he found this impossible to achieve using his new ethical ways. His heart was no longer in oil exploration, so, after much thought and discussion with Sarah, he resigned from his post at Petro-Explore NMW to become Executive Director of HASK.

Tim and Katie returned to school and normal life in Lima. It took them several months to adjust. The love and understanding of their parents helped to heal the children's emotional wounds. But their experiences had changed their lives forever too.

Tim had learnt from Miguel the importance of an education. Before the crash he was like most other teenagers, moaning about teachers and homework. Now he saw his opportunities so differently. He realised a good education would give him the right to choose his future, something that was denied to millions of children worldwide. Without education, they were condemned to poverty and all the hardship that came with it. Tim was a bright lad, but up until the accident his teachers had seen very little evidence of his true ability. After all, it wasn't cool to get good marks. But he became a conscientious pupil and studied hard. He didn't care what his classmates thought. He vowed to get the best results he could and hoped to study at university.

Katie was a little more fragile than Tim when she started back at school. However, her school was well informed of the traumas she had been through and supported her. She had always worked hard in class but now was even more determined than ever. Katie loved to help her Mum with fundraising for HASK whenever she could. Sometimes she would bake scones and cakes for the night-time teams to take out to the boys on the street.

By the time the family had decided to return to Britain, HASK was flourishing. Alex and Sarah's hard work had succeeded beyond their expectations. After a couple of years, the organisation had grown and expanded into other Peruvian cities. There were up to twenty employees supporting over forty children in hostels and several hundred youngsters living on the street. Alex handed over his directorship to a young man from Lima, but remained as chairman of the charity.

When they returned to Britain from Peru, Alex was appointed to a position at the United Nations Children Fund (UNICEF). He became the South Asia Director with a special responsibility for the street children of India. Alex and Sarah's stay in the UK was short-lived; within three months they were off to Mumbai.

Sarah returned to her previous role and became a freelance journalist. She worked alongside Alex to expose human rights issues related to the abuse of young women and girls in South Asia.

As Tim matured, he realised he didn't want to join the army as his father, grandfather and uncle had done. He couldn't help thinking about the poor in places like Amazonia. Tim believed that, if God had saved him from death several times in the jungle, it was up to him to do something worthwhile with his life. His final school exam grades were good, better than anyone expected. Tim applied to medical school and was accepted at St Thomas's in London.

Katie travelled to India with her parents and continued her secondary education in Mumbai. She hoped to study English at university and go into journalism like her mother.

In Iquitos, Miguel qualified as a teacher and worked in Nauta, which is on the Rio Amazon not far from Iquitos. He married Maria and started a family. Ronaldo found studying difficult, but fortunately he was good with his hands. Gilberto found a joinery apprenticeship for him which he enjoyed. Once a trained carpenter, he would be able to find work to support himself. Pablo worked hard at school and hoped to go to college as Miguel had done.

The Baxters remained in regular contact with Miguel, Ronaldo and Pablo through the wonders of the internet and webcams. During the summer vacations, Tim and Katie visited Iquitos to catch up with the brothers. After all, back in the jungle, the five had promised to 'always keep in touch.'

The End